PRAISE FOR E

"J.A.'s uncanny ability to place the reader at the very center of 13-year-old Evan's head captured me, from page one. Evoking 1970's America and the long reach of the Vietnam War, Evan's confused, loyal, angry, lonely, and forgiving coming-of-age as she finds her place in the heart of a colorful cast of characters at 'Eat and Get Gas' kept me from sleep right up to the perfectly pitched ending."

—JENNI OGDEN, award-winning author
of *A Drop in the Ocean* and *Call My Name*

"Storytelling at its best, *Eat And Get Gas* grabs the reader from page one and doesn't let go. Daily, life confirms for Evan that people can disappoint us even when they love us. But she has three things going for her: soothing music from the pianists next door, the skating rink, and a honeybee bracelet. The unexpected twist at the end is oh-so-worth the wait!"

—LAURIE BUCHANAN, author of the Sean McPherson novels

"It's 1972 and thirteen-year-old Evan has her hands full. Her older brother is a draft dodger; her mother is ill; her baby brother has a learning disability; and her father, a Vietnam vet, has another family overseas. When Evan's mother and brother head for Canada, Evan's father takes her to his family home in Hoquiam, Washington. As she waits for her mother's return, surrounded by a cast of quirky characters and damaged adults, Evan learns a new definition of family, the cost of untold secrets, and the value of her burgeoning self-esteem. A powerful story about a sad chapter in America's history that is thoroughly modern, relevant, and inspiring."

—ANNE LEIGH PARRISH, author of *An Open Door*

"Complex and memorable characters are at the heart of this intriguing narrative. Family, politics, and survival drive this page-turner caught in the turbulent times of the Vietnam war. Throw in DB Cooper and you've got one exciting novel! Well done!"

—MARIANNE LILE, author of *Stepmother: A Memoir*

"*Eat and Get Gas* is a compelling and affecting read that highlights experiences I haven't often seen in fiction. This masterful study of family acts as a microcosm of Vietnam War–era America and expresses extremely well the way the trauma of this war reverberates deeply and widely. The book hums with a deep sense of love, in complicated and sometimes painful situations, and describes a group of people loving each other in ways that are complicated and poignant."

—PIP ADAM, author of *Nothing to See*,
The New Animals, *I'm Working on a Building*, and
the short-story collection *Everything We Hoped For*

"Great cast of characters, a compelling story, and convincingly told."

—JOE BENNETT, New Zealand columnist
and travel writer

"J.A. Wright's second novel reprises her brilliance in creating the authentic voice of a young narrator who grips the reader in a story that is often painful but always mesmerizing . . . . The writing is lean and penetrating, with enough depth to allow the reader to feel Evan's hopes and dreams along with the searing pain of a young girl taking command of her challenging life. Evan's resilience and emerging grace is a balm amidst the wounded world she comes from, and *Eat and Get Gas* is a welcome antidote to the unremitting pessimism of our time."

—BARBARA STARK-NEMON, author of award-winning author
of *Even in Darkness* and *Hard Cider*

PAST PRAISE FOR THE AUTHOR, FOR *HOW TO GROW AN ADDICT*:

* 2016 International Book Awards—Winner in Addiction & Recovery
* 2016 National Indie Excellence Awards (NIEA)—Winner in Addiction & Recovery
* 2016 Independent Publisher Book Awards (IPPY)—Bronze Medal—Literary Fiction
* 2015 Foreward Reviews INDIEFAB Book of the Year Awards Honorable Mention for General Fiction
* 2015 USA Best Book Awards Finalist for General Fiction

"Wright deftly and insightfully describes how a life can spiral toward addiction and rehab. The story is raw and touching and I found myself rooting for Randall as she navigates redemption and sobriety. A gritty and honest read."

—SUSIE ORMAN SCHNALL, award-winning author of *On Grace* and *The Balance Project*

"Brilliant and an unstoppable read. This novel takes us right to the roots of a young addict's mind and vividly through the sights, sounds and smells of growing up. Wright radiates veracity from the tiniest of incidental details to the greatest of comic and tragic catastrophes. Part Charles Dickens part Charlie Brown, it is, in turn, thrilling and heart-breaking. She also pulls off the difficult trick of making one identify with the simple humanity of the main character, whether or not one has anything in common with her. Beautifully woven, beautifully told and deeply enthralling . . . . This is a superb and inspiring first novel."

—PETER MIELNICZEK, actor-comedian and artist

EAT AND GET GAS

EAT AND GET GAS

A NOVEL

J.A. WRIGHT

SHE WRITES PRESS

Published 2023
Printed in the United States of America
Print ISBN: 978-1-64742-481-7
E-ISBN: 978-1-64742-482-4
Library of Congress Control Number: 2022919528

For information, address:
She Writes Press
1569 Solano Ave #546
Berkeley, CA 94707

Interior Design by Tabitha Lahr
Cover Photo © Henry Hargreaves

She Writes Press is a division of SparkPoint Studio, LLC.

For my Grandma Celia.
Always cooking and always happy to see me.

Grandma's Fried Razor Clam Recipe

One large frying pan
1 to 1½ cups of peanut oil
20 cleaned and patted-dry razor clams

Pour ½ to ¾ cup of peanut oil in the frying pan before turning the heat on medium-high (the rest can be added as needed).

Mix together in a large glass dish:
    15 ground saltine crackers (use a rolling pin)
    1 to 2 cups all-purpose flour
    ½ teaspoon salt
    Dash ground black pepper

Beat together in a large bowl:
    3 large eggs
    1½ cups milk

Drop a cleaned and dried razor clam into the egg mixture, and let it sit for 10 seconds before removing and placing it on top of the flour mixture, turning once or twice until both sides are completely coated.

Put the breaded clam in the frying pan (the oil should be hot enough to make it sizzle). Turn after 30 seconds, and cook for another 30 seconds.

Eat immediately with (or without) your favorite condiment.

CHAPTER 1

I WAS SIX AND ADAM WAS THIRTEEN WHEN our brother Teddy was born. He arrived in August instead of October, and his birth caused our mother's multiple sclerosis to return.

Mom was too sick to pick Teddy up, so he slept in her bed, in the spot where I sometimes slept. "Don't be sad," she said. "It's just until I'm better."

Teddy was cute, but he wasn't fun like I thought he'd be, and he was always with Mom. I hated it. I'd had Mom to myself for years. I even went to her women's voter group meetings, where most members wore jeans and T-shirts, said terrible things about the war, and used the peace sign to say hello and goodbye.

And though I'd been scared to start school, after three weeks of playing on my own and listening to Teddy cry, I couldn't wait to go. I got up early on my first day, put on my favorite dress, and ate cereal at the kitchen table across from Mom. I pretended not to notice coffee dripping down her chin. She was shakier than usual that morning. Still, she insisted on walking me to school and had a tight grip on my hand when she lost her balance. Dad saw her fall and rushed outside, carrying Teddy. "I think you should take the pills the doctor gave you," he said and handed Teddy to me so he could help Mom.

I knew I should've followed. Instead, I leaned against our new fence and considered taking Teddy to school with me for show-and-tell. I'd just started walking away when Dad appeared on the porch and told me to bring Teddy inside.

Teddy was still drinking from a bottle and crawling when he turned three. When he turned four and Dad left for Vietnam the first time, he could drink from a cup, but he couldn't walk, and he couldn't hear the TV without the volume up. Our doctor scheduled a hearing test, but Mom didn't take him. She thought Teddy's hearing would improve once he stopped getting ear infections. But his infections persisted, and when Dad came home eight months later, he went with us to see the doctor.

"Like I told your wife, your boy might need hearing aids. And he's not walking because he doesn't have to. Put him on the floor and leave him there until he walks. Stop treating him like a baby." The doctor motioned for Dad to put Teddy down.

Teddy sat in the front seat on Mom's lap on the drive home so he wouldn't get carsick. We were almost home when Mom turned to Dad and said, "I don't think our doctor knows a thing about children. He doesn't have any."

"He's got plenty of kids. I've seen them," Dad said.

"Maybe so, but none as fragile as our boy."

"Our fragile boy needs a hearing test. Get it done!" Dad slapped the car seat so hard that Teddy jumped, and Mom stopped talking.

It was the first time I'd seen Dad slap anything. I wasn't sure what it meant, but it made my insides spin.

Before Adam and I left for school the next day, Dad turned off the TV and put Teddy on the floor. When we got home, Mom was in bed, Dad was on the couch watching TV, and Teddy was on the floor next to him, curled up like a potato bug.

"Go ahead," said Dad when I reached down to pick Teddy up. "He's been there all day like that."

It was Adam who taught Teddy to walk—by holding Teddy's arms over his head and pulling him around the living room like a rag doll. When Mom couldn't take Teddy's screaming any longer, she'd tell Adam to stop. And he would, for a few hours.

On the seventh day, when Teddy spotted Adam in the kitchen, he crawled to the coffee table, pulled himself up, and walked across the room to Mom. We all cheered, and Dad picked him up and threw him into the air the way he used to do with me when I was little.

Six months later, when Dad left again for Vietnam, Mom, Adam, Teddy, and I stood in the middle of our street, waving goodbye until we couldn't see his car. We wrote to him and watched the TV news every night, hoping to see Dad in a story about Vietnam. And when he came home a year later, we were all happy. But only for a few days, because Dad walked around with clenched fists, talked to himself, drank whiskey, yelled at the TV, and barked orders at us. Mom and Teddy ignored him, but Adam and I couldn't, so we stayed out of the house.

It was easy to do in the daytime. I had school and played on a softball team that practiced every other day and had games on Saturdays, and Adam went to college and left early in the morning. At night, though, we were at home, walking on eggshells until Dad went to the tavern or passed out on the couch.

Three months later, when I saw him packing his bags to leave, I had to pinch my arms and play steeple people with my hands to hide my excitement. Mom grinned and said I should've pinched harder.

Dad didn't say goodbye, not even to Teddy, who'd attached himself to Dad's leg like an octopus and cried when the van arrived to take him to the airport. When the van turned the corner at the end of our street, Adam clapped, and I cartwheeled around the yard. It wasn't like we were farewelling the dad who used to make French toast every Sunday and laugh at everything on *I Love Lucy*. And I don't think Mom was seeing off her high-school sweetheart, the "dreamy" senior who gave her sixteen red roses on her sixteenth birthday. Dad had become someone we didn't know, and I didn't like.

A year went by before he came home again. By then, we'd stopped writing to him, and Mom had stopped reminding us about how nice he used to be.

CHAPTER 2

IT WAS AUGUST 1971 WHEN DAD ARRIVED in a new Chevy Impala and threw the keys to Adam. "Just once around the block!"

When Teddy saw Dad, he screamed with excitement and ran to him, but I stayed seated on the porch stairs, holding my shaky knees. "Hey, Dad," I mumbled, moving to make room for him to get by.

"Hay is for horses," he said.

"Sure, sorry," I said.

"Don't you have better clothes? Your shirt is dirty," he said as he opened the screen door.

"My shirt isn't dirty—it's tie-dyed," I muttered, but only to myself.

I had lots of shirts, but this one was the coolest. I'd found it in the box of hand-me-downs Mom got from a friend at the Women's League of Voters. It had taken me two days to wash, dry, and iron seven dresses, four pairs of pants, five blouses, and sixteen T-shirts.

Mom was waiting for Dad at the door. "I expected you home two days ago. There's one piece of your son's birthday cake left."

"Oh, right? You had a birthday." Dad rubbed Teddy's head.

Dad put his bag down and handed a folder to Mom. "You'll need to fill these in so he can see a hearing specialist at the base. And what's wrong with your neck?" he asked.

"It gets stiff sometimes. Right now, I've got pins and needles everywhere. It'll go away," Mom said, tucking her chin close to her chest when Dad leaned over to have a look.

"Oh. Like how Teddy's hearing problem went away?" Dad said.

Later, when I was washing Teddy in the bathtub, Mom walked in and sat down on the toilet seat. "You know, I don't like your dad when he acts like this, but we have to get used to it. Vietnam has changed him, maybe for good. When he called me last month, he told me he'd lost nine soldiers that week. And those bumps on his face and arms are from a bomb that exploded behind a truck he was driving. He says he's going back just as soon as the army approves his request. I think he feels guilty about those soldiers. He might change his mind once he settles in. Try to be good and just do what he says, okay?"

The following day, when Dad saw me in my Jackson 5 T-shirt and Mom shuffling around in a pair of Mexican huaraches, he laughed and called us silly broads. He didn't stop laughing until he heard Mom tell Adam to take his allowance from her purse. "You take shit hand-me-downs from strangers and give money to a college student who should have a part-time job? That's screwed up, lady. These kids are spoiled." Dad threw his coffee cup into the sink.

AFTER LUNCH, ADAM AND I HAD TO HELP Dad search the garage for his missing tools. It was a sunny day, and Dad wasn't wearing a shirt, so it was easy to notice the scars, scabs, and red bumps on his head, chest, and arms. He was also missing two teeth and the top of his left ear. I knew I could learn to ignore those things, but there was no way I'd ever get used to his weird voice. Mom said it was from breathing in the chemicals they used in Vietnam to kill trees.

Whenever Dad shouted or sometimes just spoke, my heart raced, my knees went weak, and I'd get sleepy. So, I hid from him. Adam tried it, too, but Dad didn't let him get away with it. He was determined to make him earn his allowance.

One day, he showed Adam how to sharpen garden tools, then made him cut down an old apple tree, mow the lawn, and trim the hedges. The next day, from a blanket fort I'd made on the back porch, Teddy and I watched Adam wash the windows and clean the gutters. Then he climbed up a ladder to get onto the roof with Dad to replace shingles. I saw Adam slip. I also saw him reach out to Dad for help, but Dad didn't extend his hand. When Adam's feet landed on the gutter, he stopped moving, and Dad yelled, "Figure it out, boy. The sooner you do, the better chance you have of making something of yourself."

I made dinner that night because it was my turn. When Dad finished his macaroni and cheese, he pushed his plate to the side, and Mom slid an envelope across the table to him. "They revoked Adam's student deferment because he quit college. You need to do something. He can't go to Vietnam."

"Why the hell did you let him drop out? No one with a low draft number is staying stateside unless they're a cripple or in college. Surely you knew that when you let him quit." Dad was shaking the letter.

"I wasn't thinking. I wasn't well, remember? Or don't you read my letters? Never mind, I don't care if you do. The notice says Adam has to report in three days. You need to call in a favor. The army owes you a few."

"Call in a favor? Are you out of your mind? I'm not asking anyone to help Adam—no fucking way." Dad stood and tossed the notice at Adam. "And why am I just learning of this? They sent it two months ago."

"Yeah, Mom. Why didn't you give it to me?" Adam asked.

"I didn't want to upset you. I thought once your dad was home, he'd deal with it."

"Dropping out of college was a stupid move. I thought you were smarter than that," Dad said.

"I dropped out before I flunked out," Adam snapped, standing now with his arms down in front, right hand over his left, mirroring Dad. "I was coming home every weekend to help around here. I couldn't study. I didn't have time."

Dad folded his arms across his chest. "You could've called me."

Adam copied the gesture. "You could've called *me*."

Dad went into the living room to pull Teddy back from the TV. As usual, he'd been in front of the set for hours, watching cartoons and repeating commercials.

"You should've given me the notice. If you had, I'd be in Canada already," Adam whispered to Mom as he headed for the back door.

I remembered the day, more than a year ago, when Mom told Adam that nineteen was the number drawn for his birthday. I didn't know then what a draft number was, but I could tell it was bad when Adam cried.

Mom hadn't called Dad in Vietnam about the draft number. Instead, she'd called a friend from the League of Women Voters for advice, who helped to get him enrolled in college before he even graduated from high school.

"Do you have to go now?" I asked as I sat down at the picnic table next to Adam.

"I guess so," Adam said, rubbing his eyes.

"Why not run away? Join the circus or sneak onto a ship heading for South America."

Before Adam could answer, Dad opened the door and

yelled at him to come inside. "Buzz off, old man," Adam said and ran toward the alley.

"Wait up—I'm coming with you," I said.

"You'll make everything worse if you do," Adam said. "What about Teddy? Who's gonna brush his teeth and put him to bed?"

I went back inside, arriving in time to catch the end of Mom and Dad's fight. "There's no way in hell I'm letting our son become one of those baby killers I've been reading about," Mom said.

"Communist propaganda. You're still one, right?" Dad slammed the door behind him.

"I CAN'T TALK ABOUT IT RIGHT NOW. My head hurts," Mom said when I asked if Adam was going to Vietnam.

After helping Mom to her room, I made peanut butter toast for Teddy and me, and we watched TV until Adam came home.

Next morning, I waited until I heard Mom shuffling around in the kitchen before I went in. She was going through Dad's duffel bag. "Does Adam have to go to Vietnam? Are you really a Communist?" I asked.

Without looking up, Mom said, "Adam is never going to Vietnam. And your dad doesn't know the difference between a Communist, a Socialist, a Republican, or a Democrat. Most people don't. I am a card-carrying Socialist. Most Canadians are. We're also a lot smarter than most Americans, especially everyone in your dad's family."

Mom was Canadian and also American. She'd already told me about growing up in Montreal and that her name, Endura, was her mother's name, too. "It's not a sweet name like Evangeline," she said.

She'd moved to Hoquiam with her father a year after her mother died, because her dad took a job managing a paper mill there. She brought her mother's books along, and that's how she found my name, Evangeline. It was in a poem written by a man named Longfellow. Only Mom ever called me Evangeline. Everyone else called me Evan.

MOM REPACKED DAD'S BAG AND WENT back to bed, where she stayed until Dad came home. She met him at the front door, holding up the photo of a Vietnamese girl cradling a baby in her arms.

"She's a goddamn child, Gene!" she shouted. "Have you no morals? No self-control? Is the baby yours? Of course, it is!" Mom turned to show the picture to Adam and me.

Dad grabbed Mom's arm and pried the photo out of her hand. Mom slapped him and was about to do it again when Adam moved to step between them. A second later, Mom collapsed into Dad's chest. Not because she wanted to hug him—she was just too weak or too sad to keep standing. I could taste tears when Dad wrapped his arms around Mom and carried her to the bedroom.

Later, just after midnight, Mom and Adam snuck off to Canada. If I hadn't gotten out of bed to check on Teddy, I wouldn't have seen Adam putting food in a bag and Mom taking money out of Dad's wallet. She put her finger to her lips. Dad was asleep on the couch with Teddy next to him, but I knew they wouldn't wake up. Teddy never did unless someone shook him, and Dad had finished an entire bottle of Old Crow after carrying Mom to bed.

I took two pillows to the car for Mom, who held my hand and called me "sunshine."

"I know what we're doing is dangerous but taking Adam to Canada is the only way to save him from becoming like Gene, or worse," Mom said.

"Just let Adam go alone," I pleaded.

"I have a Canadian passport, but he doesn't. They'll turn him back at the border if he's on his own. And don't worry about me driving back. Once we get to the place I've arranged, I'll leave my car with Adam and take a bus or train home. You look after Teddy like you always do. I'll be back soon, I promise." She was doing her best not to look me in the eye when she kissed my cheek. "Now, go back to bed and act normal. I know you can do that."

I hugged Adam until he pulled away. He said, "Make sure Teddy doesn't forget me, okay?"

"Cross my heart." I held my breath so I wouldn't cry.

I stayed outside to watch Mom steering and Adam behind the car, pushing it. At the end of our street, she started the engine and turned the headlights on. Then Adam opened the driver's door and got in. I waved goodbye, even though I knew they couldn't see me.

NEXT MORNING, TEDDY AND I WERE watching TV when Dad woke up. It took a few minutes for him to notice Mom and Adam weren't home, and his nose was touching mine when he ordered me to tell him where they were. I stepped back to get away from his smelly breath. "I don't know. I was asleep."

Dad stomped around the house like a wild man until he found a list of numbers on the cupboard door next to the phone. He must have called twenty numbers in the next hour. Then he looked through Mom's League of Women Voters folder, before throwing it across the room.

"Are these man-haters helping her?" Dad asked.

"I don't think anyone is helping her."

"Come on. You must know something," Dad said. "What did she say? Did she leave a note? She must have. This god-damn house used to be full of her notes. Where is it?"

"Jeez, Dad, she doesn't write any longer. Haven't you noticed how hard it is for her to hold a pencil?"

"Ah, yeah. That's right," he said. "Still, she told you where they were going."

"Swear she didn't," I said.

FOR THE NEXT TWO DAYS, I STAYED outside with Teddy until it got dark. We played with our dog, Leroy, read comic books, ate the peanut butter sandwiches I made for lunch and had Cheerios with sliced peaches for dinner. Dad was on the couch the whole time, watching baseball, drinking beer, and waiting for the phone to ring.

On the third day, the day Adam was supposed to be in Seattle for his appointment, I made a fort with blankets in my bedroom so Teddy and I could hide from Dad, who'd stayed up all night drinking and yelling at the TV.

"Someone from the army is gonna call or come by today looking for Adam when he doesn't show up for his physical." Dad closed my curtains. "Do not answer the door or the phone."

Except for sneaking next door to pick peaches off the McDougalls's tree, we stayed in my room until Dad said we could come out.

There were only four hot dogs left in the refrigerator, so Dad took us to the Huff and Puff Diner. Good thing, too, because we'd used the last of the ketchup the night before.

While Teddy and I ate cheeseburgers and French fries, Dad drank coffee and talked about the League of Women Voters. "Your mom never voted until those gals got her to register. Now she votes just to cancel out my vote. They've brainwashed her. She's a terrible mother, right?"

"No," I said.

"What about her leaving you and Teddy alone? That's pretty terrible."

"Well, you're here with us, so we're not really alone."

"Oh, she's got to you, hasn't she?" Dad said. "Now you're talking like her."

A second later, Teddy accidentally blew the whipped cream off the top of his milkshake right into Dad's chest, and Dad picked up his water glass to throw it. When I panicked and pushed Teddy off the bench so he wouldn't get soaked, he fell hard and screamed so loudly that everyone in the diner stood up to see what was happening. Dad yelled, "Nice going, dumb shit!" and the waitress threw her hands in the air as if we were the worst customers she'd ever had.

I was angry about the water in my face and on my shirt, the dirty look the waitress gave me, and Dad calling me a dumb shit and then refusing to stop at the store on the way home to buy food. And I was angry with Mom for leaving us with Dad.

Still, I didn't think she was terrible, no more terrible than Dad was for not trying harder to take care of us. He didn't even know how to turn on the washing machine, and the one time he did the dishes, he used Pine-Sol instead of Joy dish soap and didn't rinse.

Teddy's screaming fit at the Huff and Puff Diner had embarrassed Dad. He left the waitress a ten-dollar tip. Then he dropped us at home and went to the tavern "to get a break from you brats."

IN THE MORNING, WHEN I HEARD THE front screen door slam shut and Dad's car start a second later, I ran outside to tell him we'd be ready soon. "Our doctor's appointment to get vaccinated isn't until 9:00 a.m. We just need to get dressed. We'll hurry."

"You can get those shots another time. I gotta go. I found a bookmark with a ferry schedule and an address. It looks like they took a ferry to Canada and drove to Calgary." Dad was rolling up his window and driving off.

I considered walking to our doctor's office, but it was too far for Teddy, so I called and canceled. Then we scrounged around the house for money, and I pulled Teddy six blocks in his wagon to the store. With the $4.32 we found, I bought bread, milk, toilet paper, Cheerios, and a bag of Ideal cookie bars. I wondered if it was enough to hold us over till Mom or Dad came home.

Teddy threw up in my bed that night. When he threw up again in the morning, I went next door to ask for help.

Mrs. McDougall wasn't happy we'd been left alone. When she saw Teddy, she gasped and then filled the bathtub with hot water. Later, she brought cinnamon-and-sugar toast to my room. "I should call the police or the army base. They need to find your dad," she said.

"Oh, no, don't do that. He'll be back soon, and besides, I'm thirteen, old enough to babysit."

Mrs. McDougall smiled, patted my hand, and said she'd be back in a few minutes. I was on edge until she returned with a box of food, including some Nestle Quik. She put clean sheets on our bed before she went home to make dinner for Mr. McDougall. "If Teddy gets worse, call me, no matter what time it is." She squeezed my hand.

"We'll be okay now," I said, squeezing back.

The second the door closed, I regretted saying it. I'd never taken care of Teddy on my own when he was too sick to walk to the bathroom. Instead of getting into bed next to him, I sat in a chair next to the bed, poking him every few minutes to see if he was still breathing. It was after midnight when I started throwing up.

"OH, LORDY," MRS. MCDOUGALL SAID WHEN she arrived the next day to check on us. She was only in our house for a minute when she called her husband for help. They bundled us up in blankets and took us to the hospital. I was so relieved, I sobbed when she handed me a warm washcloth.

The doctor at the hospital said we had ear and throat infections and needed rest and aspirin. Mrs. McDougall told him we'd been on our own for days, before Mr. McDougall said we had a hippie for a mother and a negligent army officer for a father.

They were right about Dad, but Mom wasn't a hippie. I was about to say she was a Socialist when the doctor said it might take longer for Teddy to recover because of his congenital disorder.

"What's that?" I asked.

"Something he was born with. It's the reason he's the size of a five-year-old and not a seven-year-old," the doctor said.

"Our doctor never said that," I said.

"I'm a children's doctor, and it's what I think. I'm sorry if I upset you."

Mrs. McDougall moved in and slept on our couch. She cleaned the kitchen, made bread and soup, and got Teddy to take aspirin by hiding it in a spoonful of raspberry jam. That night, when I woke and saw her beside my bed brushing my ponytail, I told her I loved her, and she squeezed my hand and said she loved me too. I don't think that was really true, but at that moment, I didn't care.

Dad was back Tuesday, without Mom and Adam, and Mrs. McDougall told him she'd call his commanding officer if he ever left us alone again.

CHAPTER 3

"**DID YOU FIND MOM AND ADAM?**" I asked Dad when Mrs. McDougall left.

"Nope, and I've got no idea where they are." Dad was pouring the last of the Hawaiian Punch into a cup for Teddy.

Teddy and I were feverish, weak, and had lumps on our necks. The following day, Dad took Leroy to Mrs. McDougall, because she'd offered to keep him for a few days. We then drove to Eat and Get Gas, my Grandma Willa's home, gas station, and roadside café in Hoquiam.

At first, I didn't think it was a good idea to leave. But I changed my mind after watching Dad try to get Teddy to swallow an aspirin in a spoon of jam, the way Mrs. McDougall had shown him. Teddy wouldn't open his mouth, so Dad pulled it open and pushed the pill down his throat with his finger. Teddy gagged and then screamed. "If you ever bite me again, you'll regret it," Dad said.

THE HOUR-LONG DRIVE FELT LIKE five, and when Dad finally parked in front of Grandma's house, I felt like throwing up. He honked until Grandma came outside with a woman who had the same round cheeks, blue eyes, and wide smile. "What a surprise." Grandma was opening the car door to help Teddy and me out. Seeing her smiling eyes made me almost as happy as when Mrs. McDougall arrived to help me with Teddy.

A second later, the woman who looked like Grandma poked her head into the car. "Hi, kids. I'm your Aunt Vivian."

I said hello, wondering if I'd met her before and trying not to throw up. I'd been sicker than Teddy that day, and I wanted to tell Grandma I was dying, but I thought it might sound stupid. I was sure I was, though. Just the month before, I saw a lady in the waiting room at Mom's doctor's office with a similar lump on the side of her neck. Mom said the woman was deathly ill.

But when Grandma saw my neck and Teddy's, she said, "You've got the mumps."

"Are you sure?" Dad asked.

"Seen it plenty of times," Grandma said.

Aunt Vivian took a few steps back, and Dad walked to Grandma's front porch. "I'll be staying in the basement room," he said, loud enough for me to hear.

Grandma pleaded with Teddy to get out of the car, but he wouldn't budge. "He'll come out when he notices I'm gone," I said. The wet grass was soaking my new Keds.

I'd just closed the car door with Teddy still under his blanket in the back seat when Uncle Frankie showed up. I hadn't seen him for years, and never with long hair, but I could tell it was him from the gap in his two front teeth. He pulled Teddy out of the car by his feet and carried him like a sack of potatoes to his old bedroom, upstairs and across the hall from Dad's old room. Teddy kicked and cried, but Uncle Frankie just laughed and said, "Special delivery on its way."

Watching Uncle Frankie goof around with Teddy reminded me of how Dad joked around with Adam and me before Teddy was born. When Uncle Frankie sat Teddy down on the bed next to me, Teddy snuggled in close, asked for

Leroy, and hid his face in my armpit. "Who's Leroy? And where's your mom?" Uncle Frankie asked.

I explained. "Leroy is our dog. He's staying with our neighbors. Mom and Adam went to Canada last week so that Adam won't have to go to Vietnam and turn out like Dad." I swallowed hard.

"Your mom is so right on." Uncle Frankie was smiling.

"You think so, do you?" Grandma stared at Uncle Frankie as she spoke.

I'd never thought of Mom as being "so right on," but I guess she was. She didn't like the war either and sometimes told strangers that we should all listen to Dr. Martin Luther King.

TEDDY DIDN'T SETTLE DOWN UNTIL Grandma made him a cup of hot chocolate. He finished it in a few gulps, and to my surprise, let Grandma undress him and put him in the bathtub afterward. While he soaked, Grandma took clean sheets out of a tall dresser in the corner of Dad's old bedroom, which she'd assigned to me.

"Jeez, you're so grown up now," she said, turning her head to look at me as I sat on the bed. "It must be three years since Gene last brought you to visit."

"I was here four years ago, on my ninth birthday," I said. She'd given me a twenty-dollar bill that day and had sent cards and money since. I felt bad about not thanking her before now.

"I'm sorry I haven't been in touch much," Grandma said. "We're just so busy here these days. After Pa died, I didn't have the will to keep the place going, but then Viv moved in and got it up and running. It's a lot of work for two old ladies. Still, it's no excuse to ignore my grandchildren." Grandma handed me a set of sheets.

"It's okay. I've been busy too. Mom is always sick, and

Teddy takes up a lot of time." I could hear him calling out to me from the bathroom.

"I can tell," Grandma said. She tossed two white pillow-cases with blue-and-yellow lace trim on the bed. "My mother made them. They're pleasant-dream pillowcases." Grandma turned to look out the window. "It's gonna rain for the next few days. Sometimes it leaks in this room. Maybe I can get Gene to fix the roof while he's here."

Fat chance, I thought. I looked around at Dad's old things and wondered if he'd left a note at our house for Mom, telling her where we were.

"Didn't you bring any clean clothes?" Grandma was holding up a shirt from the bag we'd brought. It was one of Teddy's, the one with the raspberry jam on it.

"Dad packed for us." I was praying he hadn't put dirty underwear in the bag, too.

Grandma began rummaging through the dresser drawers. "Well then, I think it's only fair you wear some of his clothes."

When Teddy was dry after his bath, Grandma slipped one of Dad's smaller undershirts over his head. It went to his ankles and fell off his shoulders, but Teddy didn't care.

"He'll just have to wear it. I'll wash all your clothes tonight," Grandma said.

"Dad's good at fixing our washing machine, but he doesn't know how to use it." I wasn't going to tell her that Dad was drunk and hadn't even tried to give us clean clothes, because I was afraid she'd tell him what I'd said. "School starts on Monday," I added. Grandma needed to know that we wouldn't be around for much longer.

"The same school?" she asked.

"No. I'll be in the eighth grade. Teddy has to repeat the first grade, because his teacher said he's slow for his age."

"I agree with his teacher. Teddy seems younger than seven. And he doesn't pay attention, does he?"

"No," I said, "but that's because he's a little deaf. Our doctor thinks he should have hearing aids, but Mom says he doesn't need them."

Grandma rolled her eyes, the same way Dad did. "She should follow the doctor's advice."

Then Grandma told me she'd only seen Teddy once before, the year he was born. "He was a perfect little cherub, and he didn't make a peep all day. I thought it was odd for a baby to be so quiet. Now I'm wondering why he's so small." She handed me some socks before putting a pair on Teddy's feet.

"He still looks like a cherub, but now he's loud." Without knowing Teddy, Grandma had got him in and out of the bathtub with no objections. It was weird, especially since she hadn't been able to coax him out of Dad's car an hour before. When Teddy was ready for bed, Grandma walked him across the hall to Uncle Frankie's old room and told him to stay put. "I have a special cookie jar for little boys and girls who behave," she said, loud enough for me to hear. My parents sometimes offered Teddy candy to stay in his bed, but he never did.

Grandma appeared at my door with clothes and an extra blanket for my bed. "This room is chilly, and it needs a good cleaning. Maybe you can sweep and dust when you're feeling better. I imagine you do a few chores at home." She dragged her finger across the top of the dresser, moving the dust around. "Endura shouldn't have run off with Adam."

When Grandma patted my arm, I pulled away. But I didn't defend Mom, because Teddy was sobbing in the other room, and it was making me nervous. "We don't let him cry for very long. He throws up if we do." I stood up to check on him.

"I'll do it. You need a bath." Grandma gave me a T-shirt with "Hoquiam High School" written on it and a pair of long underwear with a small burn hole in the right thigh. Dad must have dropped ashes on his clothes even in high school. "These will have to do. Make sure you wash your hair. It smells like cigar smoke and vomit. And hang up your wet towel when you finish."

While waiting for the bathtub to fill, I stared at my neck in the mirror, wondering if the balloon-like lump would ever go away. I waited until I heard Grandma walking down the stairs before I slid under the steaming hot water. I only stayed in the tub long enough to wash my hair, because Teddy had stopped crying, and I knew it meant he'd gotten out of his bed.

Sure enough, Teddy was asleep in my bed. I towel-dried my hair, put on Dad's clothes and snuggled in next to my brother.

Later, when Grandma arrived with aspirin and a glass of orange juice, she woke us by pulling the covers off. "What's going on?" She looked disgusted. "Take him back to his bed, now."

I couldn't look at Grandma as I carried Teddy back to Uncle Frankie's old room, pleading with him to stay put and promising to keep the lamp on and the door open. An hour later he was still sobbing and calling out to me, so I got up and went to his room.

Other than the bruises I'd get from Teddy kicking me, sleeping with him didn't bother me like it bothered Grandma and our doctor, who said he should sleep on his own. I think my parents liked Teddy being in my bed. That way, they never worried about finding him in Leroy's bed, like they did every time they'd tried to get him to sleep on his own.

In the morning, when Grandma found me in Teddy's bed, she didn't yell. She shook me awake and asked me how long we'd been sleeping together and whether my dad knew about it.

"Sure, he knows," I said. "If Teddy isn't in my bed, it's because he's in bed with Adam or Mom. And when Dad is home, Teddy sleeps on the couch next to him."

"Well, it's time he started sleeping by himself," Grandma said. "He's too old to sleep with you. He's going to learn to sleep alone. Not now, when you're sick, but the time is coming."

CHAPTER 4

"HEY, TEDDY, LET'S GO TO THE CAFÉ for breakfast. I bet Grandma will make us pancakes and scrambled eggs." I was feeling well enough to walk around for the first time since we got to Grandma's.

Teddy moaned and moved farther down the bed. "You don't have to walk. I'll carry you," I said, reaching under the bedcovers to tickle him. He bit my hand.

Five minutes later, I was in the café kitchen, sitting on the green vinyl stool I used to struggle to climb onto, picking at a cinnamon roll Aunt Vivian had rescued from a customer's plate. I was admiring the red-and-white curtains, wondering why the cupboards were all so low, and curious about who the woman washing dishes at the double sink was.

Her body was crooked, and when she turned to get a clean dish towel from a drawer, I saw her curly brown bangs, which covered all but the bottom of a black eye patch. I was about to introduce myself when Dad walked into the kitchen looking for something stronger than cream to put in his coffee. When he noticed the woman, he made a weird face and shrugged his shoulders as if to say, "What is it?"

Grandma got our attention by clearing her throat. She motioned for us to follow her to the dining room. "Staring is rude," she whispered when we got to the counter.

"I know. I'm sorry," I said as I sat down.

"You, too, Gene," she said.

"I only stare at the lookers." Dad was searching in the newspaper for the crossword puzzle.

A few minutes passed before Aunt Vivian put a plate of eggs, hash browns, bacon, and pancakes in front of me. It was more than I could eat, so I asked Dad if he wanted some.

"You eat it," Aunt Vivian said. "You look like a lollipop. Gene can drink his breakfast. He's used to it."

No one had ever called me a lollipop before. I had to put my head down so she couldn't see my red face and ate as fast as I could, knowing I should hurry back to Teddy before he did something that would get me into more trouble.

Dad was still looking at the woman through the dining room serving window when I stood up to leave.

"Ah, I see it now," he hissed. "Is she who I think she is?"

"She is." Grandma continued to read the front-page news.

"Would've been nice if you'd told me she was here," Dad said.

"Would've been nice if you'd told me you were coming," Grandma replied.

I was curious to hear more, but the bell above the café's front door tinkled, and four customers walked in.

"Who is she, Dad?" I whispered when he stood up to leave.

"No one important," he said, but I knew he was lying.

Later, after a long nap, I persuaded Teddy to eat lunch with me in the café. Even though I'd stuffed myself that morning, I was hungry. And I knew Teddy had to be hungry too, because he didn't eat any of the tomato soup Aunt Vivian had brought upstairs the night before.

When we got outside, I could see Dad on the café's back porch stairs, smoking a cigarette, drinking a cup of coffee, and watching us. "You must be a foot taller than you were last week," he said.

"Yeah, I think so, too," I said. "Who was the woman in the kitchen this morning?"

"Oh, yeah, you saw her, too. She's Frank's sister, Louanne," Dad said.

"If she's Uncle Frankie's sister, she must be your sister and my aunt, right?" I asked, letting go of Teddy's hand so he could wrap his arms around Dad's leg.

Dad was lighting a cigarette from the one he was still smoking. "Frank isn't my brother. And she's not my sister or your aunt."

"He isn't your brother? Are you kidding?"

"Affirmative. He's not related to me or us. And there's no need for you to talk to him about it or speak to Louanne, ever."

"That's weird, Dad. How come no one ever tells me anything? Anyway, I don't care if he's not related to me, I'm still gonna call him Uncle Frankie," I said as I stepped past him to get to the kitchen's back door.

"Don't know why you'd want to," Dad called out.

IN THE CAFÉ KITCHEN, SITTING AT Grandma's workbench and blowing on Teddy's chicken noodle soup, I had to fight back an urge to introduce myself to Louanne, who was now peeling potatoes at the kitchen sink. More than telling her my name, I wanted to touch her hand or her arm and tell her I was feeling better. I'd felt the same once before, when I met my dog, Leroy. I was eight when he scratched on our front door. When I opened it and saw him, I bent down and rubbed Leroy's head, and he licked my hand and then ran down the hallway to my bedroom. That was five years ago, and no one had ever come looking for him.

I didn't ask Grandma about Uncle Frankie like I'd planned to, because Dad made us eat our lunch in the dining room with him. Once we'd finished, he said we'd be going to the beach with him every morning, starting the next day at 5:30 a.m.

"Why? We hate the beach."

"The café is famous for its fried razor clams and clam chowder, and Ma always needs clams, so we're going to fill the freezer. I'll dig them, and you and Teddy can carry them to my car."

"Teddy can't walk very far, you know. Can't we just go home and wait there for Mom? I'll take care of Teddy. You won't have to do a thing," I said.

"We're staying here. No complaints!" Dad smashed his cigarette into an ashtray as he stood up.

"I should've started the eighth grade last week. My friends are probably wondering where I am."

"You can go to school here, make new friends," said Dad. "There's a junior high just down the road. The elementary school is next to it. Teddy can go there. You can take him."

"I don't want to go to that school. I want to go to my school. I want to go home."

"Talk to your mom about that," Dad said.

"I would if I could," I growled. "Welcome to 'not gonna happen.'"

Dad picked up a dish towel from the counter and twirled it until it resembled a ball. When he stepped behind the counter to pour himself a cup of coffee, he threw the dish towel my way, and I dropped to the floor to avoid getting hit.

"Whoa!" he yelled. "I wasn't aiming for you. If I had been, you'd know it."

The thing was, I didn't know. The only thing I knew for sure was that saying or doing something Dad didn't like caused him to blow his stack. And then I'd cry, and Teddy would throw a tantrum. I had ways to calm Teddy down—pushing him on his swing, making shadow puppets on the bedroom wall, putting Leroy under the covers with him—but all of these were impossible to do at Grandma's house.

After dinner, when Dad reminded me about going clam digging in the morning, I stood up, grabbed Teddy's hand, and headed up the stairs. It took everything I had to hold my tongue until I got to the top. "We're not going with you. I mean it!" I shouted.

"So what? You're going anyway." Dad spoke without looking up at us.

Grandma said, "They shouldn't be going anywhere, Gene. They've just gotten over the mumps, and it's cold at the beach now."

"My kids, Ma," Dad replied.

TEDDY WAS ASLEEP THE MINUTE HE crawled into my bed, but all I could do was pace around the room, thinking about Dad's stupid plan to pay Grandma with clams for letting us stay at her house.

I'd already heard that razor clams were better than money, which Dad said he was short on. It wasn't true, though. Adam and I had been depositing Dad's monthly paycheck for almost a year. And I'd been helping Mom balance her checkbook for months, so I knew they had money in the bank. So why wasn't he using some of it to pay Grandma?

I was still stewing when Aunt Vivian appeared at my bedroom door and whistled when she saw me in Dad's old long johns.

"They're not mine," I said, feeling my face flush.

"Teasing." She took a swig from the glass she was holding. "What are we gonna do about that jackass dad of yours?" she asked, slurring a little.

"I don't know. What should we do?"

Aunt Vivian raised her eyebrows, put her glass down, stubbed out her cigarette in the clamshell ashtray on Dad's dresser, and danced a jig.

"How about we lock him out of the house, so he has to shit outside, like all the other dogs?" She was clapping now.

She looked funny in her baggy undershirt and underwear, bouncing from foot to foot and waving her hands over her head. Any other time, I would have laughed, but I was still too angry.

Winded, Aunt Vivian sat down on the bed and took a couple of deep breaths as she moved her big boobs to the front of her chest.

"You gotta learn to tough it out with the bully, but not for long. Gene will soon tire of trying to impress everyone with his big-man attitude and clam-digging skills. And then he'll leave, back to fighting for nothing. You might miss him." She tried to wink but only blinked.

"I won't miss him. Not like I miss my dog, Mom, and Adam. I hate being around Dad, and I don't want to go clam digging, ever."

"I'm with you on that," Aunt Vivian replied.

Her joking around made me feel better. I even smiled when she slapped the back of my hand and said, "Just be happy you're here with us and not at home alone with him. You know," she said, sitting up straight, "we don't need any clams. We still have most of the ones he dug last month. And the fried razor clam special isn't as popular as it used to be. We sell more burgers now, thanks to Mr. McDonald. So how about I get Willa to tell Gene we don't need any more, certainly not three limits every day?"

"Yes, please," I replied, then I stopped. "Was Dad here last month? Or did you mean last year?"

"Last month. Willa was sixty on August 10. We had a party—lots of guests, presents, and flowers. But the thing that made Willa happiest was seeing Gene walk in the door in his uniform."

Until that moment, I thought Dad had flown back from Vietnam on August 19 and come straight home.

"Teddy's seventh birthday party was August 17. Dad could've come if he'd wanted to, right?" I asked.

"I would think so. He was at Mooch's for a week after the party, clam digging at beaches where only Indians like Mooch can go. And he had time to go to Seattle and buy that brand-new car you all arrived in," Aunt Vivian replied.

I was angry enough to kick something, but a second later, I heard Aunt Vivian in the hallway, burping and farting. The last one sounded like a lion's roar, and it made me laugh. She popped her head around the corner when she heard me. "Just letting off a bit of steam. You should try it sometime."

IT WAS JUST AFTER 5:00 A.M. WHEN DAD knocked on the door. "Reveille! Reveille! All hands on deck!"

I moaned into my pillow until Teddy kicked me. It felt wrong to get up so early, especially on a Sunday. I cried as I used the bathroom, got dressed, and begged Teddy to sit up so I could get him ready. When he saw me wipe tears away, he sat up and kissed my arm.

Grandma sighed when she saw us and handed me four pieces of peanut butter and jelly toast wrapped in a napkin and two rain hats she'd pulled out of the café's lost-and-found box. Then she walked us outside to the car where Dad was already waiting.

"Oh, Gene, I hope you know what you're doing."

"I always do," Dad said.

Teddy and I snuggled together and ate toast while Dad sped down the highway. When he parked in the beach parking lot, it was raining, and he asked why we hadn't worn raincoats.

"They're at home with our boots and umbrellas and Leroy," I replied.

"Why didn't you say so?" he asked.

"I did, Dad."

When Dad stepped out of the car, I began rocking Teddy, telling him we had to get out, but he just screamed and wouldn't budge. So, Dad pulled him out of the car. Still, Teddy wouldn't stand up. He sat down on the wet pavement, hiding his face in his hands, so Dad jerked him up and put him over his shoulder. I walked behind them with a clam bucket, shovel, and clam bags, hoping no one had seen us.

We had to wait for Dad by the shoreline, jumping back sometimes to avoid an incoming wave. After what seemed like hours but was only minutes, Dad walked to us and filled one of the canvas bags with clams from his bucket. "How about you run this bag to the car? Put it in the trunk, under the cooler. Don't let anyone see you. I'll watch Teddy until you get back," he said.

On my way to the car, I walked by the fish and game warden's patrol car, and he waved at me. I pretended not to see him, but then he got out and started walking toward me, so I stopped.

"Hey, aren't you Gene's kid?" he asked.

"Uh-huh." I hid the clam bag behind my back, hoping he hadn't seen.

"That's a nice new car your dad's driving. I guess soldiers get paid more than wardens," he chuckled.

"I guess so," I said.

"I'm in charge here. Name's Walter Brewster. Most people call me Wally or Wally Gator."

I smiled. "I gotta go. My brother needs something from the car."

"Give him one of these," Wally said, handing me two pieces of Dubble Bubble.

I COULD SEE AND HEAR TEDDY ON THE sand, screaming, and Dad standing over him, yelling for him to stand up. I reached out and pulled him up so fast, he fell silent and went limp in my arms. Then I took off his drenched coat and wrapped him in mine, pleading with Dad to carry him to the car. Dad said he couldn't take a full clam bucket, a wet coat, and a kid too. So, I carried Teddy, trying to keep him warm as he clung to my chest like a baby ape. Dad had the car engine going and the heater on, but it wasn't enough to warm up Teddy or take away my desire to smash something.

Thirty minutes later, back at the café, Aunt Vivian made a sour face when she saw me carrying Teddy from the car. The café was too full for her to tell Dad off, but we both heard her whisper, "Some men shouldn't be fathers."

"Says only you," said Dad.

Grandma couldn't leave the grill to help with Teddy, but I could see in her face when she tossed me a dish towel that she wanted to. I had Teddy's shoes off when Louanne appeared next to me with a pair of socks. "Dry between his toes before you put those on. He'll warm up faster that way." She turned back to the kitchen sink to resume washing dishes.

Teddy wasn't the only one who was cold and wet. I was, too, but no one had offered me a towel or socks. I was sobbing when I ran him a warm bath.

We stayed upstairs in bed until we heard Dad calling us to come downstairs to try on the new rain boots and jackets he'd bought in town. The things he got us were all too small or too big, but Teddy loved his new boots, and for the first time in days, he was happy.

When Grandma and Aunt Vivian arrived home after closing the café, we ate leftover chili and Jello salad and then went to the living room to watch TV. When a Coca-Cola commercial came on, Teddy stood up to sing and dance: "I'd like to teach the world to sing."

"In perfect harmony," I sang out, joining in.

When the commercial ended, we sang it again, and I told Dad that Mom loved the song, too.

"Big deal. Now be quiet."

But the commercial had broken my resolve to tough it out as Aunt Vivian had advised. "How come you went to Grandma's birthday party and didn't come home for Teddy's?" I moved to the end of the couch, out of his reach.

"I don't answer to you, and bigmouth over there should mind her own business." He turned to look at Aunt Vivian, who was mixing a drink in the kitchen.

She didn't reply, just raised her glass to him and grinned.

"They don't need more clams," I said. "Aunt Vivian said they still have the ones you dug last month."

"I don't give a shit. You're going digging. And just like today, you'll carry empty bags down to the beach and take them back to my car when I tell you to. And you'll do it every day until I say we're done."

"Jeez, Dad, even if you get us enrolled in school here, we'll never get there on time."

"When I was your age, Pa and I went digging every day, and I was never late for school, and you won't be. You're gonna learn to fend for yourself the same way I did." Dad went to get a beer from the kitchen.

I didn't get the connection between carrying bags of stinky clams to the car and learning to fend for myself. I'd only eat a fried clam if I was starving and had an entire bottle of ketchup to pour over it.

I was sick of listening to Dad. I wanted him to shut up. And like he'd heard my thoughts, Teddy began singing along to another commercial. Back on the couch, Dad squeezed Teddy's leg hard enough to make him shriek.

"If he has to get out of bed early every day, there's going to be a lot more screaming. And he might get another ear infection."

"Again, I'm teaching you two something important. If Ma doesn't want our clams, I'll sell them to restaurants, just like Mooch does. And Teddy won't get an ear infection or drenched again if you watch him like you're supposed to." Dad put his hand up to let me know he was done talking.

CHAPTER 5

THERE WERE MANY BEACHES CLOSE TO Eat and Get Gas
where people could dig for clams, but Ocean Shores was the
one Dad liked most. Maybe because his dad took him there
when he was a kid, or because cars could park close to the
shore, though he never did.

"They've got beach wardens now. Never had 'em when I
was a kid," Dad said. "I went to school with the guy at Ocean
Shores—I didn't like him then, and I don't like him now. He
hassles everyone about sticking to the one-limit-per-person
rule. Only an idiot goes digging for one limit of clams when
taking two kids means they can dig three, four if no one's
watching. Do I look like an idiot?" Dad asked, crossing his
eyes and wiggling his head.

So, we weren't going to the beach to learn survival skills
from Dad after all. We were going so he could dig his limit
and two more—so he could cheat.

"Yeah, I met Wally the other day. He was handing out
bubble gum," I replied. "He likes your car. He said soldiers
must get paid better than beach wardens," I continued, knowing I was pushing my luck.

I didn't like my dad, but I didn't think he was an idiot. Mom did, though. She said he was an idiot for voting for Richard Nixon, and because of the weird mouth sounds he made. Dad was especially loud when reading the paper or working on a crossword puzzle. Big, breathy grunts and groans shot out of his mouth and nose as fast as he tapped his pencil while trying to think of the right word. Sometimes Mom laughed, and other times she yelled out the word he needed so he'd shut up.

Grandma did the same thing. Her huhs, ums, and ahs were louder than Dad's, followed by an even louder throat clearing. I thought it was funny. So did Uncle Frankie. "The choir is alive and well today," he often said. The thing is, Uncle Frankie made weird sounds, too, and he sucked his teeth. Funnier, though, was when he'd stretch his face and hold it, like a yawn that got stuck at the top.

I knew it was a nervous thing, like my right eye twitching when I got scared, but still, I couldn't help laughing. Once, after he did it several times in a row, I got the giggles and then the hiccups. "It never used to be this bad," Uncle Frankie said, laughing too. "It got worse when the army started dumping Agent Orange everywhere."

Like Grandma and Aunt Vivian, Uncle Frankie hated the war. He also hated my dad. "You're a fucking kid killer," he shouted one morning in the café after Dad ordered him to get a haircut, put on a clean shirt, and tell his taco-eating friend, Paco, to take a hike.

ON THE EIGHTH DAY OF GOING CLAM digging with Dad, Grandma met us at the café front door when we got back and told me to run to the house, take a bath, and put on my best clothes. "We've got an appointment with the principal at Harbor Junior High to get you enrolled. Viv will take us. Gene can stay with Teddy." She glared at Dad.

Going to school in Hoquiam sounded like another bad idea. I hated the thought of being the new kid in the classroom. I wanted to wait until Mom got home and go to my school in Tacoma, where my friends were, even if it meant starting late.

"I can't be at school all day. Teddy needs me here with him—and I don't have any best clothes."

"Gene will get Teddy enrolled. And you both need new clothes. He can take you to get some after school. Isn't that right, Gene?"

Dad grunted.

After thinking about it, I decided being in school might be better than sitting around the café playing games and listening to Aunt Vivian and her customers talk about the weather and the war. So, I got dressed in the same clothes I arrived in three weeks before, and just as we were leaving, Grandma handed me a beige cashmere coat with quarter-sized gold buttons.

"A tourist left it behind two years ago. It's too long for me and too small for Viv," she said. "No one ever notices what people are wearing underneath a beautiful coat."

After slipping it on, I knew she was right.

"We haven't had our vaccinations," I said once we were in the car.

"Vaccinations for what?" Aunt Vivian asked.

"Measles and other things," I replied.

"If anyone asks, tell them you've had measles and other things," she said.

DAD GOT TEDDY INTO THE FIRST GRADE by telling the principal he was six instead of seven. Teddy didn't care, and I was happy the kids in his class were all about his size and that his school was just two blocks from the junior high.

My new school was okay for a few days. Dad had bought us new clothes, and Teddy seemed happy about taking the bus. I liked my history and English teachers, and most of the kids were friendly, except for two girls who sat in the back of homeroom class and spoke Pig Latin. I knew they ranked on everyone, because Adam spoke Pig Latin, and I'd learned a few words.

One morning, a week after starting school, we were late getting back from clam digging, and I wore my beach raincoat to school by mistake. At lunch, I heard someone yell, "Evan is a clam-scented Jolly Green Giant."

Everyone laughed, and I felt like running away. The two girls sitting across from me, Marie and Carla, who'd already introduced themselves and slid a Ding Dong across the table to me, told me to ignore them.

"They're jerks," Carla said.

"They're assholes," Marie said.

"They're jerky assholes," I said.

People had been teasing me about my height since the fifth grade, but never about how I smelled. It was hard to ignore because I knew I stank of clams. When I asked Grandma for help, she stepped closer, took a long whiff of my hair, tilted her head to the side, and said, "Oh dear, you do smell fishy. I guess we all do. Maybe this isn't the best place for you."

I got the feeling she thought I was blaming her for the way I smelled. I wasn't, and I regretted asking her. More than that, I wished Dad hadn't heard. He waited until we were alone before he let me have it. "You'd better learn to keep your mouth shut, Evan. Ma might be the only thing that'll keep you two from going to a foster home if your mom isn't back when I head back to Vietnam in December. Got it?"

"Got it." I could feel my cheeks burning. Was he going back because the army was making him or just so he could be with Hoi, the girl in the picture Mom had held up for Adam and me to see? I'd been more upset about the photo than Mom was. "I don't care anymore what Gene does over there. I just want him to keep Adam out of that goddamn war," Mom had said the night she left.

I hated the idea of living in a foster home and doing chores all day, like Anne of Green Gables. It made me want to be with Mom more than ever. But since it wasn't possible just then, living at Grandma's was better than any place else I could think of. There were five people, besides us, living at Eat and Get Gas, but not all in the same house. Uncle Frankie, Louanne, and Paco (a childhood friend of Uncle Frankie's) lived in Grandma's guest house by the gas pumps. The rest of us lived in Grandma's house, behind her café. Her home was much bigger than our house in Tacoma. It was rectangular, dark brown, with a slanted roof. There were four bedrooms upstairs and one in her basement room, which had a door that opened to the front yard, a small kitchen, and a green square bathtub. I once heard Aunt Vivian tell a customer, after he'd teased her about living in a big brown shoebox, "It's the same style house our Norwegian grandfather built for his family— Shaker style, with a porch."

Grandma's shoebox house was twenty of my giant steps (forty of Teddy's) from the back porch of Eat Café. The café was a large cabin with a high-pitched roof so steep that birds and pinecones were never on it for very long. There were two small square windows on each side of the café's double front door and several tall windows, the kind you could see traffic on the highway through, on the front and side of the building.

My room at Grandma's, Dad's old room, faced her front yard. From one of the two windows, I could see the back of Get Gas and Eat Café, a little of the state highway, and most of the gravel road, which ended at her neighbor's house. It took a while for me to get used to the sound of hard rain and traffic noise. And much longer to stop waking up when the house shook from overloaded logging trucks on the highway or when Uncle Frankie's motorcycle friends left after playing poker in his kitchen.

It wasn't just night noises I got to know. In no time at all, I knew the plumbing sounds in the house and when the gas station's underground pumps were going. I knew when an owl caught a chipmunk, the time from the whistle of a train in the distance, and if pitter-patter rain on my window was introducing a short shower or a storm.

Most of the loud noises in the daytime came from the garage, which looked like all the other gas station garages I'd ever seen, except its doors were red. It was close enough to the café that Uncle Frankie's music often caused café plates and coffee cups to rattle. It was amusing to me, but Aunt Vivian hated it and sometimes switched off the power to the garage when customers complained.

I would never have bragged about Eat and Get Gas when it was pouring down or foggy. But when the sun was out, and the trees were greener than green, it looked like it belonged on the cover of a storybook or in an enchanted forest, where the sun shone all day and animals played—not on the corner lot of a dirty, chipped-up highway that smelled of damp asphalt and something dead.

If tourists complained about the rain, traffic, or smells, Aunt Vivian told them, "We're next to a busy state highway on the edge of one of the largest rain forests in the country."

I learned to listen to the weather report in the morning like everyone else did. A sudden downpour could leave us soaking wet, and just a regular windstorm could destroy any size umbrella and make it almost impossible for me and Teddy to cross the highway to get to the bus stop. I hated the rain, but I didn't mind the wind. I liked the sound it made in the trees outside my room and how it could move me around when I was walking, as though I might fly.

Mom hated the weather in Hoquiam, and she'd stopped

visiting Grandma after Teddy's first Christmas there. It was my fault. I told her that Grandma had joked to Dad about monkeys in the zoo breastfeeding, too, and Mom flipped out about it. She told Dad it was perfectly normal to breastfeed, and that women Grandma's age should know it. Later, Dad told me I had no business telling Mom what Grandma had said. It was a private conversation, and I shouldn't have eavesdropped. He didn't shout at me, and he wasn't angry for very long. But it was before he started going to Vietnam—when he was still a nice guy.

I wouldn't have told Mom if I'd known it would put an end to us having Christmas and Thanksgiving at Grandma's. And I'd had to look up the meaning of "eavesdrop." Once I did, I knew I hadn't done that. I'd heard Grandma and Dad's conversation because they both spoke loudly enough for me to hear from across the room. I often heard what people were saying from far away. Mom said it was because of my big ears.

She might have been right. But I thought my good hearing had more to do with having to make sure Teddy was okay. At seven, along with not hearing well, Teddy struggled to do many things that came easy for other kids his age, like combing his hair, eating with a fork, and tying his shoes. I always felt bad when he tried and couldn't, and I often took the blame for his mishaps, even though both Grandma and Aunt Vivian had said Teddy's problems had nothing to do with me. When I told Aunt Vivian that Teddy didn't flush the toilet because I'd never shown him how to do it, she looked at me like I was crazy. "Let's say we file that doozy in the big brown bullshit pile!"

I was still laughing when I told Uncle Frankie what she'd said. "She don't mince words," he said, "and she don't take guff, but she sure can dish it out."

Even though I hated Aunt Vivian's teasing, I got to like the way she talked, especially to customers. She always said something nice about how they looked as she poured their coffee and took their food order. Our first week at Grandma's, when Teddy and I were too sick to get out of bed, she spoke to us the same way, like she was happy we were there and eager to feed us.

I thought Dad would move into the house once we were well, but he didn't. And when he was home, he avoided us and watched TV in the basement room. Grandma and Aunt Vivian mostly took care of us. They did everything Mom used to do but a lot faster. And sometimes, they'd invite us to sit with them under the trees next to the café. Even in the rain, Aunt Vivian put her face up to them and inhaled like she was smelling a bunch of flowers. One day, she made Teddy and me do the same thing and then told us we'd just inhaled air from a tree that was older than anyone on earth.

Grandma and Aunt Vivian's favorite trees were at the end of the café's eight-car (or one-logging-truck) parking area. They called them The Three Sisters. "Your grandpa wanted to cut them down to make a larger parking area, so Willa took him outside and made him wrap his arms around each one. You can see it changed his mind," Aunt Vivian said the day she showed me the best place to leave sunflower seeds for the chipmunks.

The Three Sisters not only smelled good, they sheltered the café from wind and rain, gave shade when the sun was out, and provided homes for owls, squirrels, chipmunks, and other critters that could keep Teddy and me amused all day. The morning smell of pine, wet asphalt, rotting leaves, and damp earth was everywhere until Grandma started cooking. From then, the place smelled of pork sausage, bacon, and buttermilk pancakes.

CHAPTER 6

EAT CAFÉ OPENED AT 7:00 A.M., Tuesday to Sunday, or when Aunt Vivian flipped the sign in the window around to OPEN and unlocked the door. Fisky and Mrs. Fine, café regulars, were always waiting on the front porch.

Occasionally, Mrs. Fine brought her sister along, and they'd ask me about school. One day, Aunt Vivian told them if my mom didn't come home soon, I'd be trying out for the school softball team. "Evan's been playing softball for years. She'll be the star player here for sure," she said.

"She must get that from you, Viv. You're a star waitress," Fisky said as he watched her carry four loaded plates on her arm and a syrup jug on a pinky finger.

Once Aunt Vivian was out of earshot, Dad whispered, "Too bad she's also a star know-it-all with a big mouth."

He meant the war; I could tell. Aunt Vivian was a war expert. She even knew about the wars from five hundred years ago. She hated them all. So did Grandma. But it was just Aunt Vivian who talked about them.

I didn't understand why they hated war so much until Uncle Frankie told me their two brothers died in a famous World War II battle called the Battle of the Bulge. Still, Aunt Vivian hated the Vietnam War more than any other. She said it was just a death trap for American boys. "There's no good reason for the USA to be in Vietnam. There was plenty to fight for in WWII. We should have gone to Europe sooner—three years sooner, if you ask me."

She talked about the Vietnam War to everyone, even tourist customers who supported it. And she kept a small chalkboard next to the café's cash register. "Number of our boys killed in Vietnam," it said. She updated it every morning.

I hated seeing the number grow. So did Grandma and Uncle Frankie. But Dad never mentioned it, though he didn't turn the board around as he'd threatened to do. He knew Aunt Vivian wouldn't have allowed it. That's the thing I liked most about her. She stood up for herself and other people when she thought they needed it. And no one ever argued with her for very long, except for Grandma—and even she would give in after a few minutes. "You're right. You're always right. It must be nice always to be right," she'd say.

Lots of things Aunt Vivian said, I'd never heard before. Some were funny, and some were just weird. Like the time she told me bushes don't do well under trees. I thought she was talking about the bushes under the fir trees. But Grandma said it was about me being teased by shorter people, like Mrs. Fine, who said if I didn't stop growing, I'd never get a husband. "How come you're so tall? Taller than your dad, I bet," she said the first time she saw me.

"Beats me," I replied, turning my head so she wouldn't see me blush, hoping Dad would provide a better answer.

"Her mother's dad was tall," Dad mumbled without looking up from the newspaper.

I was just over five-foot-ten when I started at Harbor Junior High in Hoquiam. No one else in my family was tall except for Uncle Frankie. He was six-four but, according to Dad, he wasn't my real uncle.

I was barely taller than Dad. Mom and Adam were shorter than me and so were Aunt Vivian and Grandma. Grandma was average size in every other way, and she wore a hairnet to keep her curly gray hair from falling onto café plates. Aunt Vivian was shorter than Grandma and chubby, with feet that looked like bread-dough balls. And her head was square shaped, though that could have been from her hairstyle—something Uncle Frankie called short, back, and sides.

"It's what you get for being cheap and going to a barbershop," he said when she took her hat off to fan her face one morning, and everyone in the café laughed.

"Go jump off a bridge," Aunt Vivian replied, which is what she sometimes said to Grandma, who would then remind her to watch her mouth.

Grandma didn't like rude people in her kitchen, but the café dining room was different. It was Aunt Vivian's domain, and she didn't mind people cussing or telling saucy jokes. She didn't like it, though, when people misbehaved, which included customers not leaving a tip.

If someone didn't know this, they'd find out pretty quickly—like the old couple who arrived for lunch one Saturday afternoon. I was at a table across from Dad and Teddy, filling saltshakers, when they walked in and sat down at the counter. They ordered the razor clam special with potato chips instead of French fries.

Just as their order appeared on the serving window, two Black guys with big Afros walked in, and everyone stopped talking. Aunt Vivian smiled and pointed to the two vacant seats at the counter, and the old lady gasped and moved to the edge of her stool when they sat down. Aunt Vivian quickly put the couple's clam specials in front of them and turned to ask the two men if they wanted coffee. Just then, the old man stood up and said they'd got the wrong order. He helped his wife off the stool, and they left.

When Aunt Vivian noticed they hadn't left money for the food they'd ordered, or her tip, she put the coffeepot down and ran after them, farting so loud that everyone in the café laughed. I think it was the first time anyone besides us had heard her pass gas, something she did all the time when customers weren't around.

The three truck drivers sitting at the corner table laughed. But I couldn't tell if it was because of her passing gas or how she looked running out of the café. I thought the funniest part was the way Aunt Vivian had lifted two stools that were in her way and set them down behind her before rushing through the door. It was like something Superman would do. Everyone except for Dad and the two black men clapped when she came back, waving a ten-dollar bill over her head. Right after, the two Black men stood up and walked out.

Later, when the café closed for the day and I was sweeping the floor, I heard Grandma, Dad, and Aunt Vivian arguing in the kitchen.

"And who said it was okay to let those guys eat for free?" Grandma asked.

"Coffee ain't eating. And they didn't even drink it. That old couple left because they're prejudiced, nothing else!" Aunt Vivian marched out of the room.

Dad was making fists when he told Grandma that Aunt Vivian had no business running after a decent couple to get money while letting those two eat for free. "You'd better talk with her," he said.

Grandma shrugged her shoulders, but she didn't defend Aunt Vivian. She just told Dad to take us back to the house.

No one but us ate for free. That was a rule. Grandma didn't like waste—she often reminded me to eat everything on my plate, and to use a few sheets of toilet paper and just a little shampoo. And when no one was watching, Aunt Vivian reused coffee filters and sometimes took food left on a customer's plate to use again or to feed to Teddy and me.

"Listen, Evan. Vivian isn't what anyone would call a

decent woman," Dad said on the walk to Grandma's house. "She's a women's libber. Like your mom wants to be. No one else believes women are equal to men. I tolerate Viv's bullshit because Ma says the café couldn't stay open without her help."

I had to hold my hand over my mouth to keep from saying I knew from school that everyone in America was equal—men and women; black, brown, yellow, and white; young and old—that it was the law. Then I thought I should just try harder not to let Dad get under my skin, as Mom had suggested many times.

It was hard to do, though, and later, when Dad left to play in a dart tournament at the Choker bar, I hoped he'd get so drunk, he wouldn't want to go clam digging in the morning. But he knocked on my bedroom door at 5:15 a.m., slurring, "Reveille! Reveille!" And I knew he'd keep saying it until I replied, and I didn't want Aunt Vivian to get out of bed and tell him off. So, I said we were up and began pulling Teddy's arm.

Grandma was spreading peanut butter and jam on toast when we got to the kitchen. I peeled a banana and watched Dad swallow a pill with a beer.

"Are you sick?" Grandma asked when she saw him.

"A little," he replied. "Mooch gave me one of his pills. Said it'll cure anything."

Dad wasn't in any shape to drive, but we got in the car anyway. When I closed my door, he picked up on our conversation from days ago. He was still drunk loud when he said I shouldn't get the wrong idea. "I've been fighting alongside Blacks for years. They're some of the best soldiers in the army, but I still don't want to eat dinner with them, and I shouldn't have to."

He wasn't doing a good job if he was trying to explain away what had happened in the café with the old white couple. He was just as prejudiced as them, like Aunt Vivian had said. I even looked up the word, to be sure. Maybe it didn't matter, though. Maybe Aunt Vivian and the law were wrong about all people being equal. It seemed to make the other café customers happy when the two Black guys left. I was ashamed no one had tried to stop them and embarrassed when I was the only one who'd said goodbye.

Dad perked up ten minutes after leaving Grandma's. And he wasn't loud and didn't slur when he told me about the soldiers who'd died in front of him and that he was teaching himself to speak French and Vietnamese.

Teddy had fallen asleep, and I was getting tired, but I wanted Dad to keep talking. He wasn't being mean or speeding or passing cars like he usually did. And he even laughed when I asked if I could have a pair of overalls like Aunt Vivian's to wear to the beach. "Overalls are for farmers and country-and-western singers. Vivian is neither." Dad laughed.

"Didn't Grandma and Aunt Vivian grow up on a farm?" I asked.

"Oh, yeah. Viv even married a farmer. She brought him to dinner when I was a kid. Pa called him a ten-way loser, and he was right. The guy shot someone and got twenty-five years for it. Viv was divorced and back home in North Dakota with her parents by then. When they died, she moved here to help Ma run the café and gas station. Shit, I'm talking too much. Gonna stop now. Keep your trap shut about what I told you, okay?"

"Yeah, I promise. It's a good thing Aunt Vivian moved here. Grandma said she's her best friend, and they'll live together forever."

"I'm sure it's true. Ma would be lonely on her own. Vivian takes care of her and keeps the café in order, but with that big mouth, she'd be better off working in the garage." Dad chuckled.

Dad talked again on the drive back to Grandma's. He said it had been the best digging morning in years, that all the clams were big, and it reminded him of when he was a kid and went digging with Pa.

"We had an ongoing competition about who could dig the largest clam. I won once," Dad said and then told me about the time he tried to teach Mom to dig a clam. "She waded out too far, fell over, and got soaked. Boy, was she mad." He laughed and hit his forehead with his open hand. It made me laugh, and Teddy, too.

The pill Dad got from Mooch must have been a miracle pill, because it turned Dad back into the nice guy he used to be. For the first time in a long time, I wasn't afraid to be with him.

"Do you think Mom is okay?" I asked.

Dad rolled down his window, threw his cigar out, and then gently put his hand on Teddy's leg. "I don't know. I haven't heard from her, but I've got a good idea where they are, and it ain't where I thought."

"So, you'll be bringing her home soon, right?" I asked.

"That's my plan," he replied. "I need a few weeks to figure out how."

I couldn't wait to tell Grandma and Aunt Vivian that Dad knew where Mom and Adam were. I knew it worried them that Mom wouldn't come home, because they talked about it all the time, even with customers.

When Dad said he was making a quick stop at Mooch's for more pep pills, I hoped he'd get enough to last the rest of his life.

CHAPTER 7

A HALF HOUR LATER, I WAS IN THE CAFÉ kitchen, sitting at Grandma's workbench. I was eating breakfast and trying to finish my homework when Dad walked in with Teddy. "It's 8:00 a.m. Anyone running the gas station these days?" he asked, setting Teddy down in the chair next to me.

"Those boys stay up too late playing poker," Grandma said, loud enough for us to hear over the sounds of customers talking in the dining room and sausage patties sizzling on the grill.

"Frank's always got a quick money deal going on. It's gonna do him in one day," Dad said.

Aunt Vivian, who'd been taking breakfast orders in the dining room, looked through the serving window. "I've just seen two cars pull into the pumps and drive off. Let's send Evan over to wake up Frankie. She can just knock a few times and run."

"Okay, I'll do it, but if I get caught, I'm gonna tell Uncle Frankie you sent me," I said.

"I don't mind," Aunt Vivian said, laughing now.

The gas station was supposed to open at 7:00 a.m., just like the café. It rarely did, because Uncle Frankie and Paco always slept in after a big poker game, which was just about every night. Grandma and Aunt Vivian never heard his poker buddies leave, but I did, and so did Dad. I heard him tell Uncle Frankie several times to do something about them parking their motorcycles close to the café. "Tell them to park up the road and not here and not in front of your dumpy shed, either!"

Uncle Frankie's house wasn't a shed, but it was dumpy. And from the outside, it didn't look big enough for one person to live in it, let alone three.

I finished my last pancake, took Teddy to the café dining room so Dad could watch him, and ran to Uncle Frankie's. The strings of colored lights, twisted together like a piece of red vine licorice and strung across the top of the front porch, were still on. The flower box next to the front door was over-flowing with empty beer cans and cigarette butts. I knocked three times, not expecting anyone to answer the door.

Uncle Frankie appeared. "What the . . . oh, it's you!"

"Aunt Vivian sent me to wake you up so you can open the gas station. I like your Christmas lights," I said, louder than I'd meant to, flustered at the sight of him in boxer shorts.

"Lights of Saigon," Uncle Frankie replied, scratching his armpit.

"They have Christmas lights in Vietnam?" I asked.

"Not sure. My lights are for buddies who got blown to smithereens. It's pure luck I didn't come home in a body bag too," he said, scratching faster. "Fuck! I'm so goddamn lucky, I should be in Vegas."

A few days later, Uncle Frankie told me he'd won fifteen hands of blackjack the night before and was moving to Reno as soon as he could find someone to take over the gas station and his mail route. "Maybe you could do it, or maybe Paco."

"I can't. You know that. I'll be going home as soon as Mom gets back."

"It'll have to be Paco then," he said, grinning. "He likes to pump gas and bullshit. But he's no mechanic, and he's not interested in becoming one. He spends too much time reading books and roller-skating."

"I like to skate, too, but I'm not good at it. It would be cool to skate like Big Red on the *Roller Derby Show*," I said.

"Paco can teach you. He's at the Rollarena rink every Monday, all day. It's not far from your school," Uncle Frankie said.

"I might if Dad will let me—if we haven't frozen to death at the beach by then."

WE'D BEEN CLAM DIGGING EVERY MORNING for six weeks by then. September had been rainy, but October was freezing. Even with boots, raincoats, and Teddy's Superman blanket wrapped around us, we were miserable. Dad wasn't. No matter the weather, he never wore more than shorts and a T-shirt on the beach, and his hands were always red, and his lips were always blue when he walked over to us with clams. Sometimes he'd fill a bag too full, and clams would fall out as we went to his car to hide it in the trunk. Then seagulls would swarm around, trying to get one. It was scary, but Teddy loved it so much, I occasionally dropped a few clams on purpose.

ON HALLOWEEN MORNING, GRANDMA'S neighbors—Hal and his brother, Hubert—showed up at Dad's car to help me carry the clam bags to the water pump behind the café.

"I hope you're not helping yourselves," Dad said when he saw them.

I felt like kicking Dad when the taller brother, Hal, put the clam bags down and motioned to his brother to do the same. And I picked up Teddy and ran to Grandma's kitchen when Dad began shouting at them to keep moving.

I wanted to go trick-or-treating, but there were only two houses close to Grandma's, one of them Hal and Hubert's. I knew it was no use asking Dad if we could go there, but I did anyway.

"You know kids have gone into that house and never come out," Dad said.

Grandma threw her hands up, and Aunt Vivian yelled, "Bullshit!"

I didn't believe Dad, either. Hal and Hubert looked a little scary, with their big bottom lips, pointy noses, long beards, and ears that reminded me of the kid on the front of *MAD* magazine. And they smelled funny, like burnt cream corn, even from far away. But they were friendly and helpful, especially to Grandma and Aunt Vivian.

Instead of going to Hal and Hubert's, Teddy and I went trick-or-treating at Uncle Frankie's house. Louanne gave us knitted hats and socks, and Paco gave us a box of Girl Scout Cookies to share. Uncle Frankie said he had a trick for us. "I'll flip quarters, and you call heads or tails. I'll keep doing it until you lose," he said, showing us a roll of quarters, then putting his chin up and shoulders back like he'd already won.

"Okay, why not?" I replied. I bent down, looked into Teddy's face, and explained what he had to do next.

"Tails," Teddy said, when Uncle Frankie flipped the first quarter.

Teddy called "Tails" eleven more times, and I had twelve quarters in my hand when Uncle Frankie gave up and handed me the quarter roll. "Now I'm broke. But I'll be taking Teddy to Vegas with me," he said.

Uncle Frankie was always telling Grandma he was broke. I didn't believe him, though. He'd hired Paco to work at Get Gas so he could make extra money doing a U.S. Post rural mail route. Aunt Vivian said all government jobs paid big dollars. And I knew he sold pot, because Benny and Denny Bettington, ninth graders at my school, came to the garage every Saturday morning to buy joints from him.

I WAS SURPRISED TO SEE HAL AND Hubert waiting for us in the café parking area when we returned from the beach the next day. Hal reached out to shake Dad's hand and then told him they only wanted the clamshells, not the clams, and in return, they'd clean the clams for him.

"You're gonna clean clams in return for the shells? Have at it, boys," Dad replied. When Hal and Hubert had finished, I helped Grandma serve them pancakes and fried eggs on the back porch stairs and then stayed to watch George, their peacock, chase crows down the dirt road next to Grandma's house.

Hal finished eating first, and when he stood up to leave, he shook Grandma's hand and said, "The vittles were as light as a feather and tastier than a rose." I burst out laughing. I tried not to, but I couldn't stop—not when I pinched the back of my hand or even when Grandma threw me a look that said, "Stop it." I hadn't laughed like that for months, since before Dad came home.

Later, in the café kitchen, feeling bad about laughing and upsetting Grandma, I tried to make up for it by offering to wash the pile of dishes next to the sink.

"Viv will wash them after we close, but you can take dirty dish towels to the house and start the washing machine," Grandma said.

"Sure. I'll do that," I said. "And I'm sorry about laughing. I thought Hal was joking around."

"It's okay. I forget you're not used to this place. Hal and Hubert are odd, but they're not a danger to anyone. They keep to themselves, care for injured birds and animals, and repair anything I ask them to. They've always had a peculiar way of speaking, especially Hal. I find it humorous sometimes, too, but I never laugh." Grandma reached out and ran her hands from the top of my braid to the bottom. "I sure miss having long, thick hair like yours. Not that I ever did."

"I won't laugh again. I promise," I said. "Sometimes I hear

their record player. They play old-fashioned music, like our neighbor Mrs. McDougall does," I said. Leroy was still at her house. I hoped he hadn't chewed up her shoes.

Aunt Vivian chuckled. "Once upon a time, I thought the music was from a record player, too. It's not. Hal and Hubert are pianists. And damn good ones. They play every morning and night. Lately, it's *Rhapsody in Blue*, one of my favorites."

I thought Grandma would give me a wink to let me know Aunt Vivian was teasing, but she just smiled and said, "Isn't it amazing?"

"It is," I replied and wondered if learning to play the piano was easy.

THE SUNDAY AFTER HALLOWEEN, THERE was a terrible storm. Teddy was asleep five minutes after getting into bed, but I was awake for hours listening to the rain and tree branches slam against my window. When I heard Dad in the hallway at 5:15 a.m., I was sure he'd knock on my door and say we weren't going to the beach, but I was wrong.

Dad and Mooch were the only clam diggers that morning. They dug for an hour before calling it quits and dividing up the clam haul. When we got back to the café, there were no customers, so Teddy and I got as close as we could to the wall heater. Aunt Vivian helped me take Teddy's coat and boots off while Dad went on about the glorious morning he had at the beach.

"Did you kids have a glorious morning at the beach, too?" Aunt Vivian asked in a fake, chirpy voice, glaring at Dad.

"I hated it," I said. "I still can't feel my toes or my nose."

"Don't be a bitch!" Dad said, ignoring Aunt Vivian. "Being cold never hurt anyone. Toughen up."

Dad had called me lots of names, but never a bitch. Instead of answering, I wiped my nose on my sleeve and put my chin down, and he called me a crybaby.

"Carrying smelly clam bags isn't a survival skill. Mom would never make us do it." I stuttered a little, afraid he'd throw something at me.

"Guess what? She's not here. And everything I'm teaching you is about survival. You'll thank me one day," Dad snapped. "I'm like my pa. I want my kids to be responsible, respect their parents, serve their country, and fend for themselves. He went clam digging every morning to keep his family going."

"Not after you moved out." Uncle Frankie had arrived and was pouring a cup of coffee and helping himself to one of Dad's cigarettes. "He stopped digging and started buying clams from the Meyers the day you moved out."

"Mac Meyer from Aberdeen? You sure about that?"

"From Moclips. The old man died about a year after his son John was MIA. John came home in a bag last year and had one of those fucked-up military funerals, the kind everyone is cool at because they think the kid died doing something honorable," Uncle Frankie said.

"It is an honor to die protecting your country." Dad was almost growling.

Uncle Frankie stood up. "Fucking honor, my ass!"

"Watch it!" Dad said as he folded the newspaper into a square, the way he did to kill a fly.

"You watch it, you fucking warlord!" Uncle Frankie fired back, moving toward the door.

"Frankie was never a good clam digger. Were you, Frankie?" Grandma teased from the kitchen, trying to break up the tension in the dining room.

"Nope, Ma," said Frankie, "I wasn't, but John sure was."

When Dad mumbled that POWs were reckless, Uncle Frankie made a fist right in front of Dad's face before storming out. Teddy and I didn't move an inch when Dad followed, slamming the café's double door so hard that the top panel flew back and almost hit my head.

"Hold your breath and count to ten. That's what I do when Viv upsets me," Grandma said from the grill. "Your dad hasn't always been like this."

"No, he hasn't," Aunt Vivian agreed.

"They can't help themselves," Grandma said.

"I know, I know. But it must make you mad, too. Why don't you ever tell him off?" I asked.

"I don't want mad to be the last thing I do with Gene. The war has turned him into someone I don't recognize, but he's still my son. And he's still your father. So, try a little mercy, as the song says, because you still love him." Somewhere underneath the hate, I thought I might still like Dad or maybe even love him. I knew Teddy did. I wasn't sure about Adam. But I knew Mom used to love Dad, because I'd heard her tell a woman at the voting club that the handsome and charming man she married had become somebody everyone ignored unless he stepped on their foot or blocked their way.

I disagreed. I thought Dad was hard to ignore. He had a way of making people feel uncomfortable whenever he walked into a room, like a bullfighter ready to kill.

I sat in the chair next to Teddy, watching him shuffle the deck of cards Uncle Frankie had left on the counter, braiding the bottom of my ponytail, and praying Mom would come home soon.

AFTER DAD CALLED ME A BITCH, I STOPPED complaining about going to the beach. He was still digging four limits every morning. Only now, since Grandma didn't want them, he sold them to cafés and restaurants, just like Mooch did.

By then, Teddy and I were used to being on our own after school, especially when the café was busy. Grandma had a couple of rules for us: we couldn't play by the gas pumps or be in the garage on our own. Other than that, we could play where we wanted.

That changed in November when Teddy had a tantrum on our way to the bus stop because I wouldn't let him hold the umbrella. He pulled away from me and into the path of a car driving into Get Gas. Uncle Frankie sprinted from the garage and yanked Teddy back just in time to save him. "What the fuck did you do that for?" he yelled, picking him up and shaking him.

"Stop it! You're hurting him!" I dropped the umbrella and pulled Teddy out of Uncle Frankie's grip.

Teddy put his arms around my neck and buried his face in the side of mine. "You two had better hurry or you'll miss your bus," Uncle Frankie said.

Everyone in the café dining room saw what happened and when we got home from school, Grandma was waiting for us in her living room.

"You two need to walk the other way to get to the bus stop. And I don't want you in the café when we're busy. I especially don't want Teddy hiding in here," she said with a sour face. Later, when Dad showed up an hour late for dinner, Grandma told him he needed to be home when we got home from school. "Viv and I are not available to do your job. You do it!"

Dad didn't reply. He just turned around and left the house. Then, the following day, he said he'd hire a private investigator to find Mom if she didn't show up soon.

I EXPECTED UNCLE FRANKIE TO BE ANGRY with us for at least a week, but he wasn't. He acted like he was sorry, though he never apologized for shaking Teddy. But he did give us metal plugs to play his pinball machine for free, and he invited us to come to his house the next time he cleaned it.

I hoped he'd clean it soon. I'd wanted to see the inside of his house for weeks, ever since Aunt Vivian helped me with my first English assignment, a summary of the history of bicycles and a story about my first time riding a bike.

"I could write it for you and, of course, you'd get an A, but that's not the reason you go to school," Aunt Vivian replied when I asked her to tell me what to write. "You'll find all the answers in the many encyclopedias we have around here. Frankie has a set in his house, too, but we've got a newer set in Willa's living room—the one I had to pay for after Frankie left for Vietnam without paying the bill. Don't mess up the material on the dining room table. I'm trying to make curtains for Frankie's front window. He promised he'd stop walking around in his underwear, but he's never been good at keeping promises. So, it's curtains for him." She tossed her head back and laughed.

"Is Uncle Frankie's house as small as it looks from the outside?"

"Yup, it is. Your grandpa built it to resemble his parents' house in Minnesota so they'd feel at home when they came to visit. It had shutters on the front windows then, but they fell off."

"They're on his back porch," I said.

Aunt Vivian took no notice. "The house turned out perfect, but their visit was a disaster. They died from the flu they'd caught on the train. When they passed, your grandpa emptied the house, boarded it up, and no one lived in it until Frankie got back from Vietnam."

"How come Uncle Frankie calls you Valerie sometimes, and did he really get shot in the war?"

"Frankie gets confused. The army calls it shell shock. And Valerie was a girl he dated in high school. Not as pretty as me." Aunt Vivian put her hands under her chin and tilted her head like she was a glamorous model. "And no, he didn't get shot.

He fell out of a helicopter. He was in a hospital for months after, and when he came home, he wasn't the same kid. He had a tough time remembering simple things and had such terrible nightmares that Willa and I often had to get out of bed to check on him. Once, and only once, I threw cold water on his face to wake him. He jumped up and punched me in the head, almost knocked me out. A few days later, Willa found a doctor who said Frankie wasn't crazy, just traumatized. He gave him some medicine, but Frankie continued acting crazy, and he's never returned to his old self, never been the calm, helpful kid we all knew and loved."

"Why doesn't he live in Grandma's house? There's lots of room."

"When he came home from the hospital, he had a hard time climbing the stairs, and he's too big for the couch. I recruited a few café regulars, including Fisky, to fix up the little house for him. Willa hired Hal and Hubert to build porch stairs with handrails on each side. And a friend of Fisky's brought over furniture and appliances from his deceased aunt's home. I believe Frankie still sleeps under the pink lace canopy that someone spent a lot of time making."

Talking about Uncle Frankie being too tall for Grandma's couch made me remember his time with us in Tacoma. Like me now, he was too tall for our couch, and he was twelve years old. When he finished high school, he called Mom and told her he'd joined the army and couldn't wait to get to Vietnam. Mom yelled, "No, no!" and told Uncle Frankie he was an idiot for listening to Gene. When she finished the call, she threw the phone across the room and then argued with Dad for days about him pressuring Uncle Frankie to enlist.

Eventually, Mom stopped being angry and began writing to Uncle Frankie while he was in Vietnam, sending him the occasional care package when she could. Maybe a year later, Dad called Mom from Vietnam to tell her that Uncle Frankie was in a hospital. Mom was so worried, she made Dad find a phone number so she could call him, but Uncle Frankie wasn't able to talk. So, she spoke with a nurse who assured Mom he'd survive. Months later, when they moved him to Madigan Hospital at Fort Lewis Army base, Mom took me with her to visit him. He wasn't the same Uncle Frankie I remembered. He blinked too often and too quickly, laughed about nothing, and called me "bossy Kathy."

Mom told me on the drive home that he might always get my name wrong because of how the war had changed him. When I asked if she thought the war had changed Dad, too, she said only his good parts.

CHAPTER 8

ONE SATURDAY LATE IN NOVEMBER, two weeks after Dad said he'd hire a private investigator to find Mom, and the night I discovered Uncle Frankie was using the pink lace bed canopy to cover his pinball machine, my stomach hurt. At first, I thought it was from eating the cold French fries and warm chocolate cream pie Aunt Vivian had rescued from a customer's plate. But in the middle of my second pinball game, the pain moved to my back, and I knew it was from something else.

I needed to lie down, so I unplugged the pinball machine and walked back to Grandma's house, where I met Aunt Vivian at the bottom of the staircase. She had a newspaper under her arm and her glass of tonic in her hand, and when I didn't say hi, she sang, "I dream of Evan with the dark-green hair."

I hurt too much to react.

"Why are you bent over like that?" Aunt Vivian asked.

"Something's wrong. Everything hurts. Maybe a heart attack," I said.

"Impossible. You'd be on the floor by now. I've got some Anacin in my room," she said.

I'd been living at Grandma's for three months by then, but I'd never been in Aunt Vivian's room, so I hadn't known it was full of things with wings: butterflies, moths, grasshoppers, crickets, and three stuffed owls and an eagle that hung from the place where an overhead light should have been.

"The big things are roadkill, in case you're wondering," Aunt Vivian said when she saw me looking closer at the eagle.

"They look alive," I said, my back pressed against her door.

"I knew a man back home in North Dakota who made his living stuffing dead animals and birds. I bought these from him." She took my arm and guided me over to a red wing chair.

"Here. Have a few sips of this," Aunt Vivian said, handing me her glass. "It'll make you feel better."

"What is it?" I asked.

"Just a magic tonic that cures my everythings. Anacin does, too. I know I have some somewhere." She opened the top drawer of her dresser and looked inside.

"Should I help you look?" I asked.

"No, no. You sit right there and relax. It's too dark to see now, but in the morning, I sit in that chair and talk to the firs and spruces before greeting my wall creatures," Aunt Vivian said, spreading her arms wide like she was introducing all the bugs, birds, and feathers on the walls to an audience.

I took two swallows from her glass. Through the window, I couldn't see anything except a tall metal tower in the distance, way behind Hal and Hubert's house. I'd just asked why it had a flashing red light on top, when a cramp squeezed my insides. I stayed still until it stopped, grateful it didn't get worse.

"Most of the birds are here because of Hal and Hubert," Aunt Vivian continued, ignoring my question about the tower. "You must have met their peacock, George, by now. If not, be careful. He's always looking for a mate. They also have geese, ducks, and a white swan named Dovey. And there's an eagle's nest in the big spruce behind their house. If you can't see it from your window in the morning, come back here and use my binoculars."

"From my room, I only see fir trees with drooping branches and Hal and Hubert's chimney that puffs out smoke all day and night. It smells bad." The pain in my back wasn't so bad. Maybe her tonic drink had worked its magic. I had one more sip before she took the glass away.

"I don't think your grandpa intended to build this house so close to theirs," she said. "It's good for listening to their music, not so good if smoke bothers you."

"I like the sound of the train, too," I said.

"That train is far away. You have good hearing," she said.

"I told Dad the music coming from their house was them playing the piano and not the radio like he'd said it was. He just laughed and said Polack music sounded stupid no matter who was playing it," I said.

"Gene's pretty good at putting people down. He knows they're pianists, and he knows they're not bums. They look old and tired because they used to be loggers, and it wears men out." She opened her closet door, mumbling that she must have put the Anacin in her coat pocket. "Hal and Hubert are a long story. Fisky said they were small boys when they came to the USA from Poland with their mother. They had a close relative who was a bigwig at the Steinway factory in New York, and he had their house built and then shipped two pianos here. I understand they learned English by playing American music."

"Are you my close relative?" I asked.

"Not yours. But Willa's. I'm her older sister, so that makes me your grandaunt, or the boss." She turned to me and grinned. "How's the bellyache now? I can't find my bottle of Anacin, but I'll keep looking if you still need it."

"It's not too bad now. I think your drink made it better."

"Magic!" Aunt Vivian said, patting her bed with her free hand. "Lie down here. But you still might need the Anacin when the tonic wears off."

I moved to the bed, rolled on my side, and pulled my knees to my chest as she continued searching and telling me the story of the stuffed eagle above my head.

Aunt Vivian always seemed more comfortable talking than not, and that night was no exception. "So, I suppose you know how Willa and your grandpa got this place?"

"No," I replied. "No one ever tells me anything. I just found out when we got here that Uncle Frankie isn't my real uncle."

"Frankie is as much your uncle as he is my nephew. And don't believe everything Gene says. No one else does. Anyhoo, Willa and your grandpa moved here before the war, WWII, the one you're learning about in school. Your grandpa took a job at a pulp mill in Aberdeen, and a year later, bought the gas station and café. It was the Wishkah Water Café then. Willa liked that name. Your grandpa didn't, so he changed it."

"Was this house here then too?" I asked.

"Nope. They bought the land from Hal and Hubert's mother. Your grandpa built this place with Fisky and a bit of help from Hal and Hubert, who were teenagers, and, of course, Clarence and Gene, who were just kids then," she said.

"Who's Clarence?"

"Of course. You don't know about Clarence," she replied. "I'm sure I shouldn't be the one to tell you, but now that I've said his name, you might ask Willa about him, so I'm going to tell you so that you won't ask her. He was your dad's little brother. He died in a stupid accident when he was ten. There, I've told you. Now, never mention his name."

She fished a bottle of Anacin out of the bottom drawer of her dresser. "Ah, here it is." She handed me two pills and her glass. "Swallow them with this. Just one swallow, though. You've already had too much. I can tell by your glassy eyes."

"It sure tastes good. Like licorice." I took a big swig.

"It's got orange juice with a bit of Sambuca in it," she said. "Okay, it's not a tonic. It's mostly booze. And you're not old enough to drink."

Aunt Vivian was laughing, and I was feeling well enough to walk to my room. I was about to get up when the music from Hal and Hubert's house started. I rolled onto my back to listen, and Aunt Vivian opened her window and sat down in her red chair. "It's 9:00 p.m., time for *Rhapsody in Blue*."

When the music finished, Aunt Vivian was still swaying from side to side, and I noticed the pain in my stomach was all gone. I let her help me off her bed and move me toward the door. "Go to bed. Leave your socks on, lie on your side, and put a pillow between your legs. Count sheep or ducks or whatever you want, and if the pain returns, don't think about it. Think about your toes, the big toe on your right foot, and how warm it is in the sock. If you get worse, come back, and I'll give you another Anacin. Don't knock too hard. No need to wake Willa. She needs her sleep."

"I gotta go clam digging in the morning, so I won't be able to come and look at the old eagle's nest from your window." I was marveling at the hundred or more butterflies pinned to the back of her door; I hadn't noticed them before. "Where did you get those?"

"Been collecting them since I was your age."

"I'm sorry we get in your way all the time," I said.

"I'm sorry you feel like apologizing for it."

IN THE FIRST WEEKS AT GRANDMA'S, I THINK everyone, including Dad and me, thought Mom would show up any day. Teddy and I often watched from the café table with the best view of the highway. We hoped the next car to come around the bend would be Mom's, even though she'd said she'd be coming back on a bus or a train, and even though I knew she'd never come to Grandma's house.

Then, a few days into October, Grandma told Dad he should spend more time looking for Mom and less time with Mooch. "Endura is obviously much sicker than you think she is. You'd better find her and bring her home." She was holding up the doctor's bill that Dad had mistakenly left on her couch. About the same time, Aunt Vivian began telling noisy café customers that my mom was off looking for her new knight in shining armor.

Although I thought Dad should try harder to find Mom, I couldn't say so without getting into trouble. But I got up the nerve one morning to tell Aunt Vivian my mom wasn't looking for a knight, and she shouldn't tell people she was.

"I'm just teasing. Can't you take a joke?"

When I complained to Grandma about Aunt Vivian and told her I was planning to ask her to stop calling me Too Tall, she said, "Viv has always been a teaser, and it's annoying. If you ask her to stop, it'll get worse."

I didn't know how it could. And I'd already complained so much to Uncle Frankie that he told me to shut the fuck up.

I tried. But I could never stop my face from turning red whenever Aunt Vivian threw sharp pokes, put-downs, and mean observations my way. I'd even wondered if she could see something strange about me that I couldn't. Not like Teddy's wild, curly, almost-white hair—more like something that I hadn't noticed, like a misshapen head or a giraffe neck.

Her jabs became more frequent after I confronted her about the "knight in shining armor" remarks. She even told a new customer that my ponytail would look better on a horse's ass. And yet, the same day, when the bread deliveryman arrived and asked me if I had a boyfriend, Aunt Vivian said, "You've always been a stupid shit, but I didn't know you were blind, too. Should a good-looking girl date an ugly old man?"

I was glad the delivery man laughed, because I was beet red and about to run out the door.

It wasn't the first time someone had said something like that. Many customers asked me questions, and some, primarily men, commented on the way I looked. I always responded in a smart-aleck way: I'm younger than I look, taller than I should be; my freckles could be brown M&Ms; I have to hold my ponytail up when I use the bathroom so it won't get wet.

So, I'd surprised myself when I followed Aunt Vivian into her room, and her kindness reminded me of other times when I'd been unwell and how Mom had gone to extra lengths to help me feel better, even when she was too shaky to get out of bed.

She'd relied on Adam and me more than ever after the seizure she had at my Christmas assembly the year before. It was just a month after Dad went to Vietnam for the third time, and he couldn't or wouldn't come home, so Adam quit school and moved back in. Mom was pleased about it, and not long after her third or fourth seizure, she made us learn to write like her. Adam's version of Mom's signature was perfect. Mine was just okay. I never learned to do her sweeping cursive *E*.

Knowing how to sign her name paid off like she said it would. If we hadn't taught ourselves to write like her, Dad's paychecks wouldn't have gotten deposited in the bank, and our bills wouldn't have gotten paid. We took turns signing the letters Mom typed, using a pencil to hit the keys, except for her letters to Dad—she sent them unsigned. But I didn't know this until we moved to Grandma's and I found one in the trunk of Dad's car, next to the green pillowcase containing the gun Mooch bought for him.

I wanted to know if she'd told Dad about catching me and Adam smoking, so I opened it. She hadn't. She'd only written about Teddy's new tricycle and buying new tires for her car. When I put the letter back, I saw several small, thick beige envelopes tied together with a yellow ribbon. They were from Hoi Phung Nguyen to Gene Hanson at an address I later discovered was Mooch's house. The letter on top had a postmark date of September 6, 1971, a week after we had moved in with Grandma.

I opened it, hoping to read something Mom would want to know, but the letter wasn't in English, so I put it back.

THE ANACIN HAD WORN OFF, AND IT was hard to move when I heard Dad knock on the door the next morning. I didn't get out of bed until Grandma arrived and pulled the covers off us.

"Gene's waiting. You'd better hurry. I see Teddy is in your bed again," she said with a frown. "Maybe tonight you two can try sleeping alone, huh?"

You can try all you want, I thought, *but he'll never do it.*

"Will you tell Dad I need to stay home? I don't feel well."

"Maybe you should say no the next time Vivian offers you anything half-eaten from the café," Grandma said.

A few minutes later, she was back. "I'm sorry, honey. Gene is expecting you two in the café kitchen in five minutes. You'd better get moving. He seems eager this morning."

"Okay, okay." I made my way to the bathroom, hoping the cramps would go away if I used the toilet.

Grandma had Teddy out of bed and dressed when I returned. And I felt like lying down.

"I'll be downstairs in a few minutes. I think I need to use the bathroom one more time," I said.

"Close the door this time," Grandma replied.

"I only leave it open a little, just enough so Teddy can see me. If I don't, he screams."

"Well, we don't want that. Do we, Teddy?" Grandma replied in a sweet voice, taking his hand. "Gene's gonna come upstairs soon if you don't hurry. Try to be on time today. Viv and I are counting on him to take us to bingo this morning."

I sat on the toilet for a few minutes, wondering what was wrong with me, before getting up to rinse my face with cold water, the same way I'd seen Dad do many times. I got dressed and made a quick stop at Aunt Vivian's room, hoping to get another Anacin, but when I heard snoring, I didn't knock.

"We need to be at the Eagles Hall when the doors open at 9:00 a.m. I don't want to miss claiming the front table, so don't make us late," I heard Grandma say to Dad when I opened the café's back door.

Dad made his *eee-ess* sound, the one that meant "yes," and picked up Teddy. And Grandma slid two Tootsie Pops into my coat pocket and handed me a napkin with peanut butter toast inside. "Be quick today, honey," she said.

Outside, Uncle Frankie was putting oil into his Pontiac GTO. "Jeez, you're up early," I said.

He laughed. "I'm just getting home. Nice knowing ya, kids," he said as I pulled the car door shut.

CHAPTER 9

BY THE TIME WE GOT TO THE BEACH, the pain in my stomach was almost unbearable.

"I need to use the bathroom. Right now." I was opening the car door before Dad had turned the engine off.

"They open at 6:00 a.m.," Dad said, pointing at a building twenty feet away.

"But I gotta go now."

"Go behind the building or wait here until they open. The lights will come on. Right now, I gotta get moving. Mooch is already down there getting the big ones," Dad said.

When no one showed up to open the bathrooms by 6:20, I braced myself and stepped out of the car. I knew Dad would be mad if he had to wait much longer for us to bring down empty clam bags. And since I'd already passed gas a few times, the pain in my stomach wasn't so bad. I shook Teddy awake and pulled him out of the car. Then I tied the clam bags to my belt loop, picked up the lit lantern, and dragged Teddy to the driftwood log we'd claimed after a big storm.

As I feared, Dad was waiting there for us. "What the hell took you so long?" he asked.

I ignored his question and filled the bag with clams from his bucket. "I haven't been to the bathroom yet. They still aren't open," I said.

"They are now. Someone just turned the lights on. Take your brother with you and put the clam bag in the back of my trunk, not in plain sight like you've been doing."

I tried all my usual tricks to convince Teddy to come along. I even pretended to cry, but it was no use. He wouldn't budge, and I couldn't carry him. I wrapped his Superman blanket around him and walked as close as I could to Dad without getting my feet wet. Then I swung the lantern around until he noticed me and waved. I yelled for him to watch Teddy until I got back and waited for him to nod before setting the lantern down on the log next to Teddy. I made sure his hat was on tight and gave him one of the Tootsie Pops. "I'll be back before you finish it. I promise."

In the beach bathroom, I discovered blood on my under-wear. For a few seconds, I thought I'd cut myself with the edge of a torn fingernail. But then it hit me: I'd started that thing Mom had told me about, the four-syllable word that begins with an *m*, what girls at school called "a period" or "the rag."

Suddenly, my cramps, the pimples on my chin, and even the hair growing under my arms made sense, and I wondered if there was a way to stop it.

I sat on the toilet, pushing hard, trying to get all the blood out, but it kept coming. There was plenty of toilet paper, enough to make a pad with, so I wrapped some around my hand until it resembled a catcher's mitt. Then I laid it flat in the crotch of my underwear and pulled my pants up, trying hard to keep it in place.

It was getting light out when I started back to Teddy. When I was close enough to see the lantern, I couldn't see him.

I ran to the log. Teddy wasn't on the ground, but his Superman blanket was next to the lantern, where I'd left it, only perfectly folded. I looked around, knowing Teddy wouldn't have left the blanket on purpose. My stomach turned when I noticed shoe and footprints close to the log and a trail of them going toward cars parked on the beach. Several had arrived while I was away.

I looked in the windows of the cars and asked people if they'd please check their back seats for my brother. Then I ran to the shoreline, where Dad was digging, thinking Teddy might have wandered out looking for him. I could see clam diggers, including Dad and Mooch, but no one the size of Teddy. Dad was watching the waves wash over his ankles, waiting for them to recede so he could pitch his shovel down on the far side of a clam hole. Then I remembered that he had asked me if Teddy had been to the bathroom that morning, and Teddy had shaken his head.

I headed back to the parking lot bathrooms, only to find Wally in his patrol car. My heart sank when he honked and waved me over. I didn't want Wally to know I was looking for Teddy. He might not be as nice about it as he had been on our tenth morning at the beach, when Dad broke his clam shovel and told me to get another from his trunk. I hadn't looked behind me when I walked to his car to get it. I had just assumed Teddy was close behind until I noticed he wasn't.

Wally had organized a search party, and Dad and I were on edge until the police found Teddy. He'd gotten into the back seat of a car identical to ours and fallen asleep. The car owner, Mr. Wynkoop, found him.

When we had reached Mr. Wynkoop's house, thirty miles from Ocean Shores, Dad didn't turn the engine off; he just got out and headed for the front door. Then he knocked so hard the entire front porch moved. I turned the key and followed Dad. When an old man opened the front door, Dad shook his hand. "Sir, I'm sorry for the trouble. His sister should have been watching him."

"I hope she's learned her lesson." Mr. Wynkoop handed Dad a gun. "Your kid pointed this at me when I woke him up. It's not loaded, but that's not the point."

When we got back to the car, Dad grabbed Teddy's leg, just above his knee, and squeezed hard. Teddy screamed.

"Why, Teddy? Why didn't you stay with Evan? And who said you could play with my gun? And you, missy? If you hadn't opened the glove compartment this morning, he wouldn't have seen it." Dad slid the gun under his seat, and I heard him mumble, "I'd better get rid of it."

"Teddy knew it was there before today," I said. "We both knew about it. We also know about your new gun, the one in the trunk, wrapped in one of Mom's best pillowcases. And you shouldn't let Teddy watch *The Rifleman* with you. That's where he got the idea to point a gun at that man—I'm sure of it."

Dad said I had big ears and a smart mouth, but he didn't smack my leg like I expected him to. He just lit a cigar from the one he'd been smoking, threw the old one out the window, and sped up and passed three cars.

When we got back to Eat and Get Gas, Dad took his old gun to the garage and told Uncle Frankie to sell it to one of his poker friends. And he told me to keep quiet about what had happened at the beach that morning.

I'd crossed my heart and promised Dad I'd never lose Teddy again. Now, just two months later, it was happening all over again but worse.

I ignored Wally's horn honking until he got out of his patrol car and started walking toward me. "Hello there, young lady. What are you doing?"

"Looking for Teddy."

"Is that a joke? 'Cause it's 6:58 a.m., and there are no jokes allowed on my beach until after 7:00," Wally said.

"No," I said, blinking tears away.

"Oh, come on. Don't cry. I'm teasing."

Wally told me to check the cars in the parking lot first and then the beach. I agreed because cars were still arriving.

"If you don't find him, wave to me. I'll be up on the highway looking around," Wally said.

When I reported back, Wally said, "Just keep looking and ask people if they've seen him."

So, I stood at the start of the sandy path that went from the bathrooms to the beach and asked people going by if they'd seen a little boy who looked about five, with light curly hair.

"I HAVEN'T FOUND ONE SIGN OF YOUR brother," Wally said as I approached.

"I haven't either." I felt my stomach cramp for the first time since I used the bathroom. I sat down on the side of the highway and cried.

"It'll be okay. We'll find him. But it's time to tell Gene, and you'd better do it on your own. After all these years, he still doesn't like me," Wally said.

It took a lot of yelling and arm waving to get Dad's attention and more waving to get him to walk to me.

"Teddy's gone," I said when he was close enough to hear. "I left him alone when I went to the bathroom—remember? I came out here and told you to watch him. You nodded your head."

"I got distracted. Did you look in the men's bathroom? What about those cars over there? Are there any other gold Impalas?"

"No, I checked. And I've looked everywhere. So did Wally."

"Good ole Wally, huh? Well, my guess is Teddy is off feeding my clams to seagulls like you do. Or maybe he saw a friend from school." Dad looked into my face.

"Teddy doesn't have friends. And he'd never leave this," I replied, holding up his Superman blanket.

I stepped closer until my shoulder was almost touching Dad's. He was shivering, and I could smell the salty, fishy sea on his skin. I wanted him to tell me what to do, but he just held Teddy's blanket and stared at the incoming waves. When my teeth started chattering, and I couldn't feel my feet, I asked if I could take his clam bucket to the car and get him a towel so he could help look for Teddy.

"Nope. I don't need a towel. I'm almost done here." Dad handed me Teddy's blanket, then ran the back of his hand over his mouth before reaching for the two empty clam bags still hanging from my belt loop.

"Dad! Aren't you gonna help me look for Teddy?"

"Have a look down the beach, around those stacks of driftwood, where we saw the boys throwing sticks at each other last week or last month." Dad turned away and headed back to where Mooch stood out in the water. He said something that I didn't catch. "What? What did you say?" I shouted.

But Dad was already too far away and didn't hear me.

There were boys at the driftwood pile, but none of them had seen Teddy, and I couldn't see him either. I ran to Wally's car, then bent over to catch my breath.

"Dad said he was about done digging," I said.

"What a jerk," Wally replied. "I'm calling for help, and I'm closing the parking lot. I'll get my flashlight and check the back seats of cars leaving."

DAD AND MOOCH ARRIVED AT THE PARKING lot with two full buckets fifteen minutes later. I could see Dad's bewildered expression from the open bathroom door, where I'd just been changing my toilet paper pad.

"Teddy hasn't shown up," I said.

When I got close, Dad grabbed my arm. "I said if you didn't find him to come back and tell me. I yelled it, for Christ's sake. Are you deaf, too?"

"I didn't hear you. I really didn't."

When Wally approached Dad's car, he glanced at the clam buckets. Dad said they belonged to Mooch, but I could tell Wally didn't believe him.

Behind his car, surfer-style, Dad changed from his swimming trunks into his worn-out, brown corduroy pants. He took his new gun out of the pillowcase and slid it into his front pocket, grabbed a sweatshirt, lit a cigar, and joined Mooch at Wally's patrol car.

"So what's the plan?" Dad asked Wally.

I knew if anyone could find Teddy, it was Dad. He once found soldiers who'd been in an underground hole for months.

"It's 7:45 a.m. Your kid has been missing, I'm guessing, for an hour. I've already called for help," Wally said.

Then, just when it started to pour, a state patrol car arrived and parked in front of Dad's car. Two men got out, and one asked how long it had been since anyone had seen Teddy, then used the car radio while the other questioned Dad, Wally, and Mooch. When he heard my teeth chattering, he went to his car and returned with a black Washington State Patrol jacket for me to wear. As the wind picked up, Dad made me get into our car. He started the engine, turned the heater to full, and told me to stay put and not mention his gun. "It's not exactly legal," he said.

Then I heard Mooch yell, "If he's in the water, we've only got a few more minutes!"

I got out of the car and began sprinting toward the shore. When Dad caught up with me, he grabbed my arm. "Get back to the car. Teddy's gonna be wet and cold when we find him, or when he finds the car. He'll need you."

Thirty minutes later, when the parking lot was almost empty, Wally approached our car with a policeman I hadn't seen before. "This is the sheriff. He'd like you to show him exactly where you left your brother."

It was after 8:00 a.m. and light enough to see shoe and footprints around the log. "Are any of these yours?" the sheriff asked.

"I don't know—probably." I put my foot next to one. "This one is. And some others are, too. The small ones could be Teddy's."

"What about you?" he asked Dad, who had joined us, along with Mooch and the two state patrolmen.

"I've been barefoot all morning. Mooch has, too," Dad replied.

The shoe and footprints were close to disappearing with the incoming tide, so the sheriff asked Wally to use his foot to measure them while there was still time.

Wally stood next to one of the larger prints. "Someone who wears a size eleven shoe was here."

"Why are we looking at shoe prints instead of looking for Teddy? As far as I know, no one's ever stolen a kid from this beach. It's more likely my boy wandered off," Dad said.

"It's not the first time a kid has disappeared from here. All but one showed up, though," the sheriff replied.

Back at our car, he stood in front of Dad. "I'd like to see your shoes, and my deputies are going to search your car."

"Sure, why not?" Dad replied.

The sheriff continued asking questions: "How old is your boy? When did you last see him? Can he swim? What's he wearing? How far can he walk? Just a guess will do."

Dad answered in his matter-of-fact soldier voice. "I haven't seen my boy for at least an hour. He's six, or maybe seven, and a decent swimmer. He could probably walk a mile, and he's wearing a warm coat. His sister can tell you if he knows his name. Yes or no, Evan? Answer the man."

I glared at Dad. "My brother knows his name," I said, "but he can't walk a mile, and he doesn't know how to swim. He'd never go into the ocean, and he's wearing Superman pajama bottoms under his pants. Oh, and he's a little deaf."

"So, what happened here?" The sheriff turned to me, and I told him everything.

"Could your brother have asked a stranger to take him to the bathroom?" The sheriff stepped closer, as if he knew he should have been talking to me all along.

"Maybe. Last week, he asked a customer at my grandma's café to take him to see the gorilla at the B&I store in Tacoma. It could be the person who folded his Superman blanket and left it next to the lantern."

"Maybe you stay here with us, Mr. Hanson," said the sheriff. "Wally can take your girl home. She's cold and wet, and there's nothing more she can do here."

"I can't show up at Grandma's in a police car. She'll be mad," I said.

"Not as mad as she'll be when I'm not home in twenty minutes to take her to bingo." Dad's hand was on my back, and he was edging me closer to Wally's car. "Do not say one word about Teddy to Ma. She's gonna be mad about missing bingo. Don't make it worse by telling her you lost Teddy."

"I didn't lose Teddy. We did!" Tears were falling faster than I could wipe them away. "And what am I supposed to say about being in a cop car?"

"If she asks, tell her you got a ride home with Wally because you don't feel well. It's the truth, isn't it? It's the reason you left Teddy alone. Right?"

"Yeah, but you agreed to watch him. You know you did," I sobbed.

"So, I didn't," he said.

CHAPTER 10

WHEN WALLY ROUNDED THE CORNER to Eat and Get Gas, I spotted the CLOSED sign in the café's window and exhaled. Uncle Frankie must have taken Grandma and Aunt Vivian to bingo. Or maybe he fixed the Studebaker and Aunt Vivian drove. I didn't care either way.

Get Gas was open, though, and I could see Paco washing a customer's windshield while Uncle Frankie pumped their gas. "What the hell are you doing in a cop car?" he asked when Wally parked.

When I explained as best I could, Uncle Frankie stepped forward and took my hand. "Hey, hey, stop crying. Look at me. Teddy's not missing, and he's not dead," he whispered.

"How do you know?" I whispered back.

Before he could answer, Wally said he had to get back to the beach, and he needed to take the state patrolman's jacket back with him.

"Hey, Wally, that kid's always doing things he's not supposed to. Don't worry. He'll turn up," Uncle Frankie said.

"I hope you're right," Wally said, looking up at the sky. "This sprinkle, it's the start of a storm predicted to last for days. That boy's too small to be out in this weather."

The second Wally's front tires hit the highway, Paco turned to Uncle Frankie and said, "Fuck, man, you almost blew it!"

"I know, I know!" Uncle Frankie slumped against the garage wall. "I shouldn't have smoked so much this morning. I can't think straight. Guess it's why they call it dope."

I DIDN'T WANT TO KNOW. I HEADED TO his house, hoping Louanne was there and would have the pads I needed.

"Hold on," Uncle Frankie called out. "Where are you going?"

"I need to talk to Louanne. It's private," I said.

"She doesn't know we smoke pot, so keep your mouth shut. And she's got nothing to do with your mom taking Teddy," he said.

I stopped.

"Oh, fuck, what the hell!" Uncle Frankie said. "It's no use keeping the secret now. Your mom's been planning it for weeks. She wanted to get to the beach early, when it was still dark, so Gene wouldn't see her. You two should be with her, not here. Willa's too old, Vivian's a busybody, and your dad's a savage."

I turned and followed Uncle Frankie into the garage, finding the warmest spot by the wall heater. "Mom came all the way here and took Teddy but not me?"

"Yup, looks that way," Uncle Frankie replied.

"She must have come for me, too, right?"

"Sure, she did. And she'll come back to get you when the coast is clear. But in the meantime, be happy Teddy is there and not here. You're his sister, not his mother, and you shouldn't be his minder. I've heard Willa say it lots of times. Hell, I bet when Gene finds out, he'll buy me a beer."

I shook my head. "I doubt it. He hates you."

"Mutual, mutual," Uncle Frankie said.

The heater was burning the back of my legs, so I moved forward. "Mom wouldn't have come from Canada just to get Teddy, right?"

"Like I said, she came for both of you. I met her and her cousin's son, Mike, at the Rollarena parking lot last night. They planned to get you two from the beach, stop at your house to get your mutt, and be at the Canadian border around noon. I gave them a bunch of your stuff—things I found around Willa's house," Uncle Frankie said.

"So, she's at our house now? Can I call her and tell her to wait for me? Will you take me?"

"If they left Ocean Shores at 7:15 or even 7:30, they would have made it to your house more than an hour ago. They could still be there, I suppose. If we leave now, and you don't complain about my driving, I can get you there in forty minutes." Uncle Frankie was sounding excited as he guided me toward the phone on the wall.

I tried to get some privacy, but the phone cord was too short for me to move more than a couple of feet away from them, so I pressed my body to the wall and rested my forehead on an exposed beam. I let the phone ring thirty times. "Can't you just take me to her?" I asked.

Uncle Frankie replaced the receiver. "If I knew where they were going, I'd say let's hit the road and catch up to them, but I don't even know the border crossing they're using. I asked a few times, but your mom wouldn't say. She thought Gene would beat it out of me. Unbelievable, seeing as he's so much shorter than me, but she insisted he could. Don't worry. I'll find out where they are and get you to Canada. I've taken a few friends of friends across the border. I can do it for you, too."

"It's the truth—he has," Paco said in a low whisper and patted me on the shoulder.

"How about I drive you to Tacoma anyway and buy you a

coat and a pair of sneakers at the big new mall they just built?"
Uncle Frankie asked.

"I don't need a coat. Grandma just gave me one a customer
left behind."

"I gave it to your mom last night. And I gave her your
sneakers and everything I found on top of the clothes dryer.
Also, the workbook that was on the bed in Gene's old room.
It looked important, so I grabbed it."

"It is important. But only to me." I was feeling dizzy.

The thought of Mom having my English workbook made
me want to scream. Instead of following my teacher's instructions
to write about my first time on a bike, I'd written a story about
a telephone operator who leaves her children with the Riffraff
family. It wasn't about Mom, but if she read it, she'd think it was.

"I can't believe you gave her my workbook. Now she's
gonna hate me!" I yelled. "And all my stuff—my shoes and
clothes. Does Mom have everything? What am I supposed
to wear?"

"Sorry, kid. I was just trying to help."

I wanted to run away, but I didn't have anywhere to go,
and it felt like my toilet paper pad was leaking.

Since Halloween, Louanne and I had been waving to each
other, and I had a feeling she liked me. I also thought she was
the safest person to ask for help.

I knocked three times, but there was no answer. Uncle
Frankie came up and put his hand over the doorknob. "You'd
better not snitch on me for smoking pot. She thinks I roll my
own cigarettes—don't tell her it's pot."

"I told you—I don't care, and I'm no snitch. I just want
to ask Louanne a girl question," I said.

"Oh, yeah. Okay. But hold on for a second. Before I take
you to her room, I wanna talk to you, because I don't want
you going around saying stuff that ain't true, especially to
Willa." He pointed to the bench on his porch.

"I'm okay standing," I said.

"Me, too." Uncle Frankie lit a cigarette. "Your mom called the garage a couple of weeks after she left for Canada with Adam. She'd been calling your house and not getting an answer and wanted me to drive to Tacoma to check on you. I told her Gene had brought you and Teddy here because you had the mumps. She seemed upset at first but sounded relieved when I told her you'd both recovered."

"So, Mom is just hiding from Dad?"

"That's right," he said.

"Why did she wait so long to call you?"

"She fainted or something when she got to Canada and had to go to the hospital, and I guess she's been sick ever since. She made me promise not to tell anyone, not even you. She was afraid Gene would find out and turn Adam in. Then two weeks ago, she called me again and said her cousin's son had volunteered to drive her here. She wanted to get you and Teddy before it started snowing there, while the roads were still clear."

"How'd she'd know where we'd be?"

"I told her you two went to the beach every morning with Gene and how you complained about having to stand around in the wind and rain. Let me tell you, she had a few choice words to say about that. They got to the beach this morning before you did. What I can't figure out is why you're here, and Teddy's not," Uncle Frankie said.

I wasn't about to tell him I'd started my period, so I told him I took a bag of clams to Dad's car to hide in the trunk and then used the parking lot bathroom. "I guess I was away for a long time, and she couldn't wait."

"More likely, she was scared Gene would see her. Or maybe she fell and needed medical attention. She didn't look very stable last night—she couldn't get back into the car without Mike's help. Anyway, Teddy's safe now."

Uncle Frankie walked me to Louanne's door and knocked once before opening it. "You have a visitor," he announced.

Louanne was sitting up in bed, writing in a book that she hid under a pillow when she saw us. She looked surprised to see me but not in a good way. I almost turned back, but then Uncle Frankie blurted out something about me needing a few minutes of girl talk and quickly shut the door behind him.

Louanne broke the silence. "It's okay if you don't have time to take Velvet outside this afternoon." Velvet was her flop-eared rabbit.

"It's not that," I replied. "It's just that I started my period, and I don't have the pads for it." I looked away so she couldn't see my red face.

"Oh, of course. You're that age." Louanne adjusted her eye patch, pulling her hat down to cover it. "Don't be afraid. It's not the worst thing, and it only lasts for a few days. Does it hurt? I can give you one of my pills, though it might be too strong for you. I know there's aspirin in the café kitchen cupboard."

"I just need the pads right now. I can't remember what they're called. Mom bought me some, but they're in our bathroom at home," I replied.

"I don't have any Kotex, if that's what you mean. I don't have periods. But I have a few washcloths you can have. You can cut them up," Louanne said.

"There are lots of those in Grandma's bathroom," I said.

"I'm taking the bus to the library tomorrow. You can come along and go to the drugstore. It's just across the street from the library. The cashier is helpful—she'll know what you need."

"I have an important history test in the morning," I said. I'd hidden my box of Kotex in the back of the bathroom cupboard with the list of Mom's four instructions about periods. I'd read it many times. But, just then, in Louanne's room, asking her for help, I couldn't remember even one.

"Don't worry," she said. "I'll get them. I have a friend who rides the bus on Mondays, and he'll come with me. He's a doctor," she said in a cheerful voice I hadn't heard before.

"That would be great, really great. Thanks. I have money in my bedroom. I'll bring it over."

"Thank you. I'm low on funds, unfortunately. It's costly living here with my brother," she said.

"I'm sorry we barged in. I didn't know who else to ask. My dad wouldn't want to know, and I'm not sure about Grandma. Aunt Vivian would help, but she'd tease me, too."

"I never tease. It's the evilest thing in the world, worse than murder!" Louanne spoke quickly, her usual girlish voice suddenly lower, like a dog growl. "Are you as cold as you look?" she asked.

"Yeah, I am." Then I told her what had happened.

"Oh, no, no, don't cry. It'll be okay. Your mom will come back to get you," Louanne said with a forced smile. Before I could reply, she continued, "I have something that will keep you warm."

She got out of bed and went to her closet. For a second, I thought she might fall over as she moved things out of the way to pull a crocheted poncho, with different colored squares, off a hanger.

"Here, it's yours. Now don't cry."

The poncho was the orange, pink, and navy blue one she'd worn in the café the week before. I loved it. It was beautiful and warm, and when I stood up so she could show me how to wear it, I almost leaned into her. I hugged the softness close to my body, fighting back the tears.

"How did you learn to knit and crochet? And why do you go to the library all the time?"

"So many questions." She was smiling so big that her face turned into Popeye's face. I had to look away and pinch my wrist hard to keep from laughing.

"I knitted the curtains with leftover yarn my Aunt Bethania and I used to make baby clothes for ladies at our church. My aunt taught me to knit, crochet, and sew. And I go to the library because there aren't any books around here, and I like to read. Do you?"

"Yes. And so does my mom. We have lots of books at our house, and Mom used to read to us before her hands started shaking. Teddy's favorite book is *The Wind in the Willows*. He likes Mole the best, and I like Toad. My mom likes Betty MacDonald's books. Have you read those?" I asked.

Louanne said she didn't know who Betty MacDonald was, so I told her—and that Mom met her at a bookstore and they became friends. Christmas-card friends, Mom would say.

"We have signed copies of all her books, and before Mom got so sick, she used to read out loud from one while we ate breakfast, so we'd have a Betty kind of day."

"What's a Betty kind of day?" Louanne asked.

"It's a day when something interesting or funny happens. Maybe the library has her books. *The Egg and I* is my favorite," I said and then waited for her to finish writing it down before telling her I needed to take a bath, find some dry clothes, and think of a way to tell my dad, without him going crazy, that Mom took Teddy from the beach.

"I'll be sure to lock my door when you leave, and you'd better lock yours too," Louanne replied.

BACK AT GRANDMA'S HOUSE, I USED her shampoo to make a bubble bath. Then I opened the medicine cabinet and found a bottle of aspirin. I took one before I undid my braid and got undressed. The toilet paper pad was soaked with blood. So was the crotch of my pants. It made me queasy, and once again, I sat on the toilet and tried to push it all out. That's when the thought came that having a bath isn't allowed when you had a period.

I took my chances and stepped into the hot bathwater, hoping the water didn't turn pink when I sat down. If it did, I planned to get out and have a sponge bath, but it was okay. I exhaled and slid under, staying until my hair was wet enough to wash. I imagined Mom, Teddy, and Leroy snuggled up in the back seat of her cousin's car, happy to be together and on their way to a beautiful Canadian ranch with horses, cows, and a house big enough to be a church.

The hot water made me tired, but I couldn't stop thinking about Mom and why she hadn't looked in the beach bathroom for me. I wondered if Teddy was crying when she found him, and if she noticed his clothes were dirty and that I hadn't brushed his teeth. If Uncle Frankie had just told me Mom would be at the beach waiting for us, I would have washed Teddy's face and dressed him better. I would have brought his ear drops and his good shoes, and there was no way I would have left him alone.

I moved the bathtub taps with my toes, wondering why I'd been so lazy lately, especially with Teddy. Maybe it was because my period had been coming. I'd heard girls at school talk about being on the rag and hating everything and everyone. So maybe that's what was happening to me, too. I didn't hate Teddy, but he'd been more demanding than usual in the past weeks, even insisting that I watch TV with him after school instead of doing my homework. Now I was so far behind that I knew I'd flunk history and geography if I didn't study harder.

I topped up the bath with more hot water before sliding under again, this time staying until I couldn't hold my breath any longer. Then I poured shampoo into my right palm and rubbed my hands together. I put them flat on my head and rubbed back and forth with my fingertips like Mom always did.

I should have washed Teddy's hair the same way last night. If I hadn't been in such a hurry to play pinball in the garage, maybe I would have. Instead, I rubbed Teddy's head with a slimy bar of soap. When it got in his eyes, I poured warm water over his face until he stopped crying. Then I put his dirty pj's on him and sat him on the couch next to Dad, acting like I didn't hear him chanting my name when I left for the garage.

I was kind of glad Teddy was with Mom. She'd make sure he ate vegetables and brushed his teeth. And she wouldn't let him watch TV all the time like Dad did or care if he kicked the covers off at night like I did.

Maybe it's not that bad, I thought. With Teddy gone, I'd be able to spread out in bed and use the bathroom without him sitting outside the door, whining for me. And I'd get my homework done on time, and maybe everyone around Grandma's would like me better.

CHAPTER 11

I PUT ON THE ONLY CLEAN CLOTHES I COULD find, but not the poncho Louanne had given me, because I didn't want Dad to see it. Instead, I wore the high-school letterman jacket I found in the back of his closet. "It looks better on you than it ever did on Gene!" Uncle Frankie called out as I approached the garage.

Paco took a break from changing a car tire to get me a Coke, which Uncle Frankie opened with his teeth.

"Hey, you know what tastes better with a Coke? A Marlboro, that's what."

Instead of saying no as I'd done before, I took the cigarette he held out.

"Jeez, it only took you three months to come around to the joys of smoking." He threw a book of matches my way.

"Yeah, it's also been that long since I've seen my mom, Adam, and my dog." I replied, turning toward the garage wall so I could wipe away tears without him seeing. I stuck my unlit cigarette behind my left ear and put a slug coin in the pinball machine. Maybe I should ask Uncle Frankie to drive me home right then, before Dad came back. Maybe Mom was still there.

A truck arrived before I could ask, and Uncle Frankie left the garage to pump their gas. So, I started another game, almost tilting the machine when I thought of Mom opening my workbook and reading my story. It made my head spin in the same way it had the time she caught Adam and me trying to smoke a cigar we'd found in one of Dad's old suitcases. This time, though, I wanted to scream as well because I'd mimicked Mom's scratchy handwriting, and I knew if she saw it, it would hurt her feelings.

"KNOCK IT OFF!" UNCLE FRANKIE YELLED when he came back and saw me shoving my hips into the pinball machine. "And stop worrying. I can feel it from across the room. Willa and Vivian will probably be happy you didn't go to Canada. They like having you around. They say you're good with a broom." He winked at me twice before opening the cover of his hi-fi. When the needle dropped and "California Dreamin'" filled the room, I almost smiled.

What about Louanne? Would she be happy? When I'd asked Uncle Frankie what had happened to her face, he told me she was the only survivor of a car crash that killed the rest of his family. "The crash wasn't Louanne's fault—she was a passenger. Our mother was driving, and she either didn't see the logging truck or the car slipped on ice. Louanne was pretty messed up—still is. I'm just glad I was young when it happened. I think I'd drink myself to death if it happened now."

That seemed like a real possibility. Uncle Frankie drank a lot, at least a six-pack a day, sometimes two. The first time I saw Louanne walking with him, I thought she did, too. But Grandma said Louanne didn't drink, that her aunt was very religious and forbade it. I felt better about being around her from then on. I even began wandering into the café kitchen when she was working. I just wanted to see what she was wearing. According to *Seventeen* magazine, she had a dress style known as bohemian.

She wore something cool every day. I especially liked her bell-bottomed jeans, paisley blouses, and colorful headscarves. Most of these were large enough to keep her wavy reddish-brown hair back and hide her eye patch and the jagged scar around it. Only a veil would have hidden the zigzag scar that went from the patch to the top of her lip.

The same week I started school in Hoquiam, I found out she had a man friend who was as old as Grandma. He was sitting next to her on the bus the day my geography class took the same bus to the Aberdeen library. I pretended not to see them and took a seat in front so they wouldn't see me. When my new friend Marie asked if I knew the woman who'd waved to me, I said, "No way."

Three stops later, the man paused just behind my seat on his way to get off the bus, and I froze. I didn't look up, because I thought he was going to tell me off for ignoring Louanne. But he just stood there long enough for me to feel ashamed of myself.

The next time I saw Louanne, she was on Grandma's front lawn with her floppy-eared rabbit, Velvet. Teddy and I fed Velvet a few blades of grass that day, but that's all. Then, a week before Mom took Teddy from the beach; I got to hold and play with Velvet on my own when Dad and Teddy took Grandma and Aunt Vivian to bingo. Aunt Vivian had been telling café customers all week she'd discovered a foolproof way to win, and Dad wanted to see it for himself. It had something to do with playing twenty cards at one time. Grandma laughed when she first heard about it. "This I gotta see," she said.

Grandma and Aunt Vivian played bingo at the Eagles Hall every Monday at 6:00 p.m. and sometimes on Tuesdays. Aunt Vivian was luckier than Grandma. She always won, occasionally a money jackpot, but mostly food and stuff to use in the bathroom: bags of flour and sugar, cases of Ultra Brite toothpaste and Camay soap, cans of Empress raspberry jam and Elberta sliced peaches, jars of Adams peanut butter, and just two weeks after we moved to Grandma's, a barrel of Nalley dill pickles. Aunt Vivian said it was the biggest prize she'd ever won. Grandma had won something good that day too—a green, Chinese-style ceramic teapot with two cups. I remember them well because I wanted them. Instead, she gave them to Hal and Hubert when they brought her a basket full of fresh eggs and herbs. They often left stuff on the café's back porch stairs, but apparently this was the first time they'd ever received something in return, other than a meal.

I stood under The Three Sisters with Aunt Vivian and Grandma as Hal and Hubert walked down the middle of the gravel road toward their house. Hal was in front with the teapot in his left hand and a cup in his right, and Hubert was several steps behind, holding the other cup with both hands. Aunt Vivian slapped her leg, and Grandma covered her mouth with her hand. "They think we've given them expensive china," she whispered.

The following day, when we arrived back from clam digging, I saw Hal and Hubert put two baskets on the café's back porch, then sit down on the stairs. Dad rolled his eyes and grunted when he saw them, but Grandma appeared just then with two bowls of clam chowder and a few packets of soda crackers on a tray.

Dad gave Grandma a dirty look, then snapped at me to untangle the hose and meet him at the car. On his way to the kitchen to get a pot of hot water to pour into the clam bucket, I saw him purposely bump into Hal.

Dad said a lot of mean things about Hal and Hubert as we cut clams from their shells that morning—more mean things than I'd ever heard him say about anyone. And I know they heard him because I saw them sneak away.

An hour later, when we'd finished cleaning the clams and were taking them to the café freezer, Grandma stopped us at the back door. Without taking her eyes off Dad, she told me to go to the house.

I was behind Dad when she said, "The last time I looked, Gene, you weren't in charge of me or this place. You don't get a say about who I feed."

Dad put his hand up like he was in school and started talking. "If anyone should have signed up to fight for the land of the free, it's those two."

"Where is my nice Gene? What happened to him? When did he decide every man should be in Vietnam—even his precious boy Adam?"

Dad's hand went up again, only this time, Grandma grabbed it and held it tight. "You're on the wrong side of right. If Pa were alive, he'd say so, too."

CHAPTER 12

UNCLE FRANKIE RESET THE PINBALL MACHINE. "Don't tilt it again," he said. "I'll show you how to smoke that cigarette now."

"No, thanks."

"I thought you'd want to smoke now that Teddy's gone." He gave me a smart-ass grin.

"I might be gone soon, too."

"Yeah, yeah. Until then, you're free as a bird. With Teddy gone, you might get to school on time, make more friends, eat dinner in peace, and maybe learn to skate like the roller-derby star you like so much." Uncle Frankie took the cigarette from behind my ear.

Free as a bird. *Maybe I'll do the things Uncle Frankie said. Or maybe I'll just sit on the café's porch bench until Mom comes to get me.*

"Are you sure Grandma and Aunt Vivian won't be mad that I'm still here?" I asked.

"Sure, I'm sure," Uncle Frankie replied.

But I wasn't convinced, especially about Aunt Vivian. Still, she made our breakfasts, packed our lunches, helped me with my homework, and did our laundry. And if I didn't let myself get rattled when she teased me, she could be a lot of fun. "Viv is moody like our father," Grandma had told me. "Nice as pie one second, a screeching owl the next."

IT WASN'T LONG BEFORE NOON WHEN I heard Paco yell, "Here he comes!"

Dad pulled up in front of the garage doors. I could see he was soaking wet and mad as hell. "What did you tell them?" he shouted.

Before I could answer, Uncle Frankie rushed over. "She didn't tell me jack shit. Endura has him. She was at the beach when you got there. She took Teddy without you seeing. So much for your fine soldier skills." His fists were clenched.

"What the hell? Endura was at the beach?" Dad asked.

"Sure as hell was."

That's when Dad punched Uncle Frankie in the face twice. Blood flew from his nose, and he wiped it with the back of his hand before he swung hard, landing a punch right on Dad's mouth and splitting his lip open.

When Dad lost his balance and stumbled back, Uncle Frankie jumped in his car, locked the door, and revved the engine. Then he rolled down his window and flipped Dad the bird with the hand that still had a middle finger. "Hey, Gene, I'm off to pick up your mommy from bingo and maybe buy a baseball bat."

Dad picked up a rock and threw it, missing Uncle Frankie's car by a long shot. Then he grabbed my upper arms. "What do you know about this? And you'd better not say you were in on it."

I tried to wriggle away. "You're hurting me. You're getting blood everywhere. I didn't know about Mom until Wally brought me home, I promise."

"Why the hell didn't Wally tell me when he got back to the beach?" Dad asked.

"Uncle Frankie didn't tell him. He said Mom needed more time to get across the border." I jerked my right arm from his grip.

Just then, I spotted Paco and Louanne on Uncle Frankie's front porch. Paco was smoking, and Louanne was standing with her arms crossed over her chest. When she saw me look her way, she waved and said, "Are you okay there?"

"I don't know," I replied.

Dad let go of me then, and I used the moment to take several giant steps backward, out of his reach.

"Who the hell said you could wear my jacket?" It now had blood on the front and sleeves.

"My coat's wet from the beach, and I have nothing else to wear. Uncle Frankie gave it all to Mom last night." I burst into tears. "She was gonna take me, too!"

Dad punched the palm of his left hand with his right fist over and over while muttering that Uncle Frankie had plotted with Mom to keep him from going back to Vietnam. "That fucking bitch. That's why you're still here. She left you on purpose, thinking it would stop me. You'd think she'd know me by now."

"Mom would never stop you from leaving. I'm sure of it," I said.

Still sobbing, I turned and ran to Grandma's, up the stairs to my room, sliding the dresser against the door once I shut it. My heart was going a hundred miles per hour, and when I heard Dad downstairs throwing things around Grandma's living room, I crawled under the bed and hugged the wall.

I'd only been there for a few minutes when I heard Uncle Frankie's car outside. I tiptoed to the top of the stairs and sat down to listen. Dad was just finishing a phone call when Aunt Vivian opened the front door. I only caught the end. "Sir, I realize it took a lot of man-hours to search for my boy. I did not know until recently his mother had taken him. I apologize."

Grandma was through the door by then, with Aunt Vivian right behind, carrying two bags of bingo winnings.

"Viv's the big winner this year!" Grandma shouted.

"I suppose Frankie told you Endura took Teddy?" Dad interrupted.

"He did. And we don't need to hear it again from you. Teddy is where he should be. Be thankful for once. She did you a big favor," Grandma replied.

"Hey, Gene, don't you have a clam to clean?" Aunt Vivian said, snickering.

Dad slammed the door on his way out.

Then Grandma and Aunt Vivian were knocking on my bedroom door asking me what had happened. They already knew Mom had taken Teddy, so I let them in and filled in the blanks. I also told them about starting my period and how painful it was.

"Ah, I knew your gut ache last night wasn't from eating the leftover pie. You would've thrown up in my room if it had been," Aunt Vivian said.

Grandma grabbed my hand. "You don't need to worry about Teddy. He's safe and happy with Endura. You shouldn't have been the one in charge of him. That was Gene's responsibility. I'm sorry he didn't see it that way. Viv will go to the store tomorrow and buy the things you need."

"That's okay. Louanne said she'd buy me some Kotex," I replied.

"Louanne? You told Louanne?" Grandma looked puzzled.

"I asked her for Kotex, because I thought she might have some in her room," I said.

"That makes sense. We're too old for Kotex." Grandma grinned.

Aunt Vivian put her hands in the prayer position, looked up and said, "Yup. Those days are long gone. Thank you, Jesus."

"What about Dad? I don't want him to find out."

"Men don't wanna know these things. It makes their gonads shrivel." Aunt Vivian slapped her leg and laughed, throwing her head back.

I laughed, too, even though I didn't know what a gonad was.

The next day after school, I found a paper bag on Grandma's front porch with my name on it. Inside was a box of Kotex and an elastic belt thing to hold them in place. There was also a navy blue-and-orange crocheted tie and a note from Louanne saying it would look good in my hair.

WE DIDN'T SEE DAD AGAIN UNTIL Tuesday morning when he walked into the café kitchen and went straight to Louanne. "Let's dance," he said, wrapping his arms around her waist.

"Boiled as an owl," Grandma snapped as she turned from the grill to help Louanne free herself. But Dad pushed Grandma away and held Louanne tighter. Just seconds later, Aunt Vivian arrived from the dining room with a large wooden spoon and began hitting Dad everywhere until he was forced to release Louanne and cover his head with his hands. Louanne ran to the back door, and Grandma helped her down the stairs.

Dad lurched into the café dining room, helped himself to a customer's cigarette, then took a slurp from Fisky's coffee cup and told him to go to hell.

"Go sleep it off, Gene," Fisky ordered.

When Aunt Vivian told Dad to leave and he wouldn't, I helped her and Fisky push him out the door and stayed outside to watch Dad.

"I'll be right there!" Dad called out to the woman parked at the pumps.

"The fuck you will!" Uncle Frankie said as Dad headed for the pumps, punching the air like he was boxing.

When Dad got close to the woman's car, Uncle Frankie turned the hose on him, soaking his legs with gasoline. Then he held up his lighter, threatening to set Dad on fire if he didn't back off. The woman rolled up her window and sped off, and Dad chased her car up the highway, yelling for her to come back.

Everyone was watching from the café windows as Dad stumbled to the café's parking area and sat down, but they were back to drinking coffee and talking politics when I returned to report that he was asleep under the trees.

"Let's hope he sleeps all day." Grandma met me at the swinging door and pressed two one-dollar bills into my hand. "Don't come home after school. Go skating with your friends."

On my way to the bus stop, I heard Dad yell, "Wait up," and from the corner of my eye, I saw him running at me, so I ran the other way, not stopping until he stumbled and fell.

WHEN SCHOOL GOT OUT, I DIDN'T GO skating and I didn't take the bus home, either. Instead, I walked, trying to kill a bit of time, hoping Dad was long gone.

Paco and Uncle Frankie were on their front porch, smoking a joint. Uncle Frankie told me that after I'd left, Dad had leaned against the telephone pole across from the gas pumps with his thumb out. "He had a near miss with a Mack truck that sprayed him with mud and gravel." He laughed, then howled like a wolf.

"When Willa wouldn't let Gene into the café afterward, Gene peed on the outside wall, and Vivian opened a window and threw a cup of hot coffee on him," Paco said.

"He left then, right?" I asked.

"Nope," said Paco. "The scalding coffee energized him. He got a gun from the trunk of his car and pointed it at Vivian through the window. There was a lot of yelling and a threat to call the police before Gene got into his car and left."

"I hate him!"

"Me, too," Paco said.

The café lights were out, the red-and-white gingham curtains closed, the doors locked.

"Where are Grandma and Aunt Vivian?" I asked.

"They closed up after lunch. We did, too. But they're still in there hiding, I guess."

I had to throw pebbles at the café's kitchen window to get Aunt Vivian to let me in. Grandma forced a smile. "I saw you talking to Frankie and Paco out there. I don't want you to worry. Gene's having a terrible time right now. But he's done causing trouble. I'm sure of it."

I could tell she didn't believe it any more than I did, but I went along with her and smiled, even though I could feel tears on my cheeks.

Aunt Vivian shrugged her shoulders as she handed me a napkin with two cinnamon rolls on it. "Willa and I need to finish up in here. Why don't you play pinball for a while? Lock yourself inside. If he comes back, don't let him in."

I'd just finished my fifth pinball game when Uncle Frankie opened the garage doors to move a customer's car outside. He said he would've done it sooner, but he had a nap. "I'm wiped out, man. Louanne was a mess after Gene's attack. I had to take her on my route and drive slower than usual because she was carsick." He lit a cigarette and sucked hard.

Uncle Frankie was backing the car out when I heard Dad's car coming down the highway, but not soon enough to shout a warning. Dad screeched to a stop right in front of the garage doors, blocking Uncle Frankie. With the strings of glowing lights on Uncle Frankie's porch and the lit Esso sign by the gas pumps, it was easy to see Dad was drunk when he stepped out of his car, holding his new gun. I had both hands over my mouth as Dad began weaving from side to side, yelling at Frankie to get out of the car. It wasn't safe to stay by the window any longer, so I tiptoed back to the pinball machine.

Paco was standing by the back door. I think we were both expecting Uncle Frankie to drive away in the customer's car, but instead, he turned the engine off and got out.

Dad tripped on something and fell onto his hands and knees, dropping the gun. Uncle Frankie kicked it out of his reach, though just barely.

"Get your yellow belly over here, boy!" Dad shouted.

I slipped out the garage's back door and sprinted to the café. Paco ran to Hal and Hubert's house. When I got to the kitchen, I saw Grandma and Aunt Vivian in the dining room, with the front door open.

Dad was back on his feet when Uncle Frankie kicked him hard in the stomach, knocking him back down. He kept kicking until Dad rolled onto his side and grabbed Uncle Frankie's legs, wrestling him to the ground. I screamed when Dad reached out to pick up his gun and began hitting Uncle Frankie in the face with it.

"I'm calling the police, Gene!" Grandma screamed as she stepped onto the porch. A second later, Aunt Vivian picked up a bucket of dirty clam water Dad had left by the parking area, walked over to Uncle Frankie and Dad, and drenched them. It didn't stop them from fighting, and when Hal and Hubert appeared a few seconds later, with Paco right behind, Grandma sat down on the whale-shaped bench Uncle Frankie had made in high school, looking like she might pass out. The brothers had a rope and crowbar with them.

Dad was growling like a crazed animal when he turned away from Uncle Frankie to take a swing at Hal. He missed and stumbled sideways, and Hubert knocked the gun out of his hand with one swing of the crowbar. Hal stopped Dad from jumping on Uncle Frankie's back by kicking him hard enough to knock him down. With Paco's help, they got the rope around Dad's neck and pulled him to the garage. They tried to tie his hands and feet so he couldn't move, but Dad was too strong. He got the rope off, staggered to his feet, and swung the empty bucket at Paco. "Get into the car, Evan. Right now," Dad yelled.

Aunt Vivian stepped in front of me. "She will not!" She picked up the gun and shot into the air twice. Dad ran to his car and took off so fast, he almost hit a truck that had stopped to watch the fight.

I was still sitting on my bed, holding my pillow to my chest, and listening for Dad's car, when Hal and Hubert began playing their pianos. They didn't play *Rhapsody in Blue*. They played "Lullaby" instead—three times.

I stayed awake most of the night, listening for Dad's car. When Grandma came to my room in the morning, it looked like she'd done the same thing.

"Gene's not here, and you don't have to go to school if you don't want to."

"Why do they hate each other?" I asked.

Grandma sat down and patted my legs over the blankets, just like she'd done with Teddy almost every morning.

"We adopted Frankie when his family died in a car wreck, except for Louanne, of course. The doctors said if she lived, she wouldn't be capable of caring for herself. Frankie was just eight years old and had no living relatives. At first, Pa wanted your mom and dad to take him in, as Frankie is just a couple of years older than Adam. Your mom was willing, but Gene wasn't. He only ever wanted two children, a boy and a girl, in that order. Nor did he approve of us adopting Frankie. He said we were too old and a boarding school would be a better place for him.

"And Gene was always jealous of the relationship Pa had with Frankie. Still, Frankie looked up to Gene until he returned from Vietnam, in a terrible state, as you've heard. I never dreamt they'd do what we saw yesterday, though." She wiped tears away with the bib of her apron.

"They might kill each other," I said. Grandma's crying upset me more than the fight.

"I won't let it come to that. I promise." Grandma kissed my forehead before she left.

Later, after lunch, I was in the café kitchen helping Grandma make pumpkin pies for the next day when Uncle Frankie walked in humming "King of the Road." He unpacked four bottles of booze, a quart of whipping cream, six cans of ginger ale, and a bag of nuts onto Grandma's work counter. It was already full of other stuff. Just as Aunt Vivian had predicted, she'd won big at the Bingo Gala by playing twenty cards: one hundred dollars, a transistor radio, two bottles of sloe gin, Christmas dish towels, a turkey, a ham, and a fruitcake.

"You owe me twenty bucks," Uncle Frankie said, lining up the bottles of booze in an order that seemed to make sense to both him and Grandma.

"Take it off what you're gonna owe me for the eggnog you're likely to drink tomorrow at Thanksgiving dinner," she snapped back.

"Okay—that's okay, I guess." Uncle Frankie looked past Louanne and out the kitchen window. "Looks like Gene just filled up his car and is taking off again. It must be time for him to go kill someone."

"I've about had enough of you. You need to control yourself. And you shouldn't talk that way. Not around her and not around me." Grandma tilted her head toward me but didn't break eye contact with Uncle Frankie.

"Sorry, kid." He tugged the crocheted tie at the end of my ponytail before reaching around to grab French fries from the fryer basket. "But it's true," he whispered and winked.

He winked at everyone, especially girls. Sometimes it made my insides swirl around in a good way, but not that day. Winking with a swollen eye made him look like Cyclops. And he was close enough that I could tell he hadn't showered and had been smoking pot. But I didn't care about that. I was interested in the bloody stitches around his mouth, his black eye, and the dried blood in his hair and ears.

He told Grandma he had a broken nose, a fractured cheek, and seventeen stitches in his chin. "I'm gonna report that fucker to the cops!"

"I'm surprised they didn't show up last night. Don't cause more trouble. I mean it, Frank. Just let it be."

AS THE LAST THREE CUSTOMERS GOT up to leave, Aunt Vivian reminded them that the café would be closed the next day for Thanksgiving. "Gobble, gobble," she said and locked the door behind them. Then she found a song she liked on the radio and turned it up. I swept and mopped while she cleaned the tables and counters.

When I'd finished, Grandma said I could watch *Dark Shadows* in her living room if I hurried. Then she turned to Louanne. "I know it took a lot for you to come to work today. Thank you. I'm sorry about my boys. I can't seem to get them to be nice to each other."

Louanne put her hands over her face. "I can't stay here," she sobbed.

Grandma shooed me away, motioning me to close the back door on my way out.

WHEN I GOT TO THE PORCH STAIRS, I SAW lights on in Grandma's basement room. I hoped Dad was asleep or passed out, but he was in the house, at the kitchen sink, mixing himself a drink. It was hard to keep my mouth shut when I saw his swollen eyes and the red rope marks on the front and side of his neck. He looked as bad as Uncle Frankie. And he smelled of gasoline.

It was apparent from the stuff stacked next to Grandma's dining room table that Dad had been to our house in Tacoma. It was good to see my Crissy doll again, even though I hadn't played with her since I was nine. I found my clothes in the largest box. I'd been wearing the same thing for four days. The poncho Louanne had given to me still looked okay, but the Jimi Hendrix T-shirt Paco had lent me was baggy, and I was getting tired of people asking me what my favorite Hendrix song was. I found a lot of my stuff in an old suitcase, along with Mom's yellow chenille bathrobe, tweezers, red nail polish, hair-cutting scissors, all of her Betty MacDonald books, and three photo albums.

I put everything on the floor, and even though I was still mad, I thanked Dad for bringing them, especially the cocoa-brown peacoat Mom bought for me last year. It had been way too big then but fit me perfectly when I tried it on.

I asked Dad to help me move the bed from Uncle Frankie's old room to my room. "There's a big sinkhole in your old bed. It hurts my back," I said.

He chuckled. "It's always been that way." I was afraid to ask about Mom in case it set him off, but when he said he was leaving the next day to drive to Canada, it felt like I had nothing to lose.

"But you didn't find Mom the last time. When you took a ferry to Canada. Do you know where they are for sure this time? What about taking me along? I have four days off school."

"That won't work. Don't ask again. They're not in Calgary like I thought back then. They're at her uncle's ranch in Edmonton. Frankie knew all along where they were—the prick. I didn't know Endura had so many Canadian relatives. She never mentioned them to me."

I sighed, took a few steps back, and sucked in a big breath. "Mom is gonna tell you off about your bloody face. And she'll know it's from fighting with Uncle Frankie. She always knows stuff like that."

"So what if she does?" he said in a quieter voice, like he'd just figured out I was right.

"The fight was scary, Dad. I thought someone was going to die."

"Someone should've," he grunted.

"You're staying for Thanksgiving dinner, though, right?"

"Nope," he said.

"You should. Grandma is roasting a huge turkey, Aunt Vivian is making eggnog, and I'm gonna help make stuffing with the mushrooms and herbs Hal and Hubert left on the back porch this morning. It's going to be good; I promise."

Dad stuck his chin out and mashed his puffy, bloody lips together. "It's best if I just leave. For one, I'm not interested in having dinner with veterans who played in an army band and worked in a mess hall. Two, I wouldn't eat anything made with shit those filthy bums left on a porch. And three, I'm not sure I could stop myself from stuffing the turkey down Frankie's throat."

I had to put my hand over my mouth to keep quiet, and only because he insisted, I followed him downstairs to watch TV with Grandma and Aunt Vivian. Halfway through the show, Dad cleared his throat to get everyone's attention.

"Hey, Ma, I'm letting an army buddy and his family stay at my house in Tacoma until I get back. Just so you know," he said.

"What about our stuff?" I cried. "My bed and bike and all of Mom's things?"

"They'll take care of it, and we'll all be back there in a week, maybe two, and they'll have moved out by then," Dad replied.

"Mom won't like it."

"So what?" he said.

I slid to the other end of the couch, next to Aunt Vivian, and took one of the blue cushions to hold in my lap, squeezing it hard, trying to count to twenty with my mouth shut.

"I'm staying at Mooch's tonight and leaving first thing in the morning for Canada. I'll be back when I'm back."

Even though the idea of being in a smoke-filled car for fifteen hours, listening to Dad's honky-tonk music, watching him steer with just his index finger, and being scared every time he passed a car sounded like the worst thing in the world, I still asked him one more time if I could go along.

"Again, it's a no."

"Why didn't Mom wait for me?" I threw the cushion across the room.

"'Cause she knows she would've got more than a piece of my mind if I saw her, that's why."

"For shit sake, Gene," said Aunt Vivian, "what's with the tough talk? You're not in a bar. You're in your mother's living room, talking to your child."

Dad shrugged, lit a cigarette, and told Aunt Vivian to give him back his gun. "I'm surprised you knew how to shoot it."

"Oh, you'd be surprised about the things I know, including how to use the phone to call your wife. By the way, Endura says her uncle and cousins are ready for you. Are you ready for them?" Aunt Vivian grinned. "And you won't be getting your gun back unless you fish it out of the Wishkah River."

Dad stood, shouted something I didn't catch, and slammed the door behind him.

We watched the rest of *The Odd Couple* in silence, and when Aunt Vivian stood up and headed for the stairs, I followed, waiting until we were at the top before asking if she'd called Mom to warn her, or if she was just teasing. "Don't worry. It's all taken care of. Sweet dreams, kid."

In bed, I snuggled into Mom's quilt and read from one of my favorite books, *Sounder*, until I heard the beginning of *Rhapsody in Blue*. Then I went to my window and opened it wide. When the music finished, my room was an icebox, and I was crying so hard, I could barely breathe.

When Hal and Hubert started playing their pianos in the morning, I stayed awake just long enough to listen to "Amazing Grace." Then I put my pillow over my head, spread out, and went back to sleep.

"COAST IS CLEAR, SWEETHEART." GRANDMA, wearing a bright blue apron, was standing at the end of my bed. Louanne must have made it for her. "Gene's gone. He went digging before he left to get your mom and brother. I found a bucket of clams on the porch. I gave them to Hal and Hubert."

Grandma looked tired, as usual, but there was something different about her that morning. She was exceptionally cheerful and not in a rush to leave my room. Last night, when Aunt Vivian had let Dad have it, Grandma hadn't reacted at first. But then I'd seen her clench her hands and purse her lips, and I knew that Dad had finally gotten under her skin. When Aunt Vivian had told Dad he'd have to fish his gun out of the river, Grandma had smiled. And now she was humming a song and about to rub my feet through the covers, the way she often had when I first arrived.

"Try not to worry. They'll be back soon, and your life will be normal again."

"Dad will probably want to pick a fight with Mom so he won't feel so bad about going back to Vietnam. He's got a girlfriend and a baby there, you know. Mom is furious. She says the girl isn't much older than me." I rolled over to face the wall.

"I suspected something like that was going on. Some men can't help but cause trouble. I'm sorry for Endura, and you, of course. My mother once told me that betrayal hurts the betrayer more. At the time, I didn't believe it, but I've lived long enough to know it's true. Let's not think about them today. Let's think about happy times and find a few things to be thankful for, like the sunny sky this morning and the pumpkin pie we're gonna eat later. We've got two hungry neighbors and six lonely veterans coming for Thanksgiving dinner in seven hours. It's all hands on deck." Grandma stroked my arm before pulling the quilt back. "Go easy on the hot water."

CHAPTER 13

EVERYONE WAS GLAD DAD WASN'T around for Thanksgiving—no one more than me, though. I had two reasons: he wasn't around to tell me to wash off my blue eyeshadow and he was driving to Canada to get Mom and Teddy.

In the café kitchen, as we prepared Thanksgiving dinner, Aunt Vivian sang along to the radio while Grandma made bread rolls and I chopped celery and onions for the stuffing, the same way I'd done the year before for Mom. It was my first holiday without her and my brothers. Were they missing me as much as I was missing them?

"Have you thought of things you're thankful for?" Grandma asked. "I've got eleven on my list, and Viv says she's got two."

The only thing I'd come up with was being able to go home when Dad brought Mom and my brothers back, but I didn't want to risk hurting Grandma's feelings, so I didn't say it.

"I'm still thinking," I said.

I pretended to be cheerful and didn't complain, not even when Aunt Vivian pulled on my ponytail while she danced around the room to "Red Roses for a Blue Lady." When I finished chopping celery, I peeled carrots and set the table without being asked. And when Uncle Frankie showed up late in the morning, wearing the bloody shirt and jeans he'd worn the day of the fight, I offered to do his laundry. He'd brought the mail with him, setting it down on the workbench before going to the dining room to listen to the news on the radio. I stayed in the kitchen to watch Grandma look through the stack of letters, hoping she'd find one from Mom.

"You said you paid this!" Grandma leaned back and waved an envelope for Uncle Frankie to see through the serving window.

"Yeah, but I didn't. I've got the gas pumps open today, so I should have the money later."

"You'd better," Grandma said. "Although I doubt you'll have many customers on Thanksgiving. And don't forget, I need my Studebaker fixed by Monday. We daren't miss bingo after Viv's big win last week. She says she's on a winning streak. You should come with us. Bingo is much more fun than poker."

Uncle Frankie had both hands in the air when he kicked open the swinging door between rooms and said, "You've never won fifteen hands of blackjack in a row, lady."

Then, still laughing as he tried to get close enough to the toaster to drop in two pieces of bread, he stepped on my foot and said, "Hey, how about you sort the mail for me? I'll pay."

"How much, and how long does it take?" I asked.

"I only need your help tomorrow and Saturday. It might be two hours—three if you're slow. If it works out, maybe you can sort for me every Saturday until Christmas."

"Why just Saturdays?" I asked.

"I can handle the weekdays on my own, and there's no mail delivery on Sunday. Low tides in the morning bring clam diggers to the beach, and there's been a lot of them this year. I'm sure you've seen the line of cars waiting to buy gas on weekends. Lately, it's been too busy to leave Paco on his own until 2:00 or 3:00 p.m. The past two Saturdays, I've left here with unsorted mail. Let me tell you, searching through mailbags at each mailbox isn't the best way to get the job done."

Uncle Frankie was right about Eat and Get Gas getting busy on the weekends. By Sunday afternoon, Grandma, Aunt Vivian, Louanne, and Paco were visibly tired. But not Uncle Frankie—he was always excited about his "big stakes" Sunday night poker game.

Uncle Frankie was licking the knife after putting jam on his toast. "So, what do you say? With Christmas coming up, there's lots of mail to sort. I'm already behind."

"I'm not sure I'd be any good at it. I'm still trying to figure out the Dewey Decimal System in the school library. Besides, I'll be going home when Dad comes back with Mom and my brothers."

"Sure, you will. But don't count on Adam coming back. He's a fugitive now—best if he stays where he is. In the meantime, while you're waiting, how about I teach you to sort mail? It sure would help, and Cindylee will be happy when I'm home from delivering in time to take her to dinner. Not this Saturday, though. I've plans that don't include her."

"Cindylee? What happened to that girl Judy you told me about?"

"She's still around but keep it to yourself." Uncle Frankie winked.

It was the same long slow wink I'd seen him give girls who bought gas. And I guessed it meant Cindylee didn't know Uncle Frankie was dating Judy, too.

"What do I have to do with the mail?" I asked.

"You just gotta sort my route mail when I bring it back from the post office in the morning, around 7:30. I'll make you a route map and clear off my poker platform, which doubles as my kitchen table. And I'll get clean boxes from Swanson's grocery store today. The ones on my back porch are full of garbage, which I'm gonna burn when I have time."

"Sounds okay. How much will I make?" I was eager to know.

"Then it's a deal," Uncle Frankie replied, ignoring my question again. He offered me a cigarette. "Let's smoke on it," he said.

"I'm thirteen." I sucked in my cheeks when I saw Grandma make a sour face.

"You sure 'bout that?" he laughed. "You sure you're not twenty?"

"He's just fooling around. Don't pay him any attention," Grandma said.

"Sorry, kid. I need to leave here by 12:30 p.m. I hope you're a fast learner."

"Can I deliver with you?" I asked. "I'd like to learn how to be a mailman."

"Fine by me. Bring your coat and wear your rain boots, 'cause my route roads are muddy, and you might have to get out of the car."

Sorting and delivering mail seemed important and official, something kids at school wouldn't laugh at like they did when I told them I swept the café floors and made toast for customers. I thought about the books I could buy and the cool clothes I could order from Grandma's J. C. Penney catalog. And then I thought I should ask her if it's okay to take the job, even though I'd already said yes.

"I think so," she said. "I can handle the toaster. Frankie needs help, so you might as well do it. But don't let him get away with not paying you. Keep track of your hours and remind him each week what he owes you."

"There's a lot of old mail stored in the house," Louanne said. We both turned to look at her.

"Lots of it. Some from last month." Louanne continued to slice potatoes for French fries, pushing the small ends into a bucket that Aunt Vivian would later put on the back porch stairs for Hal and Hubert's chickens.

THANKSGIVING DINNER IN THE CAFÉ dining room wasn't anything like the year before at my house. Instead of my mom's favorite folk songs, we had to listen to Aunt Vivian's Andy Williams records on a portable player she'd brought from her room. And instead of Mom and my brothers, around the table were Hal, Hubert, and six World War II veterans in military jackets adorned with medals. I sat between Paco and a musty-smelling veteran, and across from Uncle Frankie and Louanne, who'd dressed for the occasion, including a Pilgrim hat. I could tell from the crocheted collar on her dress that she'd made it. I thought it was neat, but I didn't say it out loud, because I didn't want Aunt Vivian to hear and then tease her about it.

"Lots of rum in this." I was smiling as I filled Louanne's glass with eggnog. She pushed it toward Uncle Frankie, who drank it in two swallows.

"She don't drink," he said. I refilled his glass and then poured half glasses of eggnog for the veterans, as Aunt Vivian had instructed.

It took a while for Grandma and Aunt Vivian to bring the food out of the kitchen. I'd offered to help, but Grandma told me to stay seated. Finally, fifteen minutes later, when everyone else had a plate of food and a piece of pie, Grandma put my plates down in front of me, and I saw she'd given me a whole turkey leg.

I put my head down and tackled my dinner as though I hadn't eaten in days. Louanne scooped small amounts of food onto her spoon and then chewed as if she had a piece of tough steak in her mouth rather than mashed potatoes and gravy. Between each bite, she took several sips of water. When

Uncle Frankie noticed, he signaled to me that she ate that way because of her mouth.

Then he pointed at the pitcher of water, and I put my fork down to fill Louanne's glass. "I like your dress," I said, "especially the red collar."

"Red is the only color for this place." Louanne set her glass down and wiped her mouth with a napkin.

I didn't know how to reply, so I acted like I hadn't heard and stood up to get another piece of pumpkin pie. "Fatty, fatty, two by four, couldn't get through the kitchen door," Aunt Vivian sang out. The veterans laughed, and I did too, but only to cover my shame.

When I sat back down without the pie, Louanne pushed her piece across the table. "I don't like pie, but I do like fatties and kitchen doors," she murmured and grinned a little.

Louanne and I talked more at Thanksgiving dinner than we had in the almost three months I'd been at Grandma's. I almost cried when she said she was tired and stood up to leave. As she walked to the door, Louanne said good night to everyone before bending down as she passed me. "I look forward to the day I can escape from this place," she whispered.

CHAPTER 14

IN THE MORNING, WHEN UNCLE FRANKIE arrived back from the post office, I ran outside to meet him. There were three cardboard boxes and three mailbags inside his car and more stuff in the trunk. I saw magazines, packages, and at least a dozen square boxes from the Columbia House Record Company. I carried two of the mailbags into his house, then put the empty boxes on his front porch. On my third trip, I stumbled, and the record boxes flew out of my hands, several landing in a mud puddle next to the front porch.

"Oh jeez, sorry," I said as I bent down to pick them up.

"Hey, don't sweat the boxes. It's what's inside of them that counts," Uncle Frankie said. He grabbed one and wiped the mud off with his hand.

Still feeling bad and afraid he'd fire me, I remarked that someone named George Isaac Joseph was getting a lot of records.

"Yeah, that G.I. Joe really loves music." Uncle Frankie slapped his leg with his free hand.

Once the mailbags were on his kitchen floor and stacks of packages and boxes next to his poker table, I said hello to Paco, who was on the couch that was also his bed. Then Uncle Frankie began to speak so fast about the various ways to sort mail that I could barely keep up. He picked up a bag and dumped it over the table, grabbing a letter before it slid off and holding it up for me to see. "This postmark in the corner means it's first class," he said, pointing to a black ink stamp next to a regular stamp. "First class is the most important. So is knowing the names of people on the route and what road they're on. We'll go faster if we both know."

I knew I should write it down, and a second later, when he handed me a map of the route he'd drawn on the back of an advertising leaflet, I took a pencil from his counter and made a few notes.

"I always look for the first-class mail before I do anything else," he continued. "You can try another way, but just make sure it's in the route order when you put it in the clean boxes. And it needs to be done by 12:30 p.m."

"You said it would take me a couple of hours to sort—three, if I were slow. So how come you're giving me four hours to do it?" I asked.

"Well, today it looks like a four-hour job." Uncle Frankie picked up another mailbag and tipped it out over the table, which was already full. The new stuff slid off and onto the dirty carpet underneath. There were a lot of other things under the table: moldy dishes, seashell ashtrays full of butts, empty beer cans, a pair of lady's underwear, and a green glass tube Uncle Frankie called a bong.

When I reached to grab a large envelope, I saw two dead mice and screamed. "Oh, that's nothing," Uncle Frankie chuckled. Picking them up by their tails, he opened the door and threw them off the side of the porch. "Those fuckers are everywhere. And I think there's a dead raccoon under the house. Smells like it."

When Uncle Frankie came back, he saw me staring at the kitchen sink and grabbed a filthy towel off a chair to drape over the dirty dishes piled high. "There, now you won't have to look at it. Anyway, it's Paco's turn to clean up. Hey, have a look for Eat and Get Gas's mail before you get started. Even though this place isn't on my route, the postmaster gives me the mail. Not to be helpful, but to keep that slug they've got on our route from sitting in the café all day."

"Oh, I met him last week," I said. "His name's Roy. When he finished his lunch, he ordered a milkshake and stayed in the café reading the paper until Aunt Vivian said she was closing up."

"Yeah, that's him—the slug," Uncle Frankie said. "I put the mail for Eat and Get Gas inside one of these bags. I can't recall which one, but the stack has a rubber band around it." He gave a big grin. "There's a letter on top for Mrs. Vivian Pigge. If you know what's good for you, you'll never call her that."

"Are you joking? Is that her real name?"

"No joke. She used to be married to Mr. Pat Pigge. There are no piglets." Uncle Frankie pressed the tip of his finger to his nose and pushed it in until it resembled a pig snout.

I had to run to the bathroom to keep from peeing my pants, and when I returned to the kitchen, both Paco and Uncle Frankie were snorting and laughing.

"There's also two return-to-sender letters that belong to Louanne," Uncle Frankie said. "Don't take them to the café. And don't leave them in this house. Put them in my glove compartment. I haven't decided if I'm going to tell her that her letters to our aunt are coming back."

"Why would your aunt send her letters back?" I could feel the fun leave the room.

"I'm guessing our Aunt Bethania's lousy son, Orson, is doing it. It looks that way. Every letter has 'Return to Sender' written over her address. It's not a lady's handwriting, that's for sure. Louanne's been sending letters since she got here. They only started coming back in September."

"That's so mean. Why is he like that?"

"I'm not sure," Uncle Frankie replied. "Our aunt hasn't sent a letter to Louanne. And I know she hasn't called her because my only phone is in the garage. Paco would've told me if she'd called. She could've tried to call the café or Willa's house, but those phones are on party lines with two others, including Mrs. Fine, and it's hard to get a call through."

The phone in the café was yellow with a very long cord. The one in the garage was old-fashioned and black. Someone had nailed it to the wall, and it wasn't on straight.

"Last month, I found six returned letters, so I called Aunt Bethania's house to ask why. I had to leave a message with the woman who answered for Orson to call me. He hasn't."

Suddenly, I was crying. And I couldn't tell if it was because of Louanne not hearing from her aunt for six months or because I hadn't heard from my mom for three. I leaned forward in my chair and began pulling first-class letters from the pile and moving the others to the side, grateful that Uncle Frankie was still talking and hadn't noticed my shaky breathing.

"Louanne thinks she'll be back in North Dakota by Christmas. That's not gonna happen. When I drove there last May to bring her back here, Orson called the house while we were packing, and Louanne handed the phone to me. Orson told me to make sure we took everything of Louanne's with us because she wasn't welcome back, even if his mother recovered. I've never told Louanne that. She wouldn't take it well. And I'm sure she'll go off the deep end if she ever finds out her letters are coming back here."

"I won't tell. I promise." I was trying to stay focused on the mail and not on how weird I felt watching him make what he called a two-paper, one-man joint. When Uncle Frankie stood up to light it, I turned around to watch him take a big drag and hold his breath before blowing the smoke out of his nose like a dragon. He did it twice more before Paco called out, "Save some of that for me."

"Roll your own," said Uncle Frankie. "I left for Williston the day after Orson called and said Louanne had found our aunt at the bottom of the staircase on Monday and didn't call for help until Wednesday. He wanted Louanne gone and offered to pay all my costs to move her here. When I got to our aunt's house, I had to crawl through a back window to get in because Louanne wouldn't open the door. I found her hiding in a closet."

I could see from my chair that Paco had put his book down and was listening with a sad expression on his face.

I finished the warm bottle of Fresca I found next to Uncle Frankie's stove and asked him how he got Louanne to come back with him.

"She wasn't happy about it, that's for sure. She only agreed to come after I promised to bring her back when our aunt recovered and after her doctor dropped by with a shitload of pills for her to bring along. One hundred miles west, Louanne was still clutching the door handle and yelling at me to slow down. I thought she was going to jump out of the car, so I made her take three red capsules." Uncle Frankie lit a cigarette.

"Louanne was still groggy when we got here," he continued. "My spare room already had a bed and furniture in it, and she seemed happy once I got her things in there. Her first week here wasn't good. She stayed in her room, only coming out to eat the canned fruit she'd brought, use the bathroom, and take her rabbit outside. I invited her to come to the café with Paco and me to eat, but she wouldn't. Only when she ran out of canned fruit could I convince her to have lunch in the café. Willa had just introduced herself and served us tomato soup and grilled cheese sandwiches when Vivian walked in and asked who my pirate friend was. She was a little drunk from that shit she drinks all day, but that's no excuse.

"Louanne got upset, so we left, and when we got to my kitchen, she ripped her eye patch off and threw it at me. Up to then, she hadn't mentioned going back to Williston, but after Vivian's pirate jab, she started asking me to take her home." Uncle Frankie sighed.

"That's so awful!" I felt myself rock back and forth in my chair the way I'd done when I was a kid. "Why does Aunt Vivian tease? She does it to me all the time. I hate it."

"She thinks it's funny," said Uncle Frankie. "Sometimes it is. And a few customers, including Fisky, like it. But she's worse when she's drunk, like a cat ready to pounce on a rat. The pirate remark pissed me off, and I had my bowl of soup in my hand, ready to throw, when Willa tossed a wooden spoon across the counter, hitting Vivian in the chest. Vivian screamed, and Willa told her to apologize to Louanne. But you know Vivian. She won't do anything unless she wants to. Louanne began taking the bus into town, sometimes staying away all day. Then, in mid-July, she insisted on calling Aunt Bethania to ask about going home. I shouldn't have let her, but she pleaded and cried, and I gave in."

"Was your aunt home?"

"Nope, and when Louanne got off the phone, she was hysterical. She had to repeat herself three times before I caught that our aunt would be in the hospital for months, maybe years, thanks to her. Orson also said he'd moved his family into our aunt's house permanently. That call really messed Louanne up. A few nights later, out of the blue, she opened her bedroom door in the middle of a poker game and yelled, 'How much longer do I have to live in this hellhole?'"

"She wants to go home, just like me," I said.

"Yeah, but she's got no home to go to. And right now, you don't either. But you've still got parents, a grandma, and a home you'll go back to one day. She's got crazy me."

My cheeks were hot, and I wished I hadn't asked so many questions. I began sorting again, but Uncle Frankie hadn't finished. He said he hadn't known that Louanne had nightmares until he found her hiding in her closet a week after calling Orson.

"She dreams about a man who kicks her bedroom door down, picks her up, and carries her to a burning road, dropping her in front of a speeding logging truck. She had the same night-mare every night the following week. I'm a heavy sleeper, but Paco isn't. He couldn't sleep listening to her cry and scream, and he was too chicken to knock on her door, so he slept on the porch. He and I talked it over, and he said we should replace her bedroom door with a heavier one so we wouldn't hear her scream," Uncle Frankie continued. "I got Hal and Hubert to make a solid wood door. They made it, painted it yellow, and added a peacock's tail on the top corner for good luck. Now, when she has a nightmare, we don't hear a thing."

I got up to look at the yellow door because everything he'd said sounded unbelievable. As I passed the couch, Paco looked up and whispered, "I never slept on the porch. I slept in his car."

When I returned to the kitchen, Uncle Frankie was searching through the pile for first-class mail.

"You know, Vivian apologized for the pirate remark a few weeks later, and right after, Willa hired Louanne to work in the café kitchen. The work isn't hard, and Willa pays well, but Louanne is tired after work. Still, she finds time to sew, knit, read, and write to our aunt."

Finally, there was the ding sound of a car driving over the sponge cord at the gas pumps, and Uncle Frankie jumped up and left. "'Bout time," Paco called out from the living room.

I thought the same thing. It had been hard to concentrate on the mail with Uncle Frankie talking. The room felt lighter without him, and I sorted a lot of mail as more gas customers arrived. When he got back and saw what I'd done, he smiled and grabbed two cans of beer from the refrigerator. He opened both and put one in front of me. "Drink up," he said.

"I'm gonna save mine for later." It was easier to say that than to remind him, again, that I was thirteen.

WHEN UNCLE FRANKIE WAS ABOUT TO head out again to the pumps, I saw my chance and asked him for Mom's address. "Can I have it, please? You gave it to Aunt Vivian, and you must have given it to Dad, too. Otherwise, he wouldn't know where to go."

"I'll think about it." Uncle Frankie put on his sunglasses to hide his black eye and closed the door behind him.

"All right," he said when he was back. "I'll give you the address. If I don't, you might try to put me out of my misery like Gene did."

Having Mom's address and phone number and knowing Dad wouldn't be causing trouble when he got to Edmonton, took away my urgent need to call her. But I knew I would, one day. I needed to tell her I'd started my period, received an okay report card, and still wanted to be with her and my brothers. I'd already decided I wouldn't talk about my workbook story unless she brought it up.

I waited for Uncle Frankie to leave again before I opened the fourth mailbag. I found the stack of mail for Eat and Get Gas inside and the two returned letters at the bottom. Louanne's handwriting looked like the lettering on the front of the James Bond books I'd seen on Grandma's bookshelf. I put the letters in my back pocket.

While I waited for Paco to leave for work so I could use his couch for the stacks of sorted mail, I looked around for more space. "Can I put the dirty dishes and all the stuff on the counter somewhere else?" I asked when he came out of the bathroom.

"Sure. I'll help."

Paco shoved the dirty dishes under the sink and in the cupboards. I thought he was joking around and waited for him to wink or say he was kidding, but then he stuck a dirty frying pan on top of the refrigerator and smiled as though he'd done something good.

"That's a lot of mail for one day. But there's more. Have a look around. Frankie doesn't always deliver everything."

"Why don't you just wash the pan?"

"Never washed a pan in my life. I've got sisters." He grinned.

"Jeez. Only your sisters do the dishes and clean up?" I thought about Adam and how he cleaned the kitchen at home.

"They like cleaning. So does my mom. All girls do." He puckered his lips and pointed at me like he was shooting a gun.

Paco got serious before he left the house. "Your uncle lies, you know. And he forgets stuff. I don't think he even remembers picking me up in Spokane—opening the passenger door for me to get in and Louanne falling out. I thought she was dead until Frankie nudged her awake and stood her up. She fell back to sleep right after he lifted her into the car, and I had to sit in the back seat next to her rabbit cage, sewing machine, and so much other shit, I could hardly move. What I'm telling you here is that he's a few bricks short of a load. Louanne, is too. They don't sleep much, but when they do, they both have nightmares, and sometimes they scream so loud it's like being in a horror movie. Nothing here is soundproof. I hear everything, and Frankie screams louder than Louanne. I can take his screaming because I know it's from his time in Vietnam, and it'll go away one day. But man, I feel horrible when Louanne screams. And I'm not scared of her, like Frankie says. I just don't want to embarrass her, so I don't knock on her door to see if she's okay. Maybe I should. She's my friend, and I'm sure grateful for the books she brings me from the library, because I hate playing poker."

"Really? You hate poker?" I was keen for a change of subject. "Uncle Frankie told me you were good at it—that you're the reason he plays so often."

"As I said, a few bricks short." Paco indicated a box of old mail in the living room corner and shrugged his shoulders as if to say, "Here's more proof."

I spotted another box behind the couch. Some of the mail was months old. *Maybe I should start sorting for Uncle Frankie before school every day.* That way, all the mail would

124 EAT AND GET GAS

get done, and people would get their Christmas cards and gifts. There was no reason I couldn't, now that I didn't have to go clam digging. I could sort mail from 7:00 to 8:00 a.m. and still get to school on time. And I'd earn more money, too, even though Uncle Frankie hadn't said what he was paying me yet.

Even if he didn't, it would give me something interesting to do while I waited for my family to come back. I sensed Grandma and Aunt Vivian were still angry that Dad hadn't taken me with him.

"Evan should go with you. It's that simple," Grandma had said to Dad several times as he packed to drive to Edmonton.

"It's not simple," Dad had replied. "Endura made Adam a fugitive. They're both felons now. If they get arrested, where do you think Teddy and Evan will end up?"

"Not here," Grandma had said. "We're too tired to raise kids."

WHEN I'D FINISHED SORTING THE DAY'S mail, I looked around at the stacks extending from the kitchen table to the living room and felt proud of myself. It took another half an hour for me to put it into the new cardboard boxes, in route order. Then, so I wouldn't forget, I made a list of addresses with packages in the trunk, wondering if we'd get it all delivered by 5:00 p.m.

It was not far off noon, and I was hungry and thirsty. I drank Uncle Frankie's last bottle of 7Up and hunted around for something to eat. I opened the one cupboard Paco hadn't hidden dirty dishes in and saw it was full of canned fruit cocktail and boxes of Girl Scout Cookies. I knew the cans of fruit were Louanne's, but I ate a few cookies before taking her letters to Uncle Frankie's car. When I opened his glove compartment, I saw more returned letters and a plastic bag full of joints. I counted the joints (twenty-eight) before I put the letters underneath the bag, closed it, and headed for Eat and Get Gas with the café mail. I was hoping to get something to eat while I was there, but the café was busy, so I put the mail on Grandma's workbench and helped myself to a buttermilk biscuit a customer hadn't eaten. "You shouldn't eat from dirty plates," Louanne said from across the room.

"I either eat this rock-hard biscuit or more of the stale Girl Scout Cookies I found in Uncle Frankie's cupboard. I've already had twenty," I replied.

Louanne laughed at that, and so did Aunt Vivian. "How's the new job going?" she asked.

"It's okay. Some people get lots of mail. Grandma has ten letters and five magazines, and there's a letter from Big Dave at the Walla Walla State Prison with your name on it. At least I think it's yours." I was trying hard to keep a straight face, thinking about Mrs. Pigge and no piglets.

"My pen pal." Aunt Vivian gave me a dirty look as she grabbed the letter.

"Dear Lord. Not Big Dave again," Grandma said. "Do not send him any more money, Viv. Why don't you put an apron on and help me here at the grill, Evan?" Grandma said.

"I'm not finished with the mail yet."

"There's more in his bedroom," Louanne whispered, but just to me.

"I'll look for it," I said and suddenly thought there could be old mail in her room, too, which would give me an excuse to go in. When I got back to Uncle Frankie's, I went straight to her door. When I opened it, a piece of paper fell from the jamb. I smiled, thinking about all the times I'd done the same thing to see if Adam or Teddy had snooped in my room.

I closed the door and had a close look at the Osmond Brothers poster taped on the back of it. She thinks Donny is cute, just like I do.

My eyes turned to Velvet's cage on the floor next to her dresser. I was about to take her out to pet her when I noticed a poncho hanging on the closet door. It was like the one Louanne had given me the week before, except it was navy blue and yellow, and every other square had a crocheted flower in the middle. It fit me perfectly, and I kept it on as I looked at the box of eye patches, empty cans of fruit cocktail, a denture container, and four bottles of pills on her dresser. She must be really sick—sicker than Mom.

Louanne's room was comfortable, like mine in Tacoma. I felt like stretching out on her bed, but I knew I should leave. I'd turned to go when I saw a pattern for pants and blue denim material on her sewing machine table. It looked like she was making a pair of jeans. I needed new jeans. Mine were all too short in the leg and too big in the waist. It would be cool to know how to sew like Louanne, but I wasn't sure I should ask her to teach me. Uncle Frankie had already said I was nosy and had asked her too many questions at Thanksgiving dinner.

Before I went, I ran my fingers over the gold lettering on the cover of a Bible I found on the nightstand next to her bed, on top of other books. I shouldn't have looked through her things, but I couldn't stop myself.

There was a paper pocket on the inside cover of her Bible. It held photos. One of them was of a tall woman holding a baby and two little girls beside her. The date on the back was June 14, 1950. Another photo of the same people had Eat and Get Gas in the background. This time, they were older, standing tallest to shortest, and waving. I looked at the list of names and birthdays on the back of the photo and saw that Uncle Frankie's birthday was February 7, the day before mine. When I put the photos back, I noticed writing on the inside of the Bible pocket: "When you have nowhere to go, you go nowhere." I slammed it shut, feeling my stomach turn and my face flush. It could be a curse. As fast as I could, I hung up the poncho and made sure I replaced the piece of paper in the doorjamb.

Back in Uncle Frankie's kitchen, I tried to keep calm by reading the names and streets on the route map out loud and drawing stars next to names who had packages in the trunk of the car. With time to kill, I sorted two boxes of old mail and washed the dishes. Then I skipped to the garage, yelling, "Hey, I'm ready to go. How 'bout you?"

"I'll be ready in five minutes. Just about to beat Paco's high score," Uncle Frankie said as the pinball machine's bells and chimes rang out.

I wanted Uncle Frankie to hurry so he'd have time to look over the mail, including the old stuff I'd sorted, but he seemed more interested in the clean dishes. "Hey, maybe I should hire you to do everything around here," he said.

"Today's mail is in your car already. This stuff is old mail I found around your house." I was smiling at him, waiting for a thank you. "If you take out the toolbox and spare tire, there might be room for it in your trunk," I continued as he stayed silent.

"It's all third-class shit." He took out a letter, read the postmark, and ripped it up. "There might be a first-class letter or bill in here. If so, it's probably been reported lost by now. It can't just show up in a mailbox today. Not without my boss finding out I didn't deliver it when I should've. I'll burn all this when we get back."

"Isn't it wrong to burn mail?" I asked.

"Could be. But I only burn garbage." Uncle Frankie picked up the box and carried it to his back porch.

That wasn't true. I'd seen a few letters and birthday cards in the box. It made me wonder if he'd already burned letters Mom had sent to me.

CHAPTER 15

THERE WASN'T ROOM FOR ME TO SIT in front once the boxes of the mail were in Uncle Frankie's GTO, so I balanced myself on top of the two in the back seat. "Once we get some stuff delivered, you can move up. That way, I can drive, and you can throw letters into mailboxes," he said.

We'd only just pulled away from Eat and Get Gas when he lit a joint and took a few quick puffs before throwing it out the window. Then he turned the radio up and played with the dial until he found a song he liked. Singing along to it made him drive faster, and I had to hook my toes under the back seat's right door handle and hold the other with both hands to keep from sliding around.

"Can you slow down, please?"

"Nope," Uncle Frankie said. "They made this car to go fast."

I rolled onto my left side and put my right hand against the back of the driver's seat, just beneath Uncle Frankie's head. And I put my left hand over my right to brace myself. When the song finished, he began weaving, looking for a new song. "The Guess Who," he said.

"I'm not good at guessing," I said, closing my eyes when I saw a truck coming at us.

"That's the funniest thing I've heard all year. Don't you know about the Guess Who? One of the greatest bands ever?" Uncle Frankie roared as he moved back into our lane.

"I guess not," I said.

He was still making jokes about it when he turned off Highway 109 onto Powell Road and pulled up to the first mailbox—on the wrong side. I watched him slide to the middle of the seat, roll down his window, open the Waywhins' mailbox, throw in a stack of letters, and shut it with a drumstick he kept on his dashboard. He did the same thing at other mailboxes until we got to one with its red flag up.

"Fucking families who write to each other," Uncle Frankie growled as he got out of the car to get the outgoing mail. "Here, put these somewhere safe." He handed me two letters addressed to people in Kansas. "I'll take 'em to the post office on Monday."

"There's nowhere safe to put them," I replied and dropped them on the floor behind the driver's seat.

"I should've hired you weeks ago," Uncle Frankie said. "I suppose that wouldn't have worked, though. You were too busy with Teddy. I bet you're glad he's gone."

"I'm not glad. I miss him, though not as much as I thought I would," I confessed. "I miss Mom and Adam, too, but not Dad. Do you think he's in Edmonton yet?"

"Maybe, if he even went. It started snowing there two days ago—I checked. I don't think Gene owns snow tires. I know he doesn't have tire chains with him because they're in the garage. That reminds me. I've got a letter for you." Uncle Frankie reached into his back pocket and pulled out a letter with Mom's scratchy handwriting on it.

I moved up to the front passenger seat because there was room now and took the letter from his hand, feeling happy and scared at the same time.

"It's for Paco, not me," I said.

"It's really for you. I told your mom to address her letters to Paco, just to be safe. She posted this one in Kalispell, Montana. That's on this side of the border. They must have spent the night there on the way back to Edmonton," Uncle Frankie said.

"I'll read it when we get back," I said.

"Suit yourself." Uncle Frankie turned the radio up to listen to the news.

The reporter said a man the FBI referred to as "D. B. Cooper" had hijacked a plane, using a bomb in a briefcase, and parachuted from it with an undisclosed amount of ransom money. He was last seen when the plane departed Portland, Oregon, on Wednesday, November 24.

"Right on, right on. Right fucking on!" Uncle Frankie was hitting the steering wheel with his open hand.

"It was a bad thing to do," I said.

"Think so, do you? He's got balls. A true American hero is what he is! D. B. Cooper isn't his name, though. It's Dan Blaser. He's my buddy from Vietnam, and it looks like he's pulled off a big fuck you to that fuckhead Richard Nixon."

"Really? He's your friend? You're not joking?"

"No joke! He's a lot older than me, but still, he treated me more like a brother than a friend. He told me a lot of his shit, and I told him mine. I even told him about a fishing cabin my dad and his friend Bud used to take me to when I was six or seven. It's near to where he jumped. I bet he's there now, waiting for the heat to back off."

"Maybe D. B. Cooper had a helicopter waiting for him," I said when Uncle Frankie went quiet, trying to get him talking again.

"I wouldn't count on it. Those fuckers are expensive. Dan's probably broke like me." Uncle Frankie took his foot off the brake to let the car roll to the next mailbox. "A few months before I got dumped out of a chopper, Dan told me a story about parachuting from a plane with a bag of money. I thought he was talking about a vision he saw, as we'd smoked some kick-ass hash that day. But I guess not. He always said he wanted to live near a sandy beach in Mexico, but he didn't have the cash. Shit, he didn't even own a car back then."

"But how do you know for sure Dan is D. B. Cooper?" I asked.

"Because pilots always name their Hueys." Then, seeing the confused look on my face, he said, "'Huey' is another name for a helicopter. Dan called his Cooper. It's how I put it together: D. B. Cooper equals Dan Blaser, plus his helicopter. I'm sure of it." Uncle Frankie smiled and looked pleased with himself.

The story sounded crazy to me, but I went along with it. "Shouldn't you tell the police?"

"Hell no! And you'd better not either, Miss Goody Two-Shoes," Uncle Frankie snapped.

"I won't tell anyone. I promise."

I wanted Uncle Frankie to trust me. More than trust me, I wanted him to continue to tell me about my family. So, I didn't say a word until he'd finished his cigarette.

"Do you think Dan will ever get caught?" I whispered.

"Dan is a crazy shit, but he knows what he's doing. He grew up in a survival cult and could live in the forest forever if he had to. And he's smart like me and just as pissed off about getting conned into going to Vietnam. I know Dan, and he wouldn't jump out of a plane without a plan to get away." Uncle Frankie pounded the steering wheel again.

All the talk about D. B. Cooper had wound Uncle Frankie up, and it worried me. He'd already stretched his face long twice and even stuttered a few times, and now his leg was shaking.

When I opened the next mailbox and saw it was jam-packed, I told Uncle Frankie it was too full to put more in, and he said it had been that way for days.

"I stuffed a social security check in there two days ago. I can see it on top there." He pointed with his drumstick.

"How about I take their mail to their house?"

"Nice idea," Uncle Frankie said. "And put the check under the front door. I'll just have a little nap until you get back."

The house looked haunted, like other houses on the route. I knocked once, and when no one answered, I slid the check under the door and heard a man yell, "Get off my property," so I quickly sat the rest of the mail on the porch and ran back to the car.

Uncle Frankie was resting his head on the steering wheel, singing along to the Bee Gees. When he looked up, I could tell he'd been crying. I didn't know what to do. Except for Adam, I'd never seen a man cry, and I didn't want to ask Uncle Frankie what was wrong in case I upset him more, so I told him about the man yelling.

"Sorry about that. There are too many mean old men on this route." He wiped his nose on his shirtsleeve. "Probably all mangled veterans like me. Hey, I know you think my Dan Blaser–D. B. Cooper connection is crazy. And maybe it is. But it's no crazier than some of the shit we did and saw in 'Nam, that's for fucking sure. I once held a kid's head in my hands until I couldn't feel my fingers, trying to keep it connected to his neck while Dan flew us out of a bad scene. I only let go when we were on the ground, and Dan pulled me away. That kind of shit happened all the time. It tore us up."

"I sure hope Dan doesn't get caught." I really meant it.

"If there's a way to help my friend, I'm gonna do it."

For the rest of the route, we talked about Uncle Frankie's new hi-fi and his record collection. And when he flipped off a guy who'd honked and yelled at us for being on the wrong side of the road, I asked him how he'd lost the top of his middle finger.

"Someone shot it off," he said with a grin. "It could've been me."

IT WAS ALMOST 4:30 P.M. WHEN UNCLE Frankie turned the car around. "That's it for today," he announced.

"But there's still a box of mail in the back seat, and the Columbia House Records are in the trunk," I said.

"Don't worry about those. Just call me George I. Joseph, if you catch my drift. Hey, everything we talk about in his car is between us, right?"

"Right," I replied.

"Good, 'cause I'm heading out to find Dan tomorrow when we finish the route. Tonight, I'm going to the Choker to get drunk."

CHAPTER 16

MOM'S HANDWRITING WAS WORSE THAN ever, but I could still make out the words. Once I'd scanned it to see if she'd read my workbook story—she hadn't—I reread her letter more slowly, paying close attention to her explanation for leaving me behind. She and her cousin's son, Mike, had gotten to the beach early and parked by the dunes so Dad wouldn't see them. When she found Teddy alone, he told her I'd gone to Dad's car and was coming back with a Tootsie Pop, so she folded his Superman blanket and left it next to the lantern, hoping I'd see it and look for her car. Mooch was there when she and Teddy got back to the car. They'd parked next to his van without knowing it. Mooch told her she was doing the right thing and offered to keep Dad busy digging so he wouldn't see her. Mom waited another ten minutes, but it was getting lighter, and she was sure Dad would see her if she stayed longer. Her letter ended with a sentence about Teddy being happy to have Leroy and a promise to return for me once Dad left for Vietnam.

I read it twice more, feeling better each time. Although she should have looked for me in the bathroom, it was good to know Mom hadn't left me behind because she didn't want me anymore.

AS I WALKED UP THE CAFÉ'S BACK stairs to sweep the floors, I could hear Grandma and Uncle Frankie arguing. "I need the keys to the Studebaker," he said. "Just for two days. I'll be back on Monday—in time for you two to go to bingo. I promise."

"You can't take my car," Grandma said. "If there's an emergency, Vivian can't drive your car. She's too short, too large, and her feet won't reach the pedals. Besides, your car only goes one speed, and that's way too fast."

"Five-foot-three is not short. It's average!" Aunt Vivian called out from the dining room.

"My friend might be hurt, and he can't lie down in my car. It's not big enough. But the Studebaker is. Okay, I have a spare key in the garage," Uncle Frankie said.

"I mean it, Frankie. Do not take my car," Grandma said.

"Yeah, okay. But if I get the chance, I'll be going to Mexico with Dan. It'll be short notice, so be ready!"

THE NEXT MORNING, I STOOD UP AND put my coat on when Uncle Frankie parked and then honked, but Aunt Vivian told me to sit back down and eat my breakfast. "We're not made of money here, and we don't waste food."

I'd just started eating when Uncle Frankie knocked on the café window and motioned me to come outside. Grandma sighed and said I'd better get going. So, I stuffed two pancakes into my mouth and left.

Uncle Frankie was unlocking the trunk when I got to his car. Then suddenly, his face was in my face and his hand was on my head. "We gotta start my route by 0900 to be back by 1300. I gotta head south by 1400."

His bloodshot eyes and the way he kept looking around, like he was expecting someone to jump him, told me there was something more wrong with him than being stoned.

"How about a cup of coffee? You haven't had one today." I wanted Grandma and Aunt Vivian to see him. They'd know how to calm him down.

"I don't need coffee. I need a beer and a cigarette," he said.

"I bet Aunt Vivian will give you a cigarette, and I'll get you a beer out of Grandma's refrigerator." I took his arm and guided him toward the café.

Once he was inside, Uncle Frankie said he wouldn't stay unless he could have the chair closest to the door, the one Fisky had. When Fisky refused to move, Uncle Frankie sat down on top of the table. Aunt Vivian brought him a cup of coffee, a pack of cigarettes, and the newspaper, and Grandma called out from the kitchen, "Eggs over easy coming up, just the way you like 'em, but you have to sit in a chair."

Uncle Frankie did what Grandma said, and when he finished eating, he opened the newspaper and slammed his fist on the table when he saw the headline. "It's been three days, and they haven't found him. Only I know where he is!" he shouted, pushing the paper at Fisky.

"You know where D. B. Cooper is? That's really something, Frankie," Fisky said in a voice that even I knew meant he didn't believe it.

"It is something. Something huge!" Uncle Frankie thumped the table again.

"Get a hold of yourself, Frankie. No one could survive a jump out of a plane flying that high, especially at night. Whoever the guy is, he must be dead." Fisky was staring into Uncle Frankie's face.

When the radio news said the FBI had agents searching for D. B. Cooper in a remote area of the Columbia River Gorge, Uncle Frankie mumbled something about finding Dan before the pigs did. "He's alive, just like I said."

"And Santa Claus is my brother," Fisky said, chuckling.

The other two customers laughed, too, and we all pretended

not to notice when Uncle Frankie crouched down and walked backward to the door, snapping his fingers at me until I opened it for him. It was weird and kind of funny. I stayed in the café until a couple of tourists arrived, and Uncle Frankie, still on the porch, told them it cost two bucks to get in.

Grandma looked at me with pleading eyes, so I went outside and led Uncle Frankie away. We passed Paco at the gas pumps. "Call out if you need help," he said, nodding as we both watched Uncle Frankie get into his car and rest his head on the steering wheel.

"If he gets any weirder, I'm gonna run to the Rollarena and skate," I said.

I left Uncle Frankie in his car and went inside. Knowing he wanted to leave in just over an hour, I only sorted the first-class mail. And when I found the stack for Eat and Get Gas, I searched through it until I found one of Louanne's return-to-sender letters, making a mental note to put it in Uncle Frankie's glove compartment. I also found a letter from Dad addressed to Grandma.

Paco came up the porch stairs. "You'd better be careful today," he said.

"I will. Uncle Frankie is a weirdo, but he's my uncle, and I gotta help him."

MOST OF THE FIRST-CLASS MAIL WAS READY to go when Uncle Frankie pushed the door open at 9:15 a.m. He looked at me like he'd never seen me before. I said hello, but he didn't answer, just stood with his back against the door, looking at his feet. As the seconds passed, I got butterflies in my stomach, so I told him I needed to use Grandma's bathroom.

He clapped and said, "Take Willa's mail to her. While you're there, put some coffee in a thermos, grab a blanket and whatever food you can, and take a bottle of whiskey from the cupboard above Willa's workbench and a couple of packs of Viv's cigarettes. And get me a few boxes of baking soda. And don't let anyone see you."

"I'm sure Grandma will give you those things if you ask," I said in my quietest voice, trying to keep things calm.

"With a hundred questions, which I ain't about to answer. Besides, the two cops who were here yesterday for lunch just arrived for breakfast. All eyes on me, I suspect."

I knew Uncle Frankie hated cops, more so since a state patrolman had pulled him over two weeks ago on our way home from shopping for Grandma.

"You can always count on people calling the post office looking for missing checks, cards, and presents. So, I always deliver those, no matter what." Uncle Frankie drove onto the road in his usual way, like a rocket ship heading for the moon. Squeezed into the front this time, I braced my hands on the dashboard and prayed he'd slow down before we got to the big curve. He didn't, and for a few seconds, it felt like we were on two wheels.

Even though Uncle Frankie was driving as badly as ever, he was much calmer than he'd been earlier. When I asked if he was feeling okay, he dug into his shirt pocket and took out a bottle of pills I recognized from Louanne's dresser.

"Feeling fucking great! What do you know about fire? I've got a lot of garbage on my back porch that needs burning. You can do it. I'll pay you four bits."

"Maybe I will if you slow down," I replied.

"I'm only doing seventy-five. Gene drives faster than me."

"Yeah, he does. Four bits isn't enough to burn smelly old garbage. Only a little kid would do it for that."

"Yeah, yeah, okay. Two bucks, then. But you'd better do a good job," Uncle Frankie said.

"Will you show me how to start a fire in those barrels before you leave?"

"Sure, it's easy. The trick is to put a little gas on a coiled piece of newspaper and light it when the barrel's only half full. Once the fire's going, you can add more stuff, but not too much at once. The hard part is keeping it going. Wet garbage is a bitch—it smokes like a chimney. But I've still got Pa's metal pole. It's good for stirring up the flames."

"I think I can do that. Did you like Pa more than your real dad?"

"Hell, yeah. My old man was the town drunk. The only drunk worse than him was his friend Bud. Everyone hated them, especially my mom. Maybe it's why she drove into the path of a logging truck, just to get rid of them."

"Really? Your mom did that?" I asked.

"I haven't decided. Some people think so. Pa said it was just an accident."

I wanted to hear more, but I didn't ask because he was all over the road, and six mailboxes later, he ran right into one. We both got out of the car to put it back up, and he was grumpy afterward. I waited until the song on the radio finished before asking why he didn't go to North Dakota with Louanne after the car crash.

"I didn't know for three years that Louanne had survived—until my eleventh birthday when a card arrived from her. Man, that was freaky. It wasn't a big deal to me, but Willa cried, and Pa told me to forget about the card. Said my sister was just something to worry about."

Uncle Frankie hit the steering wheel with his open palm. "He was right! Goddamn it. I didn't need it then, and I sure as hell don't need it now. Louanne being here was okay for a month, but she's getting under my skin. I should've left her in North Dakota. But I felt sorry about how fucked up she got in the accident. Willa says I have survivor's guilt. I wasn't in the car with them. I was at my friend's house. His mother had to tell me about the accident. Then she gave us potato chips and said we could watch TV all night. Willa and Pa arrived the next day to get me. To this day, I still think about my mom first thing in the morning and the last thing at night," he said.

Uncle Frankie pulled up to a big red mailbox with its flag up. "There's a package in the trunk addressed to the Grange Hall that goes in this box. Go get it," he said.

Uncle Frankie picked up where he'd left off once I was back in the car. "Willa was my mom's best friend, and we sometimes came here to get away from Dad. Just the summer before the accident, when Dad let Bud move into our garage, Mom brought my sisters and me here. We stayed for weeks, and Pa let me work at the gas station. So, after the accident, when my friend's mother told me Willa and Pa were picking me up, I was pretty happy.

"Like my parents, Willa and Pa moved from North Dakota to Washington State after the war. I was born here in 1950, but Gene and Clarence were both born in North Dakota. I think Clarence was ten or eleven when he died."

I sat up straight. "Who's Clarence again?"

"I suppose he'd be your uncle if Gene hadn't been playing around in Pa's truck and released the brake when Clarence was behind it," Uncle Frankie said.

"Oh, God. Dad must have gotten into a lot of trouble. Do you think my mom knows?"

"Shit, yeah, everyone knows. You know, Pa always called me Clarence when no one was around. He did it once when Gene was in the room, and Gene almost cried. Hey, don't tell anyone I told you all this. Especially your mom. She thinks I'm an okay guy. I want it to stay that way."

"I won't say a thing, I promise."

LATER IN THE MORNING, UNCLE FRANKIE turned onto Loggerhead Road and parked in front of a mobile home. "I'll be back in fifteen. I gotta see a man about a horse," he said.

I was glad he'd left the car running and the heater on because it was freezing. I read a Christmas story in a *Reader's Digest* magazine and played with the radio dial, looking for a song I liked. Then I remembered the returned letter in my back pocket. I opened the glove compartment to put it in but instead took out half a dozen others. I sorted them by postmark date, shuffled them a few times while admiring Louanne's handwriting, and finally convinced myself it was okay to read one. No one would care about a letter from last June.

I picked at the seal of the oldest letter, dated June 12; it was easy to open. There were two pieces of floral stationery paper with writing on both sides. There was a lot of stuff I already knew about, but some of the things she wrote to her aunt about were a surprise, like what she said about Paco: "He confided to me last week that his real name is Patrick. Frankie picked him up in Spokane after he collected me in Williston. I don't recall. I was very upset about leaving and had to take additional pills. I slept almost the entire way to Mrs. Hanson's. Patrick was drafted to Vietnam. He doesn't want to go. He's hiding here, with Frankie's help. He's friendly and almost as tall as Frankie and has a mustache that makes him look like Rhett Butler from *Gone with the Wind*."

Louanne also described a strange thing that had happened on the bus when she was going to the library. An "older gentleman," as she called him, had got on and sat next to her. "He asked me to wake him if he snored," she wrote, "and he put his coat over his head. He began snoring soon after. I tried to wake him with a fake cough. I also nudged him. He didn't move. I left him sleeping and snoring." A few days later, he was on the bus again and this time introduced himself as Dr. Lars Larson. "I didn't reply because I thought he was fibbing.

He ate two sandwiches and told me to wake him if he snored. When I told him I'd tried to wake him before and couldn't, he asked me if I'd punched his arm or pinched his leg. He said that was what his son, Erik, did. 'Are you his friend? If so, you can ask him to show you how it's done.'" When Louanne told him she didn't have friends, he said he'd be her friend and tried to touch her hand. "I moved closer to the window, and he said he was sorry. I was grateful when he put his newspaper over his head and fell asleep."

Louanne also wrote about sleeping pills: "I should have had enough to last until October, but Frankie helps himself. He has a lot of pain from his time in the war and doesn't get enough sleep. It cost me ten dollars to see Mrs. Hanson's doctor. He didn't give me pills from his cabinet like Dr. Betteridge does. I had to buy them at the drugstore. I've hidden them from Frankie."

I knew I shouldn't, but I read another letter, this one written in mid-July. She hoped Aunt Bethania was feeling better and that she would write soon. It turned out that the man from the bus was a psychiatrist, and his son, who he was staying with, was also a doctor. Dr. Lars's wife had died six years ago. "He moved here from Boston," Louanne wrote, "because he was walking into people on the street on purpose, so that someone would look at him. And he used to sit on a park bench holding up one of his wife's opera gloves and asking ladies passing by if they'd lost it. He got into trouble for hugging one who said the glove was hers."

They talked some more on the bus, and then Dr. Lars Larson told Louanne that she needed to see his son. "When he stood up to get off the bus, he handed me a card with his son's phone number and a notebook. I told him it wasn't my birthday. He said friends could give friends gifts anytime, and if he were my doctor, he'd ask me to write about how I got here. I had a bad dream and sleepwalked that night. I wrote two paragraphs this morning in the notebook and then called Dr. Lars's son's office for an appointment. It's next month."

By early August, Louanne had seen Dr. Erik Larson. "He has the same calm manner as his father. I told him about my headaches and the pain in my face and jaw. I agreed to let him examine me and answered his questions. It was uncomfortable, especially when he asked about my dreams and female problems. I told him the car accident had relieved me of female problems, but I still had bad dreams. I told him what I remembered about the accident. That it was the day after Frankie's eighth birthday, and I was holding a piece of birthday cake, sitting next to my sister in the back seat of our Buick. And then I was in a bright room, with people all around me asking my name."

Although she didn't want him to, Dr. Erik Larson kept asking her about her dreams. She described a new one that had started when she got to Eat and Get Gas. "I'm in the back of a spinning car. I'm clutching a baby to my chest with both hands. I know if I reach out to grab my sister's hand, the baby will fly out the door, so I don't, and my sister flies out the door."

I put the letters I'd read under the ones I hadn't, hoping Uncle Frankie would never notice.

CHAPTER 17

I WAS CLOSING THE GLOVE COMPARTMENT when Uncle Frankie reappeared. On the trailer porch, dressed in a blue baby-doll nightie, stood a woman who was waving and blowing kisses.

"She's the most flexible gal in town. She used to be a cheerleader. Now she's a dancer."

"Yeah," I said, "she looked like a ballerina waving to her handsome prince from the balcony of a castle." I cupped my hands over my mouth while I laughed.

"Ah, we've got a wiseass in the car," Uncle Frankie said, but he laughed too.

When he pulled up next to the Powells's mailbox and saw their red flag was up, he handed me his drumstick and told me he was tired. I didn't want him to fall asleep, so I quickly asked if the café was already there when Grandma and Grandpa moved to Hoquiam.

"Don't you know anything about your family?" he asked.

"A bit about my mom's family in Canada, but hardly anything about Dad's."

Uncle Frankie slapped his face a couple of times, lit a cigarette, and turned the radio off.

"The original café had a small kitchen and dining room. I've seen pictures. Pa, Hal, and Hubert extended those rooms and added the back porch and storage room."

"And the gas station?" I asked.

"Maybe five years after they rebuilt the café, they cleared the land and built the garage. Hal and Hubert can build or fix just about anything. And, as you've heard, they play the piano like Liberace. They look like bums, though. Willa says they stopped taking care of themselves when their mother died."

"They smell bad, too," I said.

"Yeah, they do. And they don't seem to own a razor. But they're good men, and they're helpful. You saw how they saved me from Gene the other day. They didn't have to do that. Gene could have killed them. He's a fucking animal!"

"Why is Grandma's place called Eat and Get Gas?"

"That was Pa's doing. He had to come up with a name quickly when the Esso Gas sales agent offered him a contract that included a free sign. When the sign arrived, Pa put it up over the café's front porch. Willa made him take it down a week later, but everyone was calling it Eat and Get Gas by then, and it stuck."

"It's a weird name. I've heard people call it Eat and Fart," I said.

"Yeah, Willa thought they would, even though Pa told her not everyone had a dirty mind. She wanted a new sign that said Hanson's Homestyle Café and Gas Station. But they didn't have the money for it. A week before I left for Vietnam, I climbed on the porch roof and painted 'eat' in block letters where the sign used to be. It's not my best work, and it's faded now, but it made Willa happy."

"I didn't have enough red paint to write 'gas' over the garage. Besides, Willa closed it when I left. I just opened it again a year ago. It's never been a moneymaker. The café keeps the place going. When Pa first opened the gas station, the Phillips 66 in Aberdeen was where everyone bought gas. Business here was so slow that Pa had to work for a construction company in Seattle. He died in '62 after falling from the roof of a building he was helping build for the World's Fair. It devastated Willa. She couldn't get out of bed and wouldn't take anyone's calls. The café stayed closed, and the Esso truck arrived and sucked the gasoline out from the underground tank and took the handles off the pumps."

"Jeez, no wonder Dad never told me," I said.

"I don't know if you remember, but you came here with your dad and Adam after the funeral and helped me board up the café and garage. I went back to Tacoma with you. I didn't want to go, but Willa made me."

"I remember. You showed Adam how to spit water through his teeth, and Grandma was wearing Pa's coat and hat," I said.

"You've got a good memory. Willa wore his coat and hat for years after he died."

"Why didn't Aunt Vivian help Grandma?" I asked.

"She did. She came to the funeral and stayed for a week. When she went back to North Dakota, she called Willa every morning to make sure she was still standing, and I was getting ready for school. Gene could've helped Ma more than he did. He was stationed at Fort Lewis then. He could've come on the weekends and opened the gas station. But he's always been a lazy ass."

"Really? You think my dad is lazy?"

"Have you seen him do anything around here except dig a few clams and wash his car?" Uncle Frankie asked.

I thought for a moment. "No."

"There's your answer."

Uncle Frankie turned the radio back on, and just when I thought he'd finished telling me stuff, he lit a new cigarette from the one he was still smoking and said, "It's fucked up that I went to Vietnam and came back ten months later with one less finger and a broken back. Yet, after three tours, Gene's only got a scratchy throat."

When we got back to Grandma's, Uncle Frankie told me to take the empty mailbags out of his car and meet him by the barrels in his backyard. "I'm gonna show you how to burn shit before I take off."

I got there before he did and rummaged through the four boxes of garbage and old mail on his back porch, looking for first-class stuff. When Uncle Frankie brought out the box of undelivered mail I'd sorted the day before, he also had a bottle of Jim Beam.

"Don't mention the mail. Don't even look at it. Just burn it," he ordered, taking a big swig. "There's more in my bedroom, but I think this is enough for today." Then he stepped forward and started a fire in the biggest of three barrels. "Save the boxes. I might need 'em later. And some of this shit is damp. It's gonna smoke. Just keep pushing it down with that pole by the porch, and if that doesn't work, put a newspaper coil on top." He pointed to several under the porch steps. "I drenched them with gasoline this morning. They should keep the fire going. If not, ask Paco. He used to be a Boy Scout."

When Uncle Frankie left to pack his car with supplies for D. B. Cooper, I pulled a box close, adding garbage and mail and pushing it down with the metal pole until I had to use the bathroom. There was no toilet paper in Uncle Frankie's bathroom, so I ran to the café. Lying open on Grandma's workbench, next to a check for four hundred dollars made out to Mrs. Wilhelmina Hanson, was a note from Dad: "I sold the clams you didn't want. Your son, Gene."

No mention of me, and not a word about finding Mom or when they were coming home. I could feel the tears coming as I headed back to the barrels.

Uncle Frankie's car was full of stuff. It made me think he was leaving for good, not just until Monday like he'd told Grandma.

"I guess you're gonna go find the hijacker, huh?" I asked.

"Sure as hell am. That's why I'm taking firewood and blankets," he said. "Dan's gotta be cold as a motherfucker. Hey, while you're burning shit, get those returned letters of Louanne's out of my car and burn them, too."

I put Louanne's letters in the barrel and threw a gasoline newspaper coil on top. I watched them burn to ash. In the last box of garbage, I found a birthday card Louanne had sent to her aunt. Inside was a knitted, brown flop-eared rabbit, just like Velvet. It was cute, and for a moment, I considered keeping it. It took two coils to get rid of it.

WHEN UNCLE FRANKIE WASN'T HOME ON Monday like he'd promised, Grandma didn't seem worried. But when he wasn't home on Thursday, she called the Washington State Patrol office and asked if there'd been a car accident involving an orange GTO. There hadn't.

The next morning, six days after Uncle Frankie left to find his friend Dan, the café phone rang, and Aunt Vivian answered.

"It's for Frankie, Willa. Do you wanna talk, or should I take a message?" Aunt Vivian called out to Grandma from the dining room.

"Take a message. I've got bacon on the grill," Grandma said.

"It's your postmaster friend. He's been calling the garage and not getting an answer," Aunt Vivian said.

Grandma waved me over to watch the bacon. By the time she got off the phone, the bacon was cooked, and she was fuming.

"He's got five days of route mail waiting for Frankie to pick up and deliver. I lied, Viv. I told him Frankie had pneumonia and couldn't get out of bed. I hate lying. You know that, but I had to. I told him you'd get the mail this morning and deliver it this afternoon. I'm sorry. I didn't know what else to do."

"What the hell?" Aunt Vivian said, spit flying. "Why would you tell him that, Willa?"

"I had to. You know as well as I do, the gas station barely makes enough to keep it going. Frankie can't lose his route."

Aunt Vivian moved closer to Grandma, fists on hips. "Hell's bells, how am I supposed to put all that mail in the Studebaker and find my way around his route? Christ, I'm not a goddamn magician!"

I'd never seen Grandma and Aunt Vivian so upset. I thought about skipping school to sort mail, but I had a geography test that morning, and I couldn't miss it. But then I thought of something else. "If Paco can drive me around the route," I told Grandma, "I can do the rest. I've sorted and delivered with Uncle Frankie twice, and I've got the route map in my room."

After school, instead of waiting for the bus, I ran the three miles to Eat and Get Gas. Paco was standing outside the garage, trying to put his shoulder-length hair into a ponytail. While I caught my breath, he told me Aunt Vivian had made three trips to the post office to get the mail and told him she wouldn't be delivering it. "Let me put it this way—the lady ain't happy. Neither is Willa, but she's convinced Hal and Hubert to run the gas station for the next two days. So, it looks like we'll be delivering mail tomorrow, once Vivian returns from the post office with Saturday's mail, which we'll have to unload before we can fill up the Studebaker with mail that you'll sort today—I'll help if you want."

WHEN I GOT TO UNCLE FRANKIE'S, LOUANNE was looking at the bags and piles of mail in the kitchen. She seemed surprised to see me. "Oh, yes, I remember now. You're here to sort the mail for him. I'd stay and help, but I need to go to bed before my headache gets worse."

I worked as fast as I could, and after a couple of hours, the door opened, and Aunt Vivian walked in with her glass of tonic and a paper bag containing two hamburgers and French fries. "Just hold it in your lap and eat from the bag."

"Thanks. I'm starving," I said. "I haven't gotten very far. There's so much this time, and I shouldn't have emptied two bags over the table."

"Christ Almighty, we'll never get this done." Aunt Vivian pulled up a chair and sat beside me. There was just enough room for both of us.

I showed her the different postmarks and explained the importance of looking for first-class mail, but she didn't seem to care. She muttered as she pulled magazines and mail from the pile that Uncle Frankie would have considered garbage.

I knew she was as angry about being in "Frankie's filth pit" as she was about helping with the mail. After about an hour, she began tossing letters toward the living room, saying she couldn't read the addresses. Then she opened the front door and threw the Christian Science magazines outside. I volunteered to go to Grandma's house and get her a drink, reminding her that Louanne was asleep in her room.

"That girl is a hard worker, like me," said Aunt Vivian. "Hey, make my drink a double, and bring back some goddamn toilet paper."

When I got back, she was adding letters to the pile of mail for Eat and Get Gas. "Five days with no mail is a long time for us," she said, reaching for the vodka-and-orange I was holding.

"I just heard Hal and Hubert playing a new song," I said.

"I heard it last night. It's called 'Moonlight Sonata.' I imagine they're getting ready for their recital."

"I still can't believe the music coming from their house isn't from a record."

"I didn't know for sure either," said Aunt Vivian, "until I'd been here for six months, and I found an invitation to their Christmas recital on Willa's porch. I didn't want to go for many reasons, including Hal's marriage proposals. The first time he asked, it shook me up for days."

I paused and looked at her, trying to figure out if she was kidding.

"Oh, sweet Jesus, I still can't believe it," she continued. "Even though it was five years ago, the memory's as clear as glass. It was July and a full moon. I was trying to move a log that had come off a passing truck and rolled to the front of the café. Suddenly, Hal appeared next to me and said he and Hubert would take care of it in the morning. Then he dropped to one knee, grabbed my hand, and asked me to marry him, all the while trying to put a big ring on my finger. I didn't know whether to slap him or to run, so I ran. When I got to the house, I told Willa, and she laughed until she cried. He asked a second time a few months later."

"Did you ever want to say yes?"

"Hell no! I'm too old. And I learned a long time ago that a woman doesn't need a man if she can read, write, and light a stove. The ring, well, that was something else—too much gold, too many diamonds, just too much of everything. I told him so, too."

"Was he mad?"

"I don't think so. He asked a third time, a week after the second. Only that time, he tried it with a new ring—a square emerald, I think. I told him I was a married woman, so that he'd stop asking. I'm not married. I'm divorced, but he doesn't need to know that. So, I told Willa I wasn't going to the recital, but she swore they were grand pianists, and I wouldn't regret it. She also said I had to wear something other than overalls. So, I wore the only dress I own, a black sack I made to wear to my father's funeral."

I couldn't believe Hal had wanted to marry Aunt Vivian, though maybe I shouldn't have been surprised. There were always flowers for her in the basket of eggs and herbs he left on the café's back porch. And I'd heard Fisky and Grandma tease Aunt Vivian about Hal calling her "the lovely Vivian."

"Did Grandma dress up for the recital?"

"Like you've seen on bingo nights, Willa paints her face and dresses up whenever she goes out. That night was no exception. She wore her red coat, black gloves, and our mother's pearls. You would've thought she was having lunch with the queen," Aunt Vivian said. "Hal and Hubert wore black tuxedo jackets, slacks, and dress shirts I imagine were once white. The room was an icebox, but the music was thrilling, so I didn't complain. They didn't use sheet music or even look at each other. They knew every note of every song and only paused for a few seconds between each one."

I was so engrossed in Aunt Vivian's story that I hadn't noticed Paco was in the room, until he put a bottle of Coke in front of me and a can of beer in front of Aunt Vivian. When I asked if Grandma had liked the concert as much as Aunt Vivian did, Paco tipped the contents of a mailbag over the table and leaned in to hear the answer.

"Oh, she did. I don't think either of us took more than a few breaths until they finished," she said.

"Wow," I replied. "Was it better than *The Sound of Music*?"

"Much better," Aunt Vivian said. "After the concert, when they walked us to their front door, I thought they'd just open it and say good night, but they escorted us home and gave us each a small box with a red bow. Willa tried to return hers, but I wanted to know what two piano-playing loggers would have to give to an old lady. I was expecting a petrified beetle or dried flowers. Instead, I got a gold and ivory brooch and a new respect for Hal and Hubert and their many talents."

CHAPTER 18

FOR A SECOND, I WASN'T SURE WHO I was looking at. Hal and Hubert had arrived early to start work at Get Gas, and they didn't look the same without their long hair, beards, and shabby clothes. And they smelled like pine tar soap.

"At your service," Hal said, bowing like a butler. "Do you have instructions for us?"

"You both look so young and handsome," said Grandma, "and those coonskin hats are something else."

"Those suits remind me of the one Cary Grant wore in the last scene of *An Affair to Remember*," Aunt Vivian added.

"Why, thank you much, ladies." Hal reached over to straighten Hubert's tie.

I didn't mean to snort when I said Paco was on his way over to show them what to do, and I looked away when I did it again. Grandma and Aunt Vivian looked away, too, and I sensed they were trying as hard as I was not to laugh.

When Paco walked into the kitchen, Hal and Hubert stepped forward with their hands out. "Oh, wow, nice suits, you two. Ready to work, I see." He smiled and shook their hands.

Paco and I ate toast with jam at the dining room counter while Aunt Vivian poured coffee for Hal and Hubert and told them how to run the gas station, even though she never had.

We didn't look away when Hal and Hubert dropped eight sugar cubes into their cups and, in perfect sync, stirred one way for a few seconds and then the other way for a few more before drinking it in just a few gulps.

"That's spooky," I whispered to Paco.

"Guess they like it sweet and quick," he snickered.

IN THE FRONT PASSENGER SEAT OF THE Studebaker at 9:00 a.m., I had so much mail on me and around me that it was hard to see out the windshield. And if I hadn't crawled over the seat to move a box so Paco could see out the back window, we wouldn't have seen Hal and Hubert waving goodbye from the side of the road, both hands over their heads. Paco said he'd told them three times that morning to stay away from the car in the mechanic pit.

"Between customers, they went right back to the car to fiddle around with the engine, even though I told them it had a cracked radiator and Frankie could fix it. Then, right before Hal took a break to feed his chickens, he poured gasoline into the carburetor—a dangerous thing to do. Those two are strange. I don't think they'll be able to run the gas station on their own."

"They might be strange, but even my dad says they can fix anything. Maybe they know something you don't," I replied, feeling like I should stick up for Hal and Hubert and then nervous that I'd made Paco mad.

Paco said he planned to keep track of his hours, to charge Uncle Frankie for doing his route. When I told him Uncle Frankie hadn't paid me anything yet, he said, "That sounds right—he promises lots and delivers not much. He owes me money, too. I'm not holding my breath."

"How come you're helping him, then?"

"The same reason you are. Willa asked me to, and I like her. She reminds me of my grandma. And you never know," he chuckled. "Frankie might pay us one day."

Paco was a better driver than Uncle Frankie. He could get Grandma's car close to mailboxes without hitting them, making it easy for me to put the mail in. Halfway through the route, he told me it was his birthday and invited me to go roller-skating with him that night.

"Yes, please!"

I knew Grandma wouldn't let me, but I sure wanted to. I'd seen Paco skate at the Rollarena when I went to Marie's birthday party. He had his own skates, and he was faster than anyone else and weaved between other skaters without touching them. I wanted to skate that way.

"Then it's a date. I don't mean 'date.' Just a skating thing," Paco said.

"Yeah, sure," I replied. My insides fluttered. "Grandma will make you a birthday cake if I ask her. What do you like?"

"No, don't do that. I'm not supposed to tell anyone. I mean, I promised Frankie I wouldn't," he said.

"Why?" I asked, even though I already knew.

"'Cause Frankie told everyone I was twenty-one, like him, but I'm nineteen today. I don't think I could lie to Willa and Vivian. They're pretty nice ladies, and besides, I'm not a straight-faced liar like Frankie."

"He's a good liar, for sure." Maybe I was, too. "So you're a teenager, like me?"

"Yeah, I am. And I'm not Mexican, and my name is Patrick. Frankie gave me the name Paco Lopez because he doesn't want anyone to know my real name. Paco is from a Santana song he likes."

"You kind of look Mexican, though," I said.

"My mother is from Argentina. My dad is Scottish. Man, do I miss them." Paco looked straight ahead and blinked.

I didn't want him to be embarrassed, so I opened the glove compartment and riffled around like I was looking for something. When I saw the bra, I quickly slammed it shut. It had to be Aunt Vivian's.

"Hey, I'm no childhood friend of Frankie's like he tells everyone. I just met him about six months ago," Paco said. "And I have three sisters and two brothers. My oldest brother is in the Air Force. He was MIA in Vietnam for a few weeks last year, and my mom didn't sleep until he called to say he was okay. When I got my notice to report, she took me to see a guy she knew who knew a guy who could get me to Canada. That guy was Frankie. I wrote to him, and he wrote back with a date, time, and place to meet. But the guy Frankie arranged to take me across the Canadian border didn't show up. We tried again in July, but the border I would walk across, using the fake Canadian ID Frankie got for me, was closed. So, I'm here until Frankie finds another way to get me into Canada. And it's okay, I guess. I like working at the gas station, and Frankie's a good mechanic. I've learned a lot, but I sure miss my family, especially my mom. Not my dad, though. I know he hates what I've done. I hate it, too. I should have gone to Vietnam."

"My Uncle Frankie is trying to help you get to Canada?"

Paco reached over and put his hand on my left wrist. "Yes. And like I said before, he's helped others, too. You've gotta swear to keep it a secret. There's no telling what he'd do if he finds out I told you."

I swore never to tell anyone, and he loosened his grip. And I turned my head to the left and mouthed "promise."

For the remaining few hours, we talked about café customers, Hal and Hubert, poor Louanne, the book he was reading (*Moby Dick*), and all the trouble Uncle Frankie had caused by taking off to find D. B. Cooper. "I don't know what to believe," said Paco. "It sounds true, but it could just be another one of his bullshit stories."

WHEN WE RETURNED TO EAT AND GET GAS to get lunch and pick up more mail, three cars were in line to buy gas, and Hal was making change for a customer while Hubert washed their windshield. "Well, I'll be," I heard Paco say several times under his breath.

Because many packages didn't fit into mailboxes and had to be taken to front porches, the second mail run took longer than the first. We still made it back in time to go skating, though, thanks to Aunt Vivian convincing Grandma to let me go and to Grandma for letting Paco drive her Studebaker.

At the Rollarena, I put skates on and then stood by the rails with some school friends drinking a Coke and watching Paco show off. He had been right about the best skaters coming out on Saturday night, but only one or two could skate as well as he could. When the song "Young Girl" came on, Paco sped across the floor and put his hand out to me. I took it without thinking, and when he pulled me close, I didn't pull away like the voice inside my head told me to. Instead, I let him guide me to the middle of the rink and leaned into him when he put his hands around my waist.

To my relief, I could hear Grandma and Aunt Vivian snoring louder than usual as I walked up the stairs to go to bed, so I didn't have to make up an excuse for being two hours late. But I couldn't fall asleep while thinking about Paco and how he'd kissed me on the cheek when we'd finished skating together. It was thrilling. My friend Marie said he likely kissed his grandmother the same way, and she was probably right, but I didn't care.

I WAS UP EARLY MONDAY MORNING TO weave green and red ribbons into my braids for the Twelfth Day of Christmas school assembly. I'd just started my second braid when I heard Uncle Frankie's car outside. When I got to the dining room, he was talking to Grandma and Aunt Vivian. His clothes were dirty, and he smelled sour, but he didn't look like he'd been in a car wreck, as I'd been thinking.

"Dan was alone at a back table in the Carson Tavern, looking like he'd gone ten rounds with Muhammad Ali. Man, was he happy to see me. A truck driver picked him up Thanksgiving night and dropped him off in Carson. He was looking for the old fishing cabin I'd told him about, without the map I gave him back in Vietnam. I was gonna take him to the cabin right then, but the cops had put up roadblocks going east and north."

"You sure about that? Nothing about it on the news," Aunt Vivian smirked.

"Hell, yes, I'm sure." Uncle Frankie poured a cup of coffee and took several sips before continuing. "We hid in a school storeroom and slept in my car for two days until the cops opened the roads going north. I drove us to Packwood. I was planning to leave Dan in a motel there and come home for a few days, but then I heard the motel owner tell a customer that Dan looked like the picture of D. B. Cooper on the news, so I drove to Wind River yesterday, found the cabin, and there he sits."

"And yet, for the past ten days, you couldn't find a phone to let me know you were alive?" Grandma asked with wide eyes and raised eyebrows.

"That's right. You got it," Uncle Frankie said, raising his eyebrows too.

"It's not a joke, Frankie. I've been worried—we all have," Grandma said.

"You might need to worry a little longer 'cause the only way the heat won't find Dan is by me helping him. He's gonna need more supplies. Not today or tomorrow, though. And don't give me a hard time about my mail route. I've already been to the post office this morning. Thanks for telling my boss the big fat lie about me being sick. I figured it out when he asked if I still had a fever."

Grandma was stone-faced and staring at Uncle Frankie when Aunt Vivian slapped him on the back and said, "I'm giving that story a five out of ten!"

FOR THE NEXT FEW DAYS, UNCLE FRANKIE didn't talk to any of us. He just did his mail route, worked at the gas station, and ate his lunch and dinner at the Choker bar. Then, on my way to catch the school bus on Friday, when I saw his car was full of supplies for his friend Dan and noticed smoke coming from behind his house, I walked to the burn barrels to say goodbye. "I believe you," I said, not sure if I did. "There weren't any returned letters in the mail I sorted last week."

"That's good." He was almost smiling. "I haven't found one, either. Maybe Orson stopped sending them back, or maybe Louanne stopped writing to our aunt. Last night, I dreamed she died. I bet she did, and Orson doesn't have the guts to tell us."

I stepped closer to the fire to warm my hands while he dropped things into the barrel. I saw then that he was burning more than just café garbage, including a big piece of cloth with a rope attached to it.

"I'm taking off for a couple of days. Paco said he'd get the mail from the post office tomorrow and drive you around the route. It's almost Christmas, so there's gonna be a shitload of mail to sort and lots of packages and cards. You might need to deliver on Sunday, too. I'll pay you extra, of course. And let me know if Paco lays a hand on you. I'll cut it off," Uncle Frankie said with a double wink.

ON MY WAY TO THE BUS STOP, I COUNTED five full mail-bags on Uncle Frankie's front porch. I knew there'd be just as many, if not more, the next day, so when I got home from school, I sorted it, only taking a break to sweep the café floors.

"If the grill's still on, can I have a hamburger?" I asked Grandma.

"It's still hot, but you'll have to cook. I'm not moving," she said.

"Eat the leftover fries in the basket, too," Aunt Vivian said.

Two burgers, fries, and a root beer later, I was full and eager to finish sorting the mail. When I told Grandma and Aunt Vivian that Uncle Frankie had left for the weekend, Grandma sighed. "I thought so."

Aunt Vivian motioned to me to pick up the empty ice-cream buckets and take them to the back porch, then turned the radio up to listen to the news. The announcer said that it had been more than three weeks since D. B. Cooper hijacked a plane, and there had been no reliable sightings of him or his parachute.

CHAPTER 19

A WEEK BEFORE CHRISTMAS AND TWENTY-FOUR days after he left, Dad came back. I was in the café eating breakfast when he parked at the side of the building.

"How you doing, kid?" Dad lifted a bucket of clams from his trunk and headed toward the backyard.

"Where's Mom? Where's Teddy?" I asked. He ignored me until I stamped my foot. "Why won't you tell me?"

"You can either shut your mouth or get lost." He held up a clam, threatening to throw it at me.

I ran to Grandma's house, passing Louanne on her way to the café kitchen to work. "My dad's back," I said.

When Louanne turned around and began walking to Uncle Frankie's house, I followed, but she went inside without inviting me in.

I was sitting on Uncle Frankie's whale bench when I heard the door open. "Here, while you're sitting there moping, teach yourself a card trick. Distraction is the key to survival." Uncle Frankie handed me a brand-new deck.

"I can use the deck you gave to Teddy. It's still under the bed where he left it." I was trying to stop the tears.

Even though Uncle Frankie had a terrible cold, he finished a cigarette and talked about saving his friend Dan from the FBI.

"If you want to meet him, I'll take you. I already told him I might bring you along the next time I brought him supplies. You'll like him. He's interesting. These boots I'm wearing . . . well, Dan and I were walking back to the base one night when we saw them in a ditch. They were still on the feet of a dead Vietcong, but that didn't bother Dan." Uncle Frankie grinned.

"That's disgusting." I looked away, hoping he'd go back to bed.

No such luck. He stood up to spit off the side of the porch, then lit a joint. Louanne opened the door before he finished it, so he threw it down. She was wearing a red raincoat with an oversized hood and carrying a brown canvas bag. "I'm going to the library. I will not spend one more minute around Gene the barbarian."

"I hate him, too," I said.

"Do you want a ginger cookie?" Louanne took a paper bag out of her coat pocket.

"Did you make them?" Inside were five round, brown cookies, one with nibble marks around the edges.

"No. The librarian did. I tried to eat one, but it was too hard. It'll be easy for you with those big teeth."

She smiled when I curled up my top lip and said I liked my big teeth. As the bus pulled away, I could see that Louanne and Dr. Lars were sitting together in the back.

AT DINNER THAT NIGHT, DAD SAT NEXT to me. He asked me about my school, sorting mail, and roller-skating. He didn't mention Mom or my brothers, and he didn't cut me off when I went into detail about the mail route, the geography test I passed with flying colors, or my friends Marie and Carla, who both had kittens from the same litter. It was strange and kind of nice having Dad's attention for the first time in ages, but it took restraint to keep quiet and not ask about Mom, Adam, and Teddy.

It wasn't just Dad who was being weird. Grandma and Aunt Vivian were overly cheerful and quieter than usual. When Dad sat down on the couch next to me to watch TV, he handed me a roll of cherry Life Savers, my favorite, and I practically screamed, "What is it? Is Mom dead or something?"

Dad looked at Grandma, and I saw her nod.

"No, she's not dead, but she's a lot sicker than she was back in August." Dad was still looking at Grandma. "She has no balance and gets dizzy. She's seeing a specialist next month to find out what's wrong. Her family is taking good care of her, and they treat Teddy like he's a prince. Adam wasn't around, and no one would tell me where he was living. It doesn't matter now. It's best if I don't know. He'd go straight to prison if they caught him crossing the border. So, until your mom gets better, they're staying there, and you're staying here."

"What? Are you kidding?" I threw the roll of Life Savers across the room and watched it roll toward Grandma and Aunt Vivian at the dining room table.

"I can take a bus or a train, or maybe Uncle Frankie can drive me to Edmonton. I wanna be with Mom and Teddy, not here." I was talking louder and faster than I'd meant to.

"Not possible. There's no room for you there. Your mom shares a bed with Teddy and that mutt of yours," Dad said.

"Why didn't you bring her back, then?"

"She's not well enough to travel, and she hasn't told you because it could be September before she's well enough to get a place of her own there."

I hid my face in my hands. "I don't want to stay here for nine more months. No one wants me to either," I said, sucking in a breath.

"Well, I don't want you to leave. Not now, anyway." Grandma's voice was quivering. "When you heard me tell Gene last month to take you to Edmonton, I didn't know how unwell Endura was. Now that I know, I've changed my mind."

"You've got no options," Dad said. "I'm out of here in four days."

"Why? Can't you just wait for Mom to get better and come home? What did you guys do all those weeks? Why didn't you call? You said you would. You just sent Grandma a check!" I moved to the doorway, out of his reach.

Dad rubbed his hands back and forth over his bald head, and I could tell he didn't want to answer. But I stayed put, waiting.

"I was in Edmonton for three days. Been at Mooch's the rest of the time. I needed a bit of R and R before I head back to the jungle," he replied.

"A slap on that big, bald, empty head of yours is what you need!" Aunt Vivian said. She came over and pulled me close. "Who says no one wants you here? Frankie and Paco do, and everyone knows the bread delivery man does."

I took a breath, but I didn't move until she stepped back and motioned for me to follow her up the stairs. Once in her room, I sat down in her red wing chair, and she opened the floor vent so we could listen to Dad and Grandma in the kitchen below. I didn't catch what Grandma had said. I only heard Dad say, "She's staying here. I'll send you money!" And then the back door slammed shut.

In the morning, Paco told Grandma that Uncle Frankie was sicker than ever, and he'd be going to the post office to pick up the mail. I reminded Grandma that school was out, and I could skip roller-skating with Marie and Carla that afternoon to sort the mail for Uncle Frankie.

"No, you won't," Dad said, not looking up from his crossword puzzle. "Frankie is a big sissy. He needs to get his ass out of bed and do his goddamn job."

By lunchtime, Dad had already left with Mooch to go clam digging up north. I took a couple of cheeseburgers with me to Uncle Frankie's house. I sorted mail as fast as I could until Paco closed Get Gas, and we packed it all into Grandma's Studebaker.

We didn't talk too much that day. I think we were both tired and wanted to finish the route before the rain got worse. Still, it felt good to be with Paco. He said nice things to me, didn't smoke in the car, and didn't drive like he was going to a fire, and we liked the same music.

TWO DAYS LATER, WHEN DAD GOT BACK from digging with Mooch, he told me to grab my coat and get into his car. "We're going home to get some things your mom needs. You'd better get your shit while we're there. No telling if you'll get another chance."

I sat in the back seat, behind Dad, pretending to read a book.

"Those people are still here," I said as Dad parked behind a truck in our driveway. "And those kids are playing with our toys!" I yelled, pointing to a girl and a boy on our front lawn.

"Looks like it," Dad replied.

"You said they were only renting our house for a week!"

"They're renting it for a year. Let's just get our stuff and go. Don't make a scene," Dad growled.

It took me fifteen minutes to get my clothes and books from my bedroom closet. Dad had put Mom's hope chest in his car when I approached the kids. "That's my brother's wagon. Get out of it," I said, shoulders back and hands on hips, trying to look like a grown-up.

The boy got out and ran to the porch when I turned to the girl and told her to put my bike in the garage and leave it alone. She dropped the bike and went to her brother. They both cried, and later I did, too, when I recalled how mean I'd been. We didn't have room for my bike, but we took the wagon.

Back at Grandma's, before Dad left for the base to get ready to fly back to Vietnam, he took everything except the wagon upstairs to his old bedroom. I'd already decided I'd offer it to Hal and Hubert. If they didn't want it, I'd leave it under The Three Sisters and put breadcrumbs from the bottom of the toaster in it for all the critters.

"I don't have time to go through your mom's treasure chest of junk, or whatever she calls it," said Dad. "I'm gonna stay with Mooch tonight and go to the base tomorrow. Here's her list of the things she wants and twenty bucks for the postage. Put what she wants in a box and get it to the post office, okay? And, Evan, do yourself a favor—try to think about what's best for everyone and not just you."

CHAPTER 20

THERE WERE FIVE RECITAL INVITATIONS attached to a fir Christmas wreath on Grandma's porch the next morning. One was mine.

Hubert and Haldon Kowalski request your presence
Christmas Recital
December 24, 6:00 p.m.
Program:
Gnossienne No. 1
Für Elise
Clair de Lune
In the Hall of the Mountain King
Moonlight Sonata
Nocturne in C-sharp minor
Waltzes Op. 64, No. 1
Polonaise in A-flat major, Op. 53
Bumble Boogie
Joy to the World
Carol of the Bells

RSVP by 6:00 p.m. December 23

The only songs I knew were "Moonlight Sonata" and "Joy to the World," but I still wanted to go. "Keep it. I know what it is, and I'm not interested," Aunt Vivian said.

"Well, Viv, it's not like we can say no. Those two do so much for us," Grandma replied. "Besides, we need a little Christmas cheer around here. So, I'll accept for us and let Frankie and Louanne decide for themselves. And we'd better take presents along this time. I want to make sure they feel appreciated."

"Okay, okay, I'll go, but just because you're making me. But I won't like it."

"Oh, you'll like it. You might even love it like last time!" Grandma tapped her fingers on the workbench like she was playing the piano.

UNCLE FRANKIE WAS ON HIS PORCH SMOKING when Grandma and I took the invitations to his house. I'd planned to take them on my own after lunch, but Grandma wanted to take him some soup and see how sick he was.

"Nope. No can do," Uncle Frankie said after reading his invitation. "I'll just cough through it, and Louanne doesn't like music."

"Suit yourselves. We'll have a good time, that's for sure," Grandma moved beer cans off a stove burner to make room for the pot of chicken soup I was still holding. "Do any of these burners work?" she asked.

"Wouldn't know." Uncle Frankie sneezed into his hand.

"I'll ask Hal and Hubert to fix the stove," Grandma replied. "I hope you thanked them for keeping the gas station going while you were off doing whatever it is you do."

"Yeah, yeah, I'm getting to it," Uncle Frankie said.

He was mad at them for showing him up. Lately, the talk in the café had been about Hal and Hubert and how good they were with customers. Mrs. Fine talked for days about Hubert and how he'd cleaned her headlights with his handkerchief and spit, and then kissed his two fingers and held them up as she drove away. Fisky said if he could find guys like them to work for him, he'd be a millionaire, and Paco had learned his lesson about underestimating weirdos.

CHRISTMAS EVE, THE DAY OF THE RECITAL, Aunt Vivian reminded me that Hal and Hubert's house was cold and didn't have an indoor bathroom, so I didn't drink after lunch, and when it was time to leave, I put on a sweater over my shirt, wrapped a scarf around my neck, and stuffed a hat and mittens into my pocket.

I was on the front porch at 5:45, ready to go. Grandma came outside five minutes later wearing a red coat and black gloves. Her hair was caught up with gold pins. While we waited for Aunt Vivian, she told me not to clap until Hal and Hubert finished playing and stood up. "That's how it is with classical music. You applaud at the end of the concert."

To our surprise, Louanne appeared just as Grandma was attaching a small wreath ornament at the end of my hair braid. She wanted to go with us. "My friend from the bus, Dr. Lars, enjoys classical music," she said, almost giggling.

It was nearly six when Aunt Vivian came outside. She'd had a hard time wrapping the belt sander she'd won at bingo the year before, and she handed it to me to carry. I also had a Christmas present for them, and so did Louanne and Grandma. Mine was a card decorated with feathers Peacock George had shed. Grandma had made them a gingerbread cake, and Louanne brought two red hats she'd knitted, both with green yarn balls on top.

By the time we left for Hal and Hubert's, most of the candles on the path they'd laid to their front porch were flickering, and some were out. But they looked so cool that I lingered behind to take it in.

And just like Aunt Vivian had said, Hal and Hubert were wearing black tuxedos and bow ties, and their house was cold. They led us down a hall crowded with books and newspapers, to a room with a low ceiling and two large black pianos placed in the middle of the room, like puzzle pieces.

I sat between Grandma and Louanne because Aunt Vivian didn't want me asking her questions during the performance. I moved forward to the edge of my chair because I'd only ever seen someone play the piano on TV and I didn't want to miss a thing.

Hal and Hubert sat on stools and stayed hunched over their pianos, like Schroeder from the *Peanuts* comic, for a long time before they began playing. They never looked up at each other, but their fingers moved over the keys at the same time, in the same way. It was thrilling, like watching a magic trick.

The four of us were holding hands when they started playing the last song, "Carol of the Bells." Halfway through, Hubert stood up, lifted his piano's lid, and plucked the strings in sync with Hal's piano playing. It was amazing, and I couldn't stop smiling or keep my feet from moving to the music. I wanted to stay in that room, listening to them play the piano forever.

Suddenly, the song ended, and Hal and Hubert were on their feet and bowing to each other. We stood up, too, and I waited for Grandma to clap, to ensure I didn't start too soon. The music had done something to me deep down—it was like a wave of good feelings moving through my body. It was happening to them, too. I could tell. I wanted to hug Hal and Hubert, maybe even kiss their cheeks, so I asked Grandma if that would be okay, and she wrapped her arm around me and said, "I know how you feel, but it's not what a girl your age does with men their age."

Nobody spoke on the walk back to Grandma's house. Ten minutes passed before Aunt Vivian said we didn't have to wait for Christmas to open the green boxes Hal and Hubert had given to each of us.

"I still don't feel right about taking gifts from them," Grandma said.

"Why not? You see how much they liked the gifts we gave them, especially the belt sander," Aunt Vivian chuckled.

They did like our gifts, a lot more than I thought they would. They liked my feather card, tried on the hats, and oohed and aahed about Grandma's cake. And Hal said, "Oh, me, me, me, my, my, my" when he unwrapped the belt sander.

Aunt Vivian and Grandma's gift boxes contained cameo brooches. Louanne got six small silver spoons, but I got a pearl bracelet with a gold honeybee clasp. Grandma said it was stunning, and that she thought all our gifts had once belonged to their mother.

For the rest of the night, I moved my wrist around to admire my bracelet from every angle, wondering if Hal and Hubert's mother used to do the same thing.

CHAPTER 21

IN THE MORNING, I WOKE TO HAL AND Hubert playing "Carol of the Bells." The same song that had kept me smiling for hours the night before now made me cry. Not being with Mom and my brothers at Christmas was worse than at Thanksgiving. At least back then, I had thought Dad would be back with them any day.

I stayed under the covers until I heard Aunt Vivian outside my door. "There are too many presents downstairs for a girl named Evan. It isn't fair."

"Really? Presents for me?"

Dad had brought gifts from Edmonton: a puka shell necklace, a book called *Jonathan Livingston Seagull*, and a pair of brown-and-red striped pajamas.

I also got a card from Grandma with a twenty-dollar bill inside and a double-layer box of Whitman's chocolates from Aunt Vivian. "I suppose this is the first time you've had candy that you didn't have to share with Teddy?" she asked as I studied the picture of the contents, trying to decide which one to eat first.

"I'd be happy to share with him if I could." I was thinking I'd save the dark chocolates for Teddy, until Aunt Vivian told me they were her favorites.

She and I had eaten the top layer of my box of chocolates when Grandma told me to get dressed and join them for breakfast in the café. I wasn't hungry, but I went, reluctantly taking with me the presents I'd made in art class: two clay ashtrays more oval than round, more blue than green. Aunt Vivian used hers right away, and because Grandma was trying to give up smoking, she said hers would make a lovely soap dish.

When Uncle Frankie walked in with Paco to get a cup of the Tom-and-Jerry holiday drink Aunt Vivian had been talking about for weeks, she gave us the daily dead-soldier update as she poured, and Uncle Frankie immediately started in about Dad going back to Vietnam. "You've got to be a real asshole to leave your family at Christmas to go back to hell."

"That's enough!" Grandma said. "This is Christmas Day. I want a peaceful one."

Uncle Frankie said he was sorry, but I could tell he wasn't. "Letting you all know I've been too busy to get you presents," he announced, spreading peanut butter on his pancakes before pouring syrup over them.

Aunt Vivian said, "Yuck," and then in her most smart-aleck voice, "Letting you know that we all worked like dogs for you while you were off playing 'hide the imaginary fugitive,' and yet, we all have a Christmas present for you—even Evan."

"That's pretty cool. I'll make sure I'm rich enough to send you sombreros next year then." Uncle Frankie laughed as he slid his cup across the counter for another drink.

My presents for Uncle Frankie and Paco were the same. Grandma and I had been too excited after the piano recital to sleep, so we stayed up listening to Christmas records and making iced gingerbread men. I'd wrapped each one in wax paper and tied them with green ribbon, stopping to admire my new bracelet each time the light hit the gold clasp.

I STAYED BEHIND WHEN GRANDMA AND Aunt Vivian went to her house to call friends in North Dakota. Uncle Frankie and Paco had left by then to watch Hal and Hubert install an engine part in his car. I'd promised to clear tables, sweep the floor, and set up the dining room for Christmas dinner, and it was a lot more work than I'd thought it would be. I had to carry eight chairs from Grandma's house, polish her candleholders and silverware, and iron a huge red tablecloth and matching napkins. I'd never ironed a tablecloth, and I had to do it twice. Even then, I could see lots of wrinkles when I put it over the two café tables I'd pushed together. "You know you have to turn the iron on," Aunt Vivian joked when she saw it.

Even with the wrinkled cloth, I thought the table looked great. And I'd finished in time to call Mom while it was still cheap. Dad gave me ten dollars to pay Grandma for the phone call. He said ten bucks meant ten minutes, and he warned me about mentioning Adam. "Someone might listen in on your phone call, so don't mention him."

I called three times from the garage phone, but I couldn't get through. I even called the operator for help, but she couldn't manage it, either.

I lay on my bed for two hours reading my new book. I liked it okay, but it was hard to understand. Mom's Christmas card was just as confusing: "New horizons for us all. Love, Mom." Maybe the hidden messages in the story and Mom's card meant she wanted me to stop complaining about being at Grandma's and become a better helper, like Fletcher the seagull had to do. It was kind of what Dad had said before he left—I should think about what's best for everyone and not just me.

I didn't know if I could do it, though. I didn't even know if I wanted to. Didn't somebody have to think about me?

LOUANNE DIDN'T COME TO CHRISTMAS dinner, and Uncle Frankie didn't offer an excuse for her, but I figured she was afraid Aunt Vivian would watch her eat as she'd done at Thanksgiving. I left her chair and place setting at the table in case she showed up and because I wanted more room between me and Hubert, who was left-handed and stuck his elbow out.

No one said more than "Please pass the salt" at dinner, not even Uncle Frankie. I stayed quiet because I had my period and didn't feel well, but I still ate enough food to make it hard to stand up when Grandma asked me to make a pot of coffee. When it was ready, a blue station wagon pulled up in front of the café. For a second, I thought it was a customer needing gas. But then two men got out, and one of them opened the back passenger door for Louanne. She was wearing a green dress with a matching overcoat and a bright red headscarf.

Everyone but Hal and Hubert stopped eating when Louanne introduced her friends Dr. Lars and Dr. Erik Larson, who moved around the table, saying "Merry Christmas" and shaking everyone's hand, even mine. When Dr. Lars shook Aunt Vivian's hand, she held on tight, covering his hand with her left hand and not letting go until Grandma nudged her. When he shook my hand, I shook back and said, "Merry Christmas," and I almost asked if he'd fallen asleep on the bus lately. I immediately felt my face and neck burn hot and pulled my hand away.

THE NEXT FEW DAYS WERE QUIET AROUND Eat and Get Gas, so Grandma closed the café after lunch and watched soap operas in her living room with Aunt Vivian. I spent the rest of my Christmas break skating with my friends, playing pinball in the garage, and trying to finish *Animal Farm*, a book Mrs. Fine had given to me. She was expecting a full report in a week.

On New Year's Eve day, I went to the garage early to call Mom, and Uncle Frankie was in the office with the door closed.

I could see through the window that he was taking money out of the till. Then he put money in from a stack of bills in a rolled-up towel. He didn't see me, but he kept looking outside, toward the pumps, like he was waiting for someone to arrive.

Later, when Uncle Frankie left to do his mail route, I went back to the garage to call Mom, but Paco was on the phone. He hung up the second he saw me. "Two customers today. That's it. I can't wait for closing time. There's a New Year's party at the Rollarena tonight. It's five bucks to get in. You should come. It's gonna be fun, and they have prizes."

"I don't think Grandma will let me. Besides, five bucks is a lot, and I've already made plans to watch the Lawrence Welk special with her and Aunt Vivian. But even if Grandma said I could go with you, how would we get there? She's not gonna let us use her car."

"Maybe Vivian could take us," Paco said. "Or we could walk. It's only a few miles, and it's not gonna rain tonight. We can always get a ride home. And don't worry about the money—I've got it covered."

I wondered if Paco wanted me to go with him because he couldn't get a date. That couldn't be it, though. He was a good skater and a big flirt. After I skated with him on his birthday, I thought he'd never want to skate with another girl again, but then Marie and Carla told me they'd seen him skate with a Hoquiam High School girl, and my heart sank. Even so, I still wanted to go to the New Year's party. I wanted to show him the skating moves I'd learned since joining the after-school skate club. And I didn't care if the night ended with Paco leaving with another girl. I knew I could run home in twenty minutes if I had to.

"I'll ask Grandma. Maybe if I talk Uncle Frankie into going with us, she'll say yes," I said.

"He's already on his way to visit D. B. Cooper—you know, his maybe imaginary hijacker buddy, the one the FBI can't find because he's so good at hiding him?" Paco was laughing now. "Yesterday, he was searching through mailbags for magazines to take to D. B., who needs something to read, has grown a beard, and is working at a hot-springs hotel in return for his room and board. That's what Frankie said. I don't know what to think anymore."

"Me, either. But I feel bad for him. He must miss his friends from the war," I said. "Hey, have you ever seen him take money out of the garage till and then put other money in?"

"Nope," Paco replied, "but he told me last month he was going to use garage takings to clean up some of the ransom money D. B. Cooper got. He said the FBI marked the twenty-dollar bills, and if D. B. spends them, they'll know where he is. I ain't buying it. I mean, if it's true, the FBI would have arrested the Esso gas delivery driver by now. Frankie's been paying him with those cleaned-up twenties for weeks."

I made a mental note to look at the Esso truck driver the next time he delivered gas.

"I'll ask, anyway. You never know, Grandma might say yes," I said. "Right now, I need to call my mom. Grandma said it was okay to use the phone here, for some privacy."

It took a few seconds for the call to connect, and then it rang seven times before Mom's cousin Deloris answered. She introduced herself and said she was happy to hear my voice.

My eyes stung and my throat tightened when I heard Mom say, "Hello, sweetheart." Her voice was shaky, like an old lady's. I'd been rehearsing what I would say, ever since Uncle Frankie gave me her phone number. I was planning to tell her I'd earned enough money working in the café and sorting mail to buy a train ticket to Edmonton, and I'd be coming in a week, even if she didn't have room for me. But once she said she was telling everyone there how much she missed me and what a caring and forgiving daughter I was, I started sobbing and couldn't say it. Mom talked the most, apologizing for how everything turned out, and telling me Teddy was still a handful, but learning lots of new things. "He's got hearing aids now. They've improved everything. And we're all impressed with his card skills. It seems Gene finally taught him something useful."

I didn't tell her it was Uncle Frankie who taught him. I just said I was lonely and missed her. We both went quiet then, but I could still hear her breathing hard and then sigh before she broke the awkward silence. "I'm so goddamn worn out."

When I asked if Teddy missed me, she said, "He used to talk about you all the time, but he's stopped that now. He's doing just fine."

Tears fell faster than I could wipe them away, and I had to take several quick breaths when I told her Dad had rented our house to his friend. "Rented? Hell, he sold it to them. I signed the papers when he was here last month. I also signed divorce papers. I hope this isn't news for you. He promised to tell you."

"You know he never tells me anything important," I said. "And neither do you."

When she didn't respond, I told her I'd been learning about Canada at school. "It seems like a great place to live. Better than here, that's for sure," I said.

"You'll have to learn to speak French," Mom said. "The Catholic schools here require it. But you have time. It'll be months before I'm ready to move into my own place. It could be September. If you start now, you'll have mastered French by then."

"Dad never said I'd have to learn French or that I'd be going to a stupid Catholic girls' school. They wear ugly uniforms." I closed my eyes tight to keep from yelling.

"Don't worry about it now," Mom said.

I told her I had some of her stuff from our house. "Dad and I got it the other day. He gave me a list of what you want sent there. I haven't done it yet, but I will, I promise."

"No, no, no!" Mom was practically shouting. "That was a job for Gene, not you. There's nothing I need right now. I'll get my things when I get you."

"What about the money Dad gave me to pay for the postage? Should I send it to you?" I asked.

"Of course not. Use it to buy a coat or shoes. I'm sure you need both." Mom coughed a few times and then said she needed to go.

We ended our call with "Love you" and "Have a Betty kind of day" and a promise to talk on the phone every other Sunday, although we never said who would call next.

"YOU'RE TOO YOUNG TO BE OUT ON NEW Year's Eve, especially with a man, even Paco," Grandma said. "I know he's teaching you to skate but going to a party with him is different. It's more like a date."

I knew she wouldn't change her mind, but I argued anyway until she began moving her head side to side and mouthing no.

I hated the show. Grandma and Aunt Vivian must have hated it, too, because Grandma went upstairs to use the bathroom during a commercial and didn't return. And before the show ended, Aunt Vivian was asleep in the lounge chair, snoring.

I took a big swallow from her glass of tonic and lit one of her cigarettes. I took a puff and coughed. It didn't wake Aunt Vivian, so I tried again. I didn't cough, but I got dizzy, so I put out the cigarette and had a few more sips before heading upstairs to bed, wondering how much longer I had to live with two old ladies who sat down whenever they had to sneeze, snored louder than Dad, and never stayed up past 9:30 p.m.

CHAPTER 22

UNCLE FRANKIE WAS BACK IN THE morning, but I waited a few hours before walking over to ask if I could start sorting his route mail every day before school because I needed money to get to Edmonton. I needed more than what he still owed me and what Aunt Vivian had paid me for sweeping the café floors, though I didn't want any twenty-dollar bills.

"There's never much mail after Christmas. I can handle it on my own. And I'm gonna pay you, promise," he said. "You know, Edmonton is as cold as the Arctic Circle this time of year. You might wanna wait a few months before you leave," he said.

"That wasn't in the book about Canada I read at school," I said.

"Well, you can read it in an encyclopedia. There's a set at Willa's, or you can help yourself to mine." He pointed to the stacks of five books under each corner of the couch that Paco called his bed.

I was still at Grandma's dining room table at 8:30 p.m., reading about Canada in one of her encyclopedias, when Uncle Frankie arrived with a jug of what he said was magical, healing water from a mineral spring. He poured some into glasses for me, Aunt Vivian, and Grandma while he talked about the angels he'd met while soaking in a mineral pool with his friend D. B. Cooper. He'd just said the angel's name, which sounded like "yummy," when Grandma cut him off.

"I'm going to close the gas station if you don't shape up and do something about getting more customers." She slammed her hand on the table to get his attention.

"Like what?" Uncle Frankie asked.

"To start, you can stop disappearing for days and open the gas station on time. And you could clean the garage, inside and out, and treat your customers with courtesy, the way Hal and Hubert do. And put that goddamn OPEN sign on the edge of the road. It's never out. And I think it's time for Paco to go. You don't sell enough gas to keep him on." Grandma took a big breath and dropped her shoulders.

Uncle Frankie's face turned to stone. And I knew why. If Paco got caught, Uncle Frankie would go to jail, too. I kept a straight face when he looked across the table like he wanted me to defend him. Then he yelled, "Nice friend, you are!" and took off.

I didn't care that he was mad. I needed to warn Paco, but he wasn't back from skating. The next morning, though, I was on Uncle Frankie's front porch well before seven.

"What the hell are you doing here?" he asked.

"I need to borrow pliers for a school project." I could feel my cheeks burning.

"Get in here—it's cold." He opened a kitchen drawer and pulled out pliers. "Here, take 'em."

Paco was on the couch, smoking. "Did you hear? Frankie doesn't need me to work here any longer." Paco said. "I've wanted to take the manager's job at the Rollarena since the owner, Bernie, first offered it to me in October. Bernie's going to pay me. With real money. Every Friday!"

"Really? Will you still live here? Can I skate for free?"

"Yes, and yes."

By the end of January, I could skate almost as fast as Paco, and I knew all the tricks that caught people's attention. I loved it, especially when I undid my braid and let my hair fly. People said it looked like I was wearing a long brown cape.

Paco had already stopped asking me to skate with him by then. So, it caught me by surprise when he came up behind me one Sunday afternoon and grabbed my hand. We danced to a song I love called "Band of Gold." We were dancing so well that other skaters stopped to watch us and some clapped. Four dances later, I felt like telling him never to skate, talk, or look at another girl again, but I didn't because Marie had told me older boys like Paco didn't like to be tied down.

WHEN I LEFT TO CATCH THE SCHOOL BUS on the first Friday in February, it was windy and raining hard. After school, it was worse. I considered going home instead of walking to the Rollarena, but I'd worked hard to get Grandma to agree to let me join the after-school skate club, and I didn't want to miss a Friday free-for-all. It was the only day we could show off, and I wanted to see Paco, who was alone when I arrived.

"Haven't you heard? No skate club today," he said.

"I don't care. I want to skate."

After I'd skated on my own for an hour, Paco hit the rink and challenged me to a race. When he finally caught up to me, he grabbed my waist, and I turned to wrap my arms around his neck. Then we twirled like a top for so long, I fell over when he let me go.

It was the most amazing day, and except for the rink roof shaking a little, we hadn't noticed the storm outside. It wasn't until his boss, Bernie, arrived to help him close early that we found out.

Bernie couldn't give us a ride home because he had to stay and watch for roof leaks.

"We can hitchhike," Paco said.

"Okay, but you can't tell Grandma we did it," I replied.

We tried hitchhiking, but there weren't many cars on the highway, and those that were didn't stop. We were getting soaked and had to dodge falling tree branches as the wind pushed us around. It was fun until the thunder started. We were halfway home when Hal and Hubert's truck pulled up next to us. Hubert rolled his window down and yelled, "Willa sent us. Get in."

The next day at breakfast, Paco told us three giant fir trees had come down and were lying across the Rollarena's parking lot, and it would be closed until Bernie removed them. Then Grandma told me it would be a quiet Saturday, and she didn't need my help in the café. "You've got the day to yourself."

I had a bubble bath, cleaned my room, and wrapped the birthday present I'd made for Uncle Frankie at school. I took it to his house in the morning when I saw him packing his car. Since Paco had stopped working at Get Gas, Uncle Frankie didn't open on Sundays and sometimes left to visit his friend Dan late on Saturday, after finishing his mail route.

"Happy birthday for tomorrow."

He laughed about the funny pages I'd used for wrapping paper and invited me in. Louanne was there, too, pouring a can of fruit cocktail over a bowl of puffed rice. When she saw me looking at the water dripping from the ceiling onto the kitchen counter, she grimaced. "Frankie promised he'd fix the leaks," she said, loud enough for him to hear.

"You gotta be back here by five tomorrow," I said. "Grandma's making you a birthday dinner—fried chicken and chocolate cake. And get this—they're not going to bingo. Instead, she wants you to teach her to play poker."

"I'll be home for that, for sure," Uncle Frankie said.

"Wow, this is pretty cool." He was holding up the leather belt I'd made for him in shop class. I'd even stamped it with red and turquoise peace signs.

"Thanks. I got the idea from a picture I saw in a magazine you threw out. And I got my teacher to help me make the stamp."

"It's good work. I hope you get a good grade," Louanne said.

"You're still taking me to Lee's Chinese for dinner Tuesday night for my birthday, right?" I asked Uncle Frankie.

"Yeah, yeah, of course. I promised, didn't I? Turning fourteen is a big deal. Eating egg foo young for the first time is a bigger deal!"

"Your birthday is Tuesday, the eighth of February, the day after Frankie's birthday, and you'll be fourteen?" Louanne whispered so slowly and evenly that I thought she was talking to herself.

"Yeah, that's me."

Louanne put her bowl in the already-full kitchen sink and left the house, slamming the door so hard on her way out that Uncle Frankie and I looked at each other with wide eyes.

"Maybe she's mad because I was gonna take her to Lee's Chinese last month on her birthday, and I forgot. You just reminded her of what a fuckup I am."

"You're not a fuckup," I said. "Aunt Vivian says you get lost in your head because of the war."

"Well, if she said it, it must be true."

"Why didn't you tell me about Louanne's birthday?" I asked. "I would have made her something, and I know Grandma would have baked her cake. You should have said something."

"She didn't want me to. And you know me, I always do what the women around here tell me to do," he continued in his smart-aleck tone.

Just then, a piece of plaster fell to the floor outside of Louanne's bedroom door, and I jumped.

"It's from that fucking storm," Uncle Frankie said. "A couple of tree branches landed on the roof. I've got every spare bucket from the garage in her room. That's where it's leaking the most."

"It's leaking over there, too." I pointed to the wall behind his giant Seagram's Whiskey bottle and a box of damp mail he hadn't delivered. On closer inspection, I could see the letters were all outgoing.

"Pretend you don't see those!" Uncle Frankie said when he saw me looking.

But I couldn't pretend. There were two cards on top with "Happy Birthday" written in crayon addressed to Grandpa Morty. It made me think of Louanne's returned letters and letters that Mom might have sent me that I never got. I wanted Grandpa Morty to get his cards.

I'd wait for Uncle Frankie to leave, then take the bus to town with a bag of letters and put them in the US postal box outside of the library. That way, at least the envelopes with cards inside would get delivered.

WHEN I WENT INTO THE CAFÉ KITCHEN TO find a bag strong enough to hold the seventy-two letters, Grandma was busy trying to convince Louanne to move into her "bone-dry" basement room. It wasn't the first time Grandma had made the offer. She'd done the same the week Dad left, after a late-night poker game got out of hand, and Uncle Frankie's friend Chuck shot his rifle at the telephone pole outside the café.

Back then, Louanne said she didn't need to move, because Uncle Frankie swore it would never happen again. I sensed she was considering the offer this time because she was on the verge of tears when Aunt Vivian handed me a brown canvas bag from the back porch. "I don't have enough money to pay rent for my room at Frankie's and a room at Mrs. Hanson's," Louanne whispered to me. Grandma heard her, too, and turned to Louanne with arms open wide.

DR. LARS LARSON WAS ON THE BUS. He was sitting in the back and waved me over. When I took the seat next to him, he told me old guys like him could ride the bus free on weekends, and he'd been past Eat and Get Gas three times already.

I stayed quiet until he asked where I was going and what I had in the bag. I fixed my eyes on the seat in front of me and told him the truth. Once that was out, I couldn't stop talking.

"He burns mail he's supposed to deliver, and he plays poker in his kitchen with scary-looking men who arrive on motorcycles. And he's been helping the hijacker D. B. Cooper hide from the FBI, and he uses a fake name to get free records from the Columbia House Record Club. Oh, and there's a draft dodger living in his house."

I breathed out and felt calm for the first time in ages. I was smiling when I turned to look at Dr. Lars. He didn't seem shocked, and for a second I thought he hadn't heard me. But then he pressed his hands together and lifted them to his chin. "Is that all?" he whispered.

"He sells pot to boys at my school," I whispered back.

"Well, he sounds like a very troubled young man." Dr. Lars spoke in the same comforting way Mrs. McDougall had done when I was sick.

"Maybe you and Louanne should come to Boston with me. It's peaceful there. I have a big house with six bedrooms in a friendly neighborhood—plenty of room. And there are many excellent schools in Boston, if that interests you."

I didn't know what to say. I'd never imagined going any-where except for Edmonton. I knew nothing about Boston, but his offer was still in my head when I put the letters in the mailbox outside of the library, rubbed blusher on my cheeks at the Rexall drugstore, drank a root-beer float at Farrell's Ice Cream Parlor, and caught the bus back to Grandma's.

CHAPTER 23

UNCLE FRANKIE DIDN'T COME HOME FOR his birthday dinner, so I ate fried chicken and chocolate cake with Grandma and hoped he'd be home the next day for my birthday.

There was no card from Mom, which made me sad until Grandma presented me with a short stack of pancakes with whipped cream and fourteen flickering candles, and everyone in the café dining room sang to me. I tried not to think about my birthday party the year before, with Mom, Teddy, Adam, ten of my friends, balloons, banners, and lots of presents.

"If my mom calls before I get home from school, can you tell her to call back at four? I'll be home by then for sure," I said to Grandma.

When I passed Uncle Frankie on my way to catch the school bus, he began singing "Happy Birthday" in his Elvis Presley voice. When he finished, I clapped and then made him promise to be home from his route in time to take me to Lee's Chinese. "I'll even call and make a reservation," he said, crossing his heart.

Then Paco appeared from the garage holding up a pair of black leather skates. "They're not new, but they're your size and in good shape. Happy birthday."

I almost missed the bus because I had to try them on.

"HEY, BIRTHDAY GIRL," GRANDMA called through the serving window that afternoon.

"Did my mom call?" I asked.

"Not yet. How about locking that door? It's almost four, and I don't want any more customers."

"Sure, okay," I said.

"And how about you finish the French fries in the cooker here, so they don't go to waste?"

"I can't. I'm going to dinner with Uncle Frankie in two hours, and I want to be hungry when I get there."

"About that—Frankie just left to do his route an hour ago. He won't be back in time to take you to dinner or us to bingo. I'm sorry, Evan. Maybe he'll take you another night." Grandma looked sad.

I was sorry, too. Sorry I'd done what Aunt Vivian had warned me about, counting on Uncle Frankie to keep his word. And he wasn't the only one: I'd been counting on Mom to keep her word since the night she left with Adam. She'd forgotten my birthday, too.

I headed for the back door. "These came for you the other day," Grandma called out, waving envelopes over her head when I turned around. "Viv had put them in the drawer for safekeeping and just remembered."

My birthday card from Mom had a rose on the front and fourteen one-dollar bills inside. Teddy's card had a clown on it. He must have picked it out himself. It read "Happy Birthday Evangeline Gene Hanson from your brother Theodore Gene Hanson."

Knowing Mom hadn't forgotten was great, but Teddy's card was even better. In November, when Mom took him, he could only write Ted.

After bargaining with Grandma and Aunt Vivian, I agreed to forgo *The Mary Tyler Moore Show* and drive them to bingo, because Grandma didn't know how to drive, and

Aunt Vivian had lost her glasses the week before. I'd been driving the Studebaker for weeks by then, just on the gravel road next to Grandma's house. I still wasn't very good, but Aunt Vivian said she'd sit next to me to make sure I didn't wreck the car.

While they got dressed, I went outside to warm up the car and tripped over a box on the porch. It had a pink-and-blue yarn bow and a card on top. "I hope they fit. Happy Birthday, Louanne." Inside was a pair of size 28/34 Seafarer jeans with yellow daisies embroidered on the hems.

AUNT VIVIAN YELLED FOR ME TO CHANGE gears and speed up the entire way to the bingo hall. And once there, she made me responsible for ten of her twenty-two cards. Four games later, she reached over and took them back. "Go sit at the slow-poke table with Willa."

I used some butcher paper from the five pounds of bacon Grandma had already won to write a thank-you note to Louanne. When I told Grandma about my plan to give it to her in the morning, she told me Louanne had already left to stay with her friend Dr. Lars at his son's house.

"Why? For how long?" I swallowed hard.

"Until Frankie gets the leak in the roof repaired. She took her things, so I guess she doesn't trust he'll do it. Neither do I."

"Did she take Velvet?" I was starting to sob.

"No need for tears," Grandma said. "They'll be back. And I don't blame her for leaving. Viv and I went to Frankie's house today. For the life of me, I can't understand why Louanne stayed in that wet room for four days. Even the wallpaper has peeled off."

WHEN I GOT HOME FROM SCHOOL THE next day, Hal and Hubert were on Uncle Frankie's roof. Grandma had hired them to repair it, and it turned out to be a big job because of something called wood rot. They were still putting a new roof on when Louanne came back a few days later. Grandma's basement room door was open, and Louanne and Dr. Lars were inside whispering to each other. They hadn't seen me, so I went to find Grandma, who was upstairs, taking sheets and clean towels out of the linen closet. "It's just Louanne who's moving into the basement room, not the doctor. She's my guest for as long as she wants."

I went to the basement room five times that evening to ask Louanne if she needed anything and to show her how perfectly the jeans fit. "With a long body and legs like yours, you can wear almost anything. Even this," she said and held up a bright orange tank top she'd just finished making.

"I can clean out the refrigerator. All the beer in there is from Dad." I wanted to do something nice for her in return.

"Maybe you can do it tomorrow. It's been an exhausting week, and I need to sleep. If you have clothes that need alterations or embroidered flowers, bring them here. I'll see what I can do."

I left two pairs of jeans next to the basement door on my way to catch the bus in the morning. When I got home from school, they were on Grandma's couch. Not only had Louanne embroidered red and pink roses around the bottom, but she must have noticed they were too short for me, because she'd taken down the hem on both pairs.

They were the coolest clothes I'd ever had, and when I saw Louanne outside with Velvet that night, I thanked her again. Then, without thinking, I stepped forward and put my arms out to hug her. I knew I'd made a mistake when she jumped back and almost fell. When she got her balance, she tipped her head toward me, like she'd changed her mind about hugging. But the moment had passed.

"Would you like to see the tapestry I've been working on? It's a gift for Mrs. Hanson—for letting me stay. I didn't have to wear socks and a hat to bed last night."

"I've been wearing a hat and socks and sometimes a sweatshirt to bed since Teddy left," I said. "I wish I knew how to knit and sew and all the other things you do."

"I can teach you." There was excitement in Louanne's voice. "I have a bit of time before I go to Boston, if I go at all. I'm still not sure it's the right thing to do. It's more expensive to get to Williston from Boston than from here. I'm afraid I'll get to Boston just as my aunt is ready to go home from the hospital."

"My mom never calls me." I wanted Louanne to know I was in the same boat, waiting for someone to change my life.

"My guess is that they're both unwell right now and can't do anything for us just yet. But that will change soon; I'm sure of it." Louanne handed me a Kleenex.

I hoped she was right. More than that, I hoped her aunt wasn't dead like Uncle Frankie suspected. Maybe she was and he knew it.

"Did Dr. Lars tell you he invited me to come to Boston?" I asked.

"Yes, he did. If you want to, you should. A summer in Boston might be something you'd treasure your whole life."

Grandma patted my shoulder when I told her about Louanne's offer to teach me to knit, sew, and maybe embroider. "There wasn't a blanket or pillowcase in my childhood that didn't have embroidered flowers on them. I have my mother's sewing baskets, and Viv brought three bags of our mother's material with her. It's all in the café storeroom. You're welcome to it."

MOM CALLED GRANDMA'S HOUSE AFTER school on February 21. It was the first time I'd heard her voice since we talked on New Year's Day. "I've been calling Frankie's phone. I called on your birthday and every day after for a week. I'm sorry. I don't have my address book with me, and it took me a while to realize that I could ring our house and get the new owner to read me Willa's phone number from the phone cupboard door."

Since Paco had stopped working at Get Gas, there wouldn't have been anyone in the garage to answer the phone after lunch while Uncle Frankie was delivering mail. Still, I couldn't help but wonder why Mom hadn't called our house in Tacoma sooner.

"Someone wants to speak with you," Mom said. The next second, I heard Teddy yell, "Happy birthday, sister Evangeline Gene Hanson. I'm sending a hug and a kiss through the telephone."

"Can you believe it?" Mom said. "He speaks so well. Did I ever tell you that my cousin Anne is a special education teacher? She's worked a miracle with Teddy. And hearing aids have made him a very happy boy."

IT HAD BEEN WEEKS SINCE AUNT VIVIAN lost her glasses, and she still hadn't bought new ones. "They'll turn up," she insisted.

Before I agreed to drive her and Grandma to bingo again, I made them promise to find someone who would pick them up and bring them home from then on. "And you both have to sit in the back seat, and you can't yell at me."

I drove with both hands on the steering wheel at two and ten and tried to stay calm when drivers honked or passed us because I was going too slowly. I could sense that Aunt Vivian wanted to yell at me, but she didn't. And she didn't complain when I took up two parking spaces in the parking lot.

Fisky was the bingo caller that night. He was just filling in, though. During the break, he brought a cup of coffee to Grandma. "Willa, I know it's not my business, but has Frank seen a doctor about his obsession with D. B. Cooper?"

"Oh, I've called the VA hospital several times now. They won't make an appointment for him unless he asks for one." Grandma looked in her purse for a long time before taking out a Kleenex.

I knew Fisky worried about Uncle Frankie, too. He'd been inviting him to go fishing for weeks, and just a few days ago, I stopped to listen when I saw them in the garage talking. Fisky had his arms crossed over his enormous belly and was shaking his head in disbelief as Uncle Frankie told him how he'd gotten D. B. Cooper a cleaning job at a motel that provided room and board. "Hiding in plain sight. That's how it's done, old man, that's how it's done!" He had punched the air with both fists.

THEN, TWO WEEKS LATER, JUST AS LOUANNE arrived for work in the kitchen, Uncle Frankie strode in, waving a piece of paper and yelling that she'd fucked up his life. He went straight to her, holding the paper in front of her eye. "Can you see it?"

"Yes, I see it," Louanne stuttered and stepped back.

"Read it!"

I could see from across the room that Louanne was shaking, so I went and stood next to her.

"I was in the garage Saturday afternoon, getting some oil to use on my sewing machine. I answered your phone twice. The first guy asked for Mary Jane. I told him there was no one by that name here. The second caller asked for you, and when I said you weren't available, he told me to give you a message. That's all." Louanne read the message out loud: "Leaving for the land of tamales on the eighth. See you soon, Dan."

"I put it with all the other messages under the phone," Louanne said.

"The hell you did! You threw it on the floor so I wouldn't find it in time to split!"

"We have customers, and they can hear you. Leave now," Aunt Vivian said, spit flying.

But Uncle Frankie wouldn't go. "I called the motel already. Dan took off last night."

Just then the news came on the radio. Based on new information, the FBI were upping their search for D. B. Cooper near the Columbia River Gorge. Uncle Frankie leapt down the back porch stairs and ran to his house. When I caught up to him, he said he had to get to Wind River before the FBI found the cabin and all the shit they'd left behind when Dan moved to the motel.

When he didn't come back the next day, Paco said he must have hijacked a plane to Mexico to be with D. B. Cooper. "Yeah, they're probably floating around with turtles, talking to angels," I said.

"Dog's balls! I bet he's at the Choker getting sauced," Aunt Vivian added.

But Grandma was wiping her eyes. "I'm scared to death for my boy. He's not in his right mind. What are we going to do?"

IT WAS SATURDAY, MARCH 11, WHEN UNCLE Frankie parked in front of the garage and jumped out of his car like it was on fire. "If you don't help me right now, I might never see the light of day again," he shouted, pushing the café's front door open and pointing at me.

He pulled me by the hand to his car. It was full of stuff: empty beer bottles, bags of garbage, a stained army blanket, an old brown briefcase, a tent, sleeping bags, and undelivered mail. "Help me get this shit to the backyard."

While Paco and I burned the stuff from his car, Uncle Frankie sat on his back porch, smoking. He thanked us a few times for helping him and made us promise not to tell anyone about Dan. "Swear it," he said.

Before I did, I reminded him of the people he'd already told. "Yeah, well, everyone around here knows I'm full of shit. They don't know you are, too."

CHAPTER 24

MY LESSONS WITH LOUANNE DIDN'T GO well at first. I talked too much and kept dropping stitches and having to start over. She was patient, though, and she seemed interested when I talked about Mom and Teddy, my friends at school, and skating at the Rollarena. "Once Paco kissed me on the cheek after we dance skated together. Maybe he could be my boyfriend." I made a kissing sound and giggled.

Louanne stood up suddenly. "You need to leave. I've got a bad headache. Just remember, perverts like Paco and Frankie can turn girls like us into wayward whores."

I ran to Grandma's living room and took her dictionary off the bookshelf. First, I looked up "wayward." Then "pervert." I already knew what "whore" meant.

It took a lot of encouragement from Grandma to convince me to continue my lessons with Louanne. "She probably didn't know how to react and just repeated something her mother had said to her. 'Wayward' is a word from my generation."

When I knocked on Louanne's door three days later, she seemed happy to see me and invited me inside. There was a hat pattern and several balls of yarn set up in my place, so I dived in. I never mentioned Paco again, and neither did she.

The more I knitted, the better I got—and quieter, too. Louanne sometimes broke the silence to tell me something she'd learned from her aunt. "In a pinch, you can use newspaper to make a dress pattern. Make sure it's old and faded, though, so the ink doesn't stain your fabric."

A week later, when I finished knitting a hat and a scarf, we moved on to crocheting. It was when Louanne bent down to show me how to hold a crochet hook so it wouldn't leave a dent in my finger that she saw me looking at the long pink scar on her face. She ran her finger down it. "My aunt says people choose to live in heaven or hell. I chose hell," she whispered.

"No, you didn't," I said. "It was just an accident. Everyone says so."

I MADE THE SCHOOL SOFTBALL TEAM, as a shortstop, at the end of March. I'd played third base for three years on my team back home by then, but Uncle Frankie said I'd be a better shortstop. "You're too tall to play third base."

Playing softball meant I couldn't work in the café on Saturday mornings or have a lesson with Louanne in the afternoon. When I told Louanne, she said I didn't need more lessons, just more practice and then handed me a bag of yarn. "I don't need it. I'm almost sure I'll be going to Boston with Dr. Lars. First, though, I need to call home to find out if my aunt is there or still in the hospital. I don't want Mrs. Fine knowing anything about me, so I'm going to call my aunt's house from Dr. Erik's office. They both think I should find out what's going on at home—that it would be helpful to know, even if the news isn't good," she said.

"**YOU'RE THE DEVIL,**" **LOUANNE WAS SHOUTING** as she hobbled into the garage where I was looking at album covers with Uncle Frankie. She stepped right up to him, putting her finger on his chest and keeping it there until he swatted it away. "Orson said he sent me a letter three weeks ago, telling me that Aunt Bethania had died. Did you see it? You must have it. You're the mailman, for God's sake!"

"Never seen a letter from Orson." Uncle Frankie shrugged and grabbed her hand when she raised it again.

"How would you even know? It could be under your bed or in one of those boxes on the back porch. I'm gonna look for it!"

"Sure, but you won't find it. If it ever was there, it's long gone. Burned with the other garbage," said Uncle Frankie, this time with an evil grin.

"Why are you like this? Don't you care that our aunt is dead?"

"I met her once. She told me I looked like the scarecrow in *The Wizard of Oz*. So no, I don't care."

"I know you got the letter!" Louanne was sobbing now. "What did I ever do to make you hate me? Live through the accident or take a phone message you didn't find in time to leave Mrs. Hanson in the lurch?"

Uncle Frankie stood up straight and beat his chest with his fist like he was King Kong. "Dan was my ticket to freedom—now I'm trapped here forever. Fuck!"

His flying spit hit Louanne's cheek, but she didn't move. Her voice was strong. "You made the whole thing up. You're no friend of D. B. Cooper's. You're a liar, just like our dad. Every bad thing was because of him. Just remember that."

"No way to prove it now, thanks to you," Uncle Frankie called as Louanne turned and walked out of the garage.

I followed her, saying I could look through the boxes on his back porch for Orson's letter. But she just put her hand up and shook her head.

Later, when I saw her carrying Velvet's cage to the lawn, I rushed outside. She didn't say hello or even look at me, just picked pieces of grass to feed to the rabbit. "I'm a pretty good shortstop now," I said. "And I'm expecting a great report card, thanks to Uncle Frankie helping me with American history."

She looked up at me then and smoothed her bangs over her eye patch. "I'm surprised to hear it. I've yet to see him read anything other than the funny papers."

Louanne's tone was like my history teacher's when he was trying to get his point across. I reached out to pet Velvet, but Louanne grabbed my hand and held it. "I'm going to Boston with Dr. Lars. We're leaving tomorrow. I'm gifting you my sewing machine, the sewing box, and all my yarn. And I'm leaving Velvet with you. I think it's best."

"But it's almost Easter," I pleaded. "Don't go before Easter. Grandma's making hot-cross buns with orange icing."

"You have one for me, okay?"

Tears were running down my cheeks as I promised to take good care of Velvet.

"And you can always come to Boston, even for just a week or two. Dr. Lars says you're welcome anytime," Louanne said.

"There's a big picture book of Boston city in my school library. It's nice, but I don't think my mom will let me go."

"In case she does, I'll leave the address and phone number next to the sewing machine." Louanne picked up Velvet and held her to her chest. "I'll leave the quilt I just finished with you, too. You need something extra warm on your bed. I made you several nightgowns and bought you two bras. They're in my room. They're your size, so wear them, okay? Boys and men like to stare." She paused and grinned. "And don't forget about the distant neighbors; they are as annoying as their chickens."

It was more or less a line from *The Egg and I*. I was glad Louanne had read it, though, and embarrassed about the bras.

The next morning, Louanne and I were sitting on the café porch bench, waiting for the Larsons, when Uncle Frankie drove past us with his window down. "Adios, amigo!" he shouted in a fake Mexican accent, revving up his engine and peeling out.

"How soon can you get to Canada?" Louanne asked.

"As soon as my mom finds a place for us to live," I said.

"The sooner, the better," she said, patting my leg.

Aunt Vivian and Grandma came outside when the Larsons parked. They both bent down to look into the back seat, the way they had when Teddy and I arrived, and Grandma handed Louanne a bag of hot-cross buns. "It's been a joy getting to know you, Louanne. Safe travels." The three of us stood on the porch and waved goodbye until the car was out of sight. "It's like she's going home with Marcus Welby, MD," Aunt Vivian said in disbelief.

By eleven o'clock I had a bra on, Velvet on my lap, and the sewing machine going.

CHAPTER 25

I WAS MORE UPSET ABOUT LOUANNE leaving than I ever imagined I'd be. I avoided Uncle Frankie and Paco as much as possible, staying busy on weekdays with school and softball. On weekends, I worked in the café, doing Louanne's old job, and playing gin rummy with Aunt Vivian when the café was slow. I also knitted scarves, because they were easy, and once Grandma showed me how to change the broken sewing machine needle, I moved it to my bedroom and made pillowcases and dish towels at night after Aunt Vivian and Grandma went to bed.

Three weeks to the day after Louanne moved to Boston, I walked to the Rollarena to skate the afternoon session with Marie and Carla. Paco was at the counter, helping a little kid untie his shoelaces, but he waved me over.

"I'll skate with you after I warm up," I said.

Paco didn't want to skate, though. He just wanted to tell me about Uncle Frankie and how much worse his nightmares had gotten since Louanne left. "Last night he pulled me off the couch and onto the floor and tried to choke me. Then he made me crawl on my belly to the front door. Luckily a passing logging truck rattled the house enough to wake him up. If it hadn't, I don't know what would have happened to me. He's one-hundred percent cuckoo!"

The next day, when Paco left for the Rollarena, I put a deck of cards in my back pocket and picked up four dish towels from the pile I'd made for Grandma.

"Who is it?" Uncle Frankie yelled when I knocked on his door.

"I've got a present for you," I said.

"The door's unlocked."

"What are you doing here? Aren't you Louanne's friend?" he asked in a smart-aleck voice while continuing to roll a joint.

"I just came over to say hi and to give you these dish towels. And I thought you'd like to know I can shuffle cards now. I've been practicing, and I see what you mean about not holding the deck too tight."

"Show me. Right here." Uncle Frankie pushed baggies of pot and joints to the side to make room on the table.

His seriousness scared me, but I shuffled and dealt five cards to four imaginary players. Uncle Frankie leaned back in his chair, crossing his arms over his chest. "Not bad, not bad. So, deal me in. But here, use these." He reached behind him and took a new deck from his poker chip wheel.

In just thirty minutes, I lost ten hands of heads-up and owed him $2.50. Still, the good feeling I got from playing cards with him again was worth it.

"Gotta go. Mail route is calling. I'll take the $2.50 in cash or you can roll joints. There's enough weed in that bag for forty—fifty if you roll 'em thin. Or you could do my laundry instead. I haven't changed my sheets since Christmas, and Cindylee says sleeping with me is like playing in a sandbox." Uncle Frankie slapped his leg.

Rolling joints sounded much better than doing laundry. Besides, I didn't have time. Wendi Whip It, the best girl skater on *Roller Derby*, was appearing at a special Rollarena event in a few hours, and I wanted to get there early.

I had a quick look at the mail Uncle Frankie had sorted that morning and a much longer look at the mail he'd put in the burn box under the table. There was a yellow envelope on top. "It doesn't have an address or a postmark," I said, when he saw me staring at it.

"It's from Louanne. She left it on my porch before she took off with her grandpa boyfriend."

"Aren't you going to open it before you burn it?" I asked.

"Maybe, if I ever want to know what she thinks of me. I think I already do, though. That's why it's in the burn box. Maybe I'll burn it now," Uncle Frankie said.

He spent fifteen minutes teaching me to use his rolling gadget. Then he said he'd run out of time to burn and would do it when he got back. The second I heard his car drive away, I held Louanne's letter up to the kitchen window, but the envelope was too thick to see through. I went to Uncle Frankie's bedroom and found what I needed, a razor. It was on a piece of broken mirror on his dresser, next to a shoebox so full of cash that the lid wouldn't close. Using the tip of the razor blade, I cut along the top seam of the envelope. The two pieces of paper were easy to pull out.

March 30, 1972

Frank,
You should have given me the letter Orson sent last month. At the very least, you should've told me that our aunt had died. It would have been the decent thing.

With help from Dr. Lars, I now recall many things about my past. Things that our aunt, my doctor in Williston, and even Willa Hanson kept from me.

Our mother drove into the logging truck on purpose. I know it for sure. It happened on the way to take me back to a home for pregnant girls, where I'd been living for three months. It was the day after your birthday party. Mom had insisted you stay with your friend and that Dad and Bud come along. They were drunk, and she said she wanted to keep her eye on them. I know now she wanted them to die.

She didn't like Dad, and she hated Bud. She blamed him for my situation. But it wasn't Bud who got me into trouble. I don't know who it was. I snuck out one night and got drunk with my friends. That's all I remember. I couldn't tell Mom what I'd done, and I already knew she hated Bud, so I let her think it was him.

It had just started snowing when Mom turned onto Highway 14 and collided with the truck. Everyone was screaming. I grabbed my door handle and reached out for Kathy, but she flew out the door, right behind Dad.

The car spun for a long time before crashing into something and stopping. I remember rolling on the ground and smelling smoke. Then I couldn't move or breathe. I was under something heavy and hot. I could see Kathy, though. Her eyes were open. They were bleeding. When I grabbed her hand, she told me to come with her. I was going to, but someone was lifting me and yelling at me to keep my eyes open.

She was born (cut out of me) the same day. I've enclosed a copy of her birth certificate. My doctor in Williston sent it to Dr. Erik Larson at my request. She may need or want it one day.
—*Louanne*

I looked at the Oregon State birth certificate. There were tiny ink footprints on the back. On the front were the details.

Mother's name: Louanne Elizabeth Stewart. Live birth: Yes. Sex: Female. Weight: 6 lbs. There was no father or child's name anywhere, but a doctor had signed it on both the front and back. I reread the date and time: February 8, 1958, 2:22 p.m. Her baby and I shared a date of birth, but not a place or time. I was born in the middle of the night in Tacoma, Washington.

With the letter and birth certificate in my hand, I ran to Grandma's house and up the stairs to look in Mom's hope chest, which was still in my closet. I found the birth certif-icates for Teddy, Adam, and myself and placed them on the floor. Adam and I were both born at 3:14 a.m. and weighed eight pounds, five ounces. It seemed odd. I turned them over to look at the footprints on the back. They were identical, with the same ink smear above the right big toe. Mine was an altered copy of Adam's birth certificate. Someone had erased his name and typed my name over it. And they'd added "Fe" to the word "male."

I was gasping, sucking hard, trying to pull in air; then I curled up like a cat among the papers and stayed still until I thought I could stand without falling. I counted every one of my steps out loud from Grandma's front porch to the café. When I opened the door, I could see that Grandma was cleaning the grill, and Aunt Vivian was moving the last two customers out the front door. I waited until she locked it before I went up to Grandma and handed her the two birth certificates and the letter. "The 'she' is me, right?" My voice was shaking.

"Hold your horses, honey," Grandma replied. "Let me get my glasses and sit down."

Aunt Vivian joined Grandma at her workbench, and they took turns looking at the papers while I stood by the sink.

"Oh, Willa. It was inevitable," Aunt Vivian sighed. "I've been saying it since she arrived, and we figured out she didn't know."

Grandma was weeping when she walked up to me, grabbed my hand, and led me to her chair. Aunt Vivian motioned for me to sit down. "Just one swig," she said, handing me her glass of tonic.

"No one ever expected Louanne to survive," Grandma began. "She was in the hospital for eight months, in a coma for three. Your parents drove to the Portland hospital a week after the accident, at my urging. Frankie was already living with us, and I didn't want you to go to a foster home, and neither did they. When Louanne woke from the coma, she had no memory of anything after the age of ten, and her doctors said she never would."

"Yeah, but why?"

"Hold on, I'm getting there." Grandma wiped her mouth and forehead with a café napkin. "When Louanne was well enough to leave the hospital, her Aunt Bethania, who was my childhood friend, went to Portland to take her back to Williston to live. You'd been with your parents for eight months by then, but they didn't legally adopt you until Bethania and Louanne's doctor signed the adoption papers on Louanne's behalf. I think you were two. Then, maybe a year after Teddy was born, Bethania called and said Louanne was getting her memory back and dreaming about a baby. At that point, Bethania and I, along with your parents, decided not to tell Louanne the truth, to let her believe it was just a dream. It was the wrong thing to do. I knew it then, but I went along to keep the peace, hoping your parents would tell you when you turned twelve, as they said they would. I realized they hadn't the day Mrs. Fine asked you why you were so tall and didn't look like Teddy or Gene." There were tears in Grandma's eyes.

Her explanation sounded like something Uncle Frankie would make up, and I wasn't sure what to think. "So, Louanne just found out, too?" I asked.

"She's likely known for a couple of months. She hasn't spoken to me about it, but the medical records she received from her doctor back home would have revealed the truth."

"Why didn't she tell me?" I was shouting now, ready to run.

"I'm not sure, but I imagine she was trying to digest the information. When the big storm soaked her room at Frankie's, I offered her my basement room. But she wanted to stay with her friend Dr. Lars at his son's place. I thought it was strange, but it makes sense now. She must have known then and wanted time away from us to deal with the revelation. She was much calmer when she returned and moved into the basement. And she told me, that same day, she couldn't work in the café any longer—that she wanted to spend her time teaching you what Bethania had taught her."

"Louanne was calmer and friendlier, too. I thought it was because she wasn't living in close quarters with Uncle Frankie. But why didn't she tell me who she was?" I asked.

"I want you to know, Endura was sick and very unhappy before they got you. She told me once you were the best medicine." Grandma was looking straight at me.

"Well, that's a big fat lie, isn't it? She's sicker than ever now. She'll never come back!" I felt like kicking something hard enough to break my foot. Instead, I picked up a stack of dishes and dropped them on the café's back stairs on the way to my room to get my coat. I hitchhiked to the Rollarena, knowing, but not caring, that I'd get into big trouble if I got caught.

Wendi Whip It had come and gone by the time I arrived. I got my skates from Paco's locker, where I'd been keeping them, and hit the floor like a cannonball. Paco yelled three times over the loudspeaker for me to slow down. When I didn't, he skated onto the floor and chased me for two laps before he caught up and pushed me into the rails.

"Louanne is my real mother. Did you know? Did Uncle Frankie tell you?" I burst into tears.

"Are you sure?" Paco asked. "Seems kind of fucked up that no one told you until now."

"No one told me. I read about it in a letter Louanne left for Uncle Frankie. She left my real birth certificate, too. Grandma confirmed it." I pulled away from him.

"Yeah, I saw that letter, too. I thought he burned it. That's what he said, anyway," Paco replied.

"Who cares about him? Didn't you hear me? Louanne is my mother. It sucks."

"Okay, okay. I get it. And yeah, it sucks, but it's not like you're five years old with nowhere to go. My sister's adopted. She's always known it, and she's happy my parents wanted her bad enough to fill in a ton of paperwork and travel to New York to pick her up. Some kids never get parents."

I was still crying when Paco guided me off the rink floor to the front desk and got me a Coke. I sat behind the counter with him and, between customers, complained about my family and how they all kept secrets for no good reason. "Even I do it. And I know it's wrong. Don't you think Louanne should have told me who she was or left me the birth certificate instead of leaving it for Uncle Frankie to give to me? I hung out with her every day for weeks—she had plenty of opportunities to tell me."

"Would you have believed Louanne if she'd handed you a birth certificate or said, 'Oh, and by the way, I'm your mother?' I don't think so," Paco said.

I hadn't thought about that. He might be right; maybe I wouldn't have believed Louanne. And maybe some kids didn't care about being adopted. But I did. If Dad had just agreed to call in a favor, Mom wouldn't have had to sneak Adam into Canada, and the secret would still be a secret (from me anyway), and I wouldn't know I was the daughter of a one-eyed, crooked woman.

At 7:30 Aunt Vivian called the Rollarena, and Paco told her he'd walk me home later. At his suggestion, I hit the rink. It took a few laps before I stopped crying and realized I was taller than my parents and looked more like Uncle Frankie than anyone else because he was Louanne's brother. Then I tried to recall the pictures from her Bible, wondering if I looked like Louanne before the accident.

I WAS ALL CRIED OUT WHEN PACO AND I rounded the curve and saw the Esso sign was still on. I was hoping Grandma had gone to bed so I wouldn't have to talk. But she opened the door when she saw me on the porch, and I could tell she'd been crying, so I didn't flinch when she reached out and touched my face, then hugged me. "I've been so worried. Oh, honey, I'm sorry I didn't tell you when I first realized you didn't know. Gene wouldn't let me. He said he'd take care of it. But he didn't. Then, when he was packing to leave for Edmonton, I urged him to take you along so that he and Endura could tell you together. But he's too hardheaded these days, and there was no way to convince him."

"I was a glass of eggnog away from spitting out the truth when I saw you and Louanne at Thanksgiving," Aunt Vivian yelled out from the dining room. "You've got the same god-damn beautiful hair."

"Did you know her aunt had died?" I asked Grandma.

"The letter you showed us is the first I've heard of it. When Louanne moved here, I sent a couple of letters to Bethania's son Orson, asking for news. He's never gotten back to me. I'll call him tomorrow."

It was hard to get comfortable in bed. My legs twitched, and I couldn't stop thinking about Dad and how he knew about Louanne all along. I wanted to call him in Vietnam to ask why he'd never told me the truth. But then I thought it wasn't Dad I wanted to ask—it was Mom.

I WAS DOWNSTAIRS AT 5:30 A.M., AS SOON as I heard Grandma and Aunt Vivian moving around. "I want to call Mom—from the garage, not here."

"Sure, honey. And don't worry about the long-distance charge. Your dad will pay it," Grandma said.

"You know, there's a silver lining in all this," Aunt Vivian said as I passed her. "You'll never worry about being short, dumpy, and ugly like us, because you'll always be tall, thin, and beautiful."

"Haven't you noticed my nostrils flare out like a horse when I talk?" I pulled the door shut before she could answer.

When I dialed the number in Edmonton, a girl answered and then went to get Mom.

I couldn't even say hello. "Louanne Stewart is my mother, isn't she?"

Mom gasped. "What? Who told you about Louanne?"

"She lived here until a few weeks ago. She's gone to Boston now."

"Louanne Stewart was living at Willa's, and no one bothered to tell me?"

"What do you care? You only care about your secrets." I bit the back of my hand.

I heard Mom sob, and a few seconds passed before she spoke again. "She was a silly girl who got herself into trouble. She's not even supposed to be alive. She was the one with the secret. I'm the one who made everything okay for everyone. I'm your mother. The one who's taken care of you, the one who's on your side. Not her!"

Mom was bawling then, and I was on the verge of doing the same, but I told her I'd call back the next day. I didn't, though. I didn't want to hear more excuses. As the days went by, I lost interest in talking to her—even when Grandma asked me to please return Mom's calls. By then, I had a voice inside my head that kept telling me no one was on my side, especially my mother.

It took me a week to get up the nerve to return Louanne's letter to Uncle Frankie. He looked angry when he answered the door.

"Here's your letter. Sorry, I took it."

"Don't need it. Don't want it. Get rid of it." Uncle Frankie threw a book of matches at me. "You know how to burn."

"Have you known about Louanne and me all along?"

"Didn't know until you helped yourself to a letter not addressed to you. Bet you'll never do that again." He kicked the door shut.

The next day, when Velvet and I were on the front lawn, I saw Uncle Frankie coming my way. I tried to ignore him as he flapped his arms like a bird and attempted to imitate Peacock George's crow. He was only a few feet away when he fell and couldn't get up. When he noticed he was eye to eye with Velvet, he rolled onto his back and laughed so hard that I had to join in.

"Hey, I'm not the bad guy here. I didn't know about Louanne and you. If I had, I wouldn't have told you. What good would it do? What good has it done?"

"Yeah, maybe no good at all. But Paco said something good would come out of it. I hope he's right. Grandma called her cousin in North Dakota to ask about your aunt. She told Grandma she'd seen her obituary in the Williston newspaper."

"Well, there you go. Louanne was right about her being dead. But there was no letter from Orson, that's for fucking sure," Uncle Frankie replied.

"Are you sure? I've seen you throw letters in the burn box without looking at them."

Uncle Frankie laughed like I'd said something funny. "I should be madder than shit about you taking my stuff, but now that I'm officially your uncle, I'm gonna make an exception. You're sneaky, like me. It runs in our family."

"I hope it's the only thing that does," I said quietly.

CHAPTER 26

THE ROAR OF V-8 ENGINES ON THE highway woke me early on Monday morning, May 22, but I didn't open my eyes until I heard gravel spraying the café. That's how I knew they'd fishtailed off the highway and onto the dirt road next to Grandma's house. I got out of bed and reached my window in time to watch two men in blue jackets with the letters "FBI" on the back step out of a sedan and signal the cops in the car behind to follow them. When I raised the window sash to get a better view, they all turned around and looked up, one with his gun raised.

I dropped to the floor and waited for the pounding in my chest to slow down. At first, I thought they'd arrived with news about Dad, but they wouldn't need guns for that. Then I thought about the bags of pot in Uncle Frankie's house and got to my knees to look out the window again. All four men were walking toward the narrow path between the café and gas station. I knew for sure then that they'd come for Uncle Frankie, but it wasn't until I heard him shout, "Fucking pigs" that I got the courage to change into jeans and a T-shirt and run to Aunt Vivian's room. Ignoring her naked body starfished across the bed, I said, much louder than I'd meant to, "The cops are here, and they've got guns!"

"The hell you say!" She rolled out of bed. "Hand me my overalls. Are we being robbed? Has someone broken into the café?"

"I don't know. Maybe Uncle Frankie knows. They're at his house right now. Oh God, they're gonna shoot him, aren't they?"

"Calm down! Where's that gun your dad used to keep in his car? The one Teddy pointed at that old man?"

"He gave it to Uncle Frankie to sell," I replied.

"Stupid gives dum-dum a bone," she muttered. "There's a baseball bat in the hall closet. Get it. Where's Willa?"

Before I could answer, we heard Grandma calling for us to come downstairs. She said one of the FBI agents had told her to stay inside, that they'd had a tip about a draft dodger hiding around here and he might be dangerous.

"It's bullshit, Willa. Nothing but bullshit!" Aunt Vivian tightened her grip on the handle of the baseball bat, then opened the door. Grandma yelled at her to put it down. That's when a cop turned and shot Aunt Vivian.

She fell to the ground with a thud, just a few feet from Grandma's front porch.

A second later, Uncle Frankie and Paco appeared on the pathway, yelling and trying to kick the FBI agents who had a hold of their arms and were pushing them toward the FBI sedan. Grandma shoved me out of her way, then dropped to her knees and began patting Aunt Vivian's cheeks and telling her to wake her. "I need your help here, Evan," Grandma said.

I couldn't move. My feet were like cement blocks on the ground. And then, suddenly, Hubert was pulling Grandma away, and Hal was ripping open the leg of Aunt Vivian's overalls with his bare hands. Then Hubert took off his rope belt and tied it around her thigh. Hal covered her ears with his hands and began moving them in circles. "Stop it! You're hurting her," Grandma cried. But Hal kept going like he hadn't heard, and a few seconds later, Aunt Vivian opened her eyes.

With both hands flat on her chest and looking as if she might fall over, Grandma looked right at me and told me to get a blanket. When I didn't move, she said, "Right this god-damn minute!"

I forced myself to obey but dropped the blanket when I saw the blood all around Aunt Vivian's leg. Hal caught it before it hit the ground and covered Aunt Vivian from chin to toe while telling her about a new song he was learning, a sparrow's nest in his woodshed, and their new chicken coop he was planning to paint red. I'd never heard him talk so much; later I learned he'd done it to keep Aunt Vivian awake.

The cop who shot Aunt Vivian called for an ambulance from his patrol car, then came over to Grandma. He cleared his throat a few times before he apologized. "Honestly, ma'am, I thought an angry old farmer was coming at me with a shotgun."

"That's understandable," Grandma said.

By the time the ambulance arrived, there was blood every-where, and the FBI agents were still struggling to get Uncle Frankie and Paco into the back seat of the sedan. "Burn every-thing, Evan!" I heard Uncle Frankie say before the car door slammed shut.

When the ambulance left with Aunt Vivian, and the FBI drove off with Uncle Frankie and Paco, Grandma fell to her knees on the grass and cried as I'd never seen a grown-up cry. I sat down and cried too, until Hal put his hand out to help Grandma stand up. "Do not fret. We are here to help."

Once they'd led her into the house, Grandma asked Hal and Hubert to take her to the hospital. "I need to see my sister. She'll know what to do. You can drive my Studebaker. Frankie changed the spark plugs just the other day."

"Of course, of course," Hal replied.

I didn't have to go to school, but Grandma insisted I stay in the house until she returned, and she didn't expect to be back before lunch.

As soon as the Studebaker drove off, I grabbed a dish towel and a book of matches from the kitchen drawer and ran to Uncle Frankie's house. There was blood on the porch, and the cops had left the front door wide open. I slammed it shut, pulled the box of undelivered mail out from under the kitchen table, and dumped it out onto the floor. As fast as I could, I scattered the letters to see the postmarks and make sure I wasn't about to destroy anything important. It would take a while to burn it all, and I prayed the cops weren't on their way back to search his house.

I wasn't confident I could start a barrel fire without one of the gasoline-soaked coils that Uncle Frankie used, but I tried. I was on the verge of giving up and hiding the box in the barely visible old truck in the field behind the house, when Hal and Hubert appeared.

"We know about the marijuana cigarettes Frank sells," said Hal. "We met several of his customers when we worked here. We need to burn whatever he has in his house."

"Yeah, sure. I'll get it," I replied. "But it's not just marijuana we need to burn. Do you know about the undelivered mail?"

Hal frowned. "We'd rather not know."

"Then don't watch." I picked up a handful of letters and hurled them into the barrel.

Hal stepped forward and stirred the fire up. "You should get the marijuana now, and anything else in the house he shouldn't have."

I found Paco's wallet under the couch. Inside was his driver's license and high school ID card. I found Uncle Frankie's shoebox of money on the top shelf of his closet, behind a blanket. The blanket hid a blue folder with army papers that looked important and two stacks of twenty-dollar bills held together with thick, yellow rubber bands. I found a Columbia House record box that had once contained a Three Dog Night album. It was full of joints. I went to the refrigerator next and took out two bags of pot. Then I grabbed his rolling gadget, cigarette papers, and an ashtray filled with cigarette and joint roaches and took everything outside.

I handed the twenty-dollar bills to Hal, and they both chuckled when I told them it was part of the ransom money D. B. Cooper got when he hijacked the plane. "I read about it," Hal said with no expression.

Hal and Hubert took turns holding the stacks of twenties like they were trying to guess what they weighed. "Must be marked," Hal said as he took the rubber bands off and fed the bills to the flames one by one. I'd never seen money burn before. When the corners of the bills caught fire, they curled up, and the green melted into shades of a rainbow.

When they'd finished burning the twenties, Hal picked up Paco's wallet.

"Oh, don't burn that." I reached for it. "He'll need it when he comes back."

Hal grinned, opened Paco's wallet, and had a quick look at the driver's license before taking out seven one-dollar bills and handing them to me. "He won't be back," he said and dropped the wallet into the barrel. When I complained, Hal told me to sit on the stairs.

Next, Hubert showed the blue folder and the shoebox of cash to Hal. They whispered to each other for a few seconds, and then Hubert brought them to me. "Willa is going to need these."

"What about the joints and the bags of pot and stuff?" I asked.

"We'll get to those," Hal replied.

"And there's a gun in Uncle Frankie's bedroom. He was gonna sell it to one of his friends, but he didn't."

"Bring it here." Hal sounded excited now.

I found the gun underneath some shirts in the bottom drawer of Uncle Frankie's dresser. I checked to make sure it wasn't loaded, the way Dad had shown me, before taking it outside. "I'll take that," Hal said. He motioned Hubert to throw in all the dope stuff and the ashtray. He was still holding the gun when the smoke from the burning pot began making me tired.

Once the fire had died down, Hal and Hubert left to pick up Grandma from the hospital, and I went to the house to have a bath and calm down. But all I could see and hear was Paco, begging the cops to leave him alone, his nose and mouth bleeding, and the FBI agents kicking him before shoving him into their car. Uncle Frankie's face was just as bloody, but he kept spitting and calling the cops "fucking pigs." I saw Aunt Vivian, too, blood flowing like lava from a hole in her right thigh, and Grandma on her knees telling her to wake up.

It was as if I had a View Master in my head and couldn't stop clicking to the next screen. I dressed and went downstairs to watch TV. When that didn't work, I found a bottle of vodka and poured some into a glass of orange juice. I drank it at the sink and had another before going outside to sit on the front porch and wait for Grandma. I thought about cleaning up Aunt Vivian's blood, but I was too woozy. I don't know what time it was when I fell asleep.

I woke up to Grandma rocking me with her foot. "Vivian is going to be okay, and so are we," she said.

"Am I supposed to call you Mrs. Hanson now?" I could hear myself slurring and felt as if I might throw up.

"Oh, honey, I'll always be your grandma."

THE "CLOSED" SIGN STAYED ON EAT CAFÉ'S front window on Tuesday, but Get Gas opened on time. Hal and Hubert showed up to get the keys, and Hal told Grandma they'd work for just lunches and cinnamon rolls this time. "As recompense for not coming to your aid sooner."

"Oh, you two. I can pay and provide lunch," Grandma said. "I'm not sure about the cinnamon rolls, though. I'm not opening the café until Vivian recovers. It could be a long, long time."

"Good thing we have a long, long time," Hal replied with a mischievous grin.

When Grandma asked Hal if he wouldn't mind driving her to the hospital that afternoon, he took a step forward, bowed, and tipped his hat. "Madam, it would be my pleasure."

I put a hand over my mouth, but Grandma still heard me giggling and threw me a look.

Before I left for school, she said, "I have to call the postmaster today to tell him Frankie won't be available to do his route for a while. He's an old friend of Pa's, and I know he's kept Frankie on because of it, but I'm sure he'll fire him now. Then he'll send someone here to get the mailbags and the sign in his back car window. If that someone arrived today, would they find any undelivered mail in his house?"

"No, they would not," I replied with confidence. "I know it was wrong, but I burned some undelivered mail yesterday after Hal and Hubert drove you to the hospital. I thought Uncle Frankie might get into more trouble if the police came back to search his house and found it. It was all bulk class, I promise—what Uncle Frankie considers garbage. And the other things I found and didn't burn, I put on the floor in your kitchen closet. There's a file with papers and a shoebox full of cash."

Grandma was quiet for a few seconds, and I thought I was in big trouble until she smiled and said, "I thought I told you to stay in the house."

"You did." I smiled back.

"This place is a pigsty," Grandma said once we were inside Uncle Frankie's house. "I might have it torn down. Not today, though. Today, I need to cancel my bread and milk order and get to the hospital to see Viv. And I might need to find a lawyer for my poor Frankie. I imagine I'll know soon why they arrested him. If *Perry Mason* is right, he gets one phone call." She began to weep. "I can't run the gas station and café and care for Viv and worry about Frankie and everyone else. It's too much."

"Is it okay if I stay home from school today? I can clean the café," I said.

"I don't need a phone call from the principal asking where you are—not on top of everything else. You can do it when you get home from school."

THE NEWS ABOUT THE FBI AT EAT and Get Gas spread fast. Everyone at school thought it was about the pot Uncle Frankie sold, and I went along with them. It sure made me popular. Even kids I didn't know asked me to get Uncle Frankie's autograph for them.

For the next two days, I was on my best behavior. I did my homework and anything Grandma asked me to without complaining. She split her time between the hospital and sitting by the phone, waiting for Uncle Frankie to call. She'd tried calling him at the jail in Seattle, but they wouldn't let her speak to him. Then, on Thursday afternoon, three days after the FBI took him to jail, the phone rang just as I got home from school. Grandma answered on the first ring.

"What for? What has he done? Are you sure?" I heard her ask. She hung up after saying she'd be at his arraignment the next day.

Between wringing her hands and pulling curlers out of her hair, she told me she had to see Aunt Vivian right away, and she couldn't ask Hal because he'd already driven her at lunchtime. "You'll have to take me, Evan."

When I told her I couldn't drive that far, she put a finger under my chin and kept it there. "Our boy is in big trouble.

He could go to prison for a long time. He's been helping draft dodgers, and he's going before a judge in Seattle tomorrow at 1:00 p.m. I need to be there. You're going to take me. Understand?"

I nodded. "What about Paco?" I asked.

"They've moved him to another jail," Grandma said. "He's the reason the FBI came to my house. He's a draft dodger. I never bought Frankie's story about them being childhood friends. Did you?"

"No, not really," I replied in a steady voice.

While Hubert filled the Studebaker gas tank, Hal cleaned the car windows, stopping at the passenger door when Grandma rolled her window down. She told him everything she knew about Uncle Frankie and Paco while I tried to untangle the two curlers still in the back of her head.

"We would be grateful to take you to the hospital now and to attend the arraignment with you tomorrow," Hal said. "A departure time of 9:30 a.m. should be adequate."

I saw Grandma smile and heard her exhale. "I think Evan can drive me now, but I'll take you up on your offer to get to Seattle in the morning—thank you."

I WAS ESPECIALLY NERVOUS DRIVING WITH Grandma in the front seat. We almost went off the road when she grabbed the steering wheel, and she let out a big sigh when I finally pulled into the hospital parking lot. "You're off the hook for tomorrow. You can go to school and skate after. We'll pick you up from the Rollarena on our way home." Grandma released her grip on the dashboard to pat her forehead with a tissue.

When we got to her room, Aunt Vivian was sitting up in bed, drinking coffee and reading the newspaper with a magnifying glass. She looked paler than usual and seemed surprised to see us. She waved us over, and Grandma sat down in the chair next to her bed and told her about the arraignment.

"I want to go, too," I said. "I need to see Uncle Frankie."

To my surprise, Aunt Vivian agreed that I shouldn't go. When I complained, Grandma clapped her hands. "Enough is enough! You might not look like a child, but you are a child, and you don't need to be involved. I'll give Frankie a message from you, that's all."

IN THE MORNING, I HUGGED GRANDMA for a long time and told her I was sorry for being a brat. Then I gave her the note I'd written for Uncle Frankie, telling him I'd burnt everything. I'd used words from songs Uncle Frankie and I both liked and folded it in a triangle, the way I'd seen him fold small papers. Only he would understand.

CHAPTER 27

WHEN GRANDMA DIDN'T TURN UP AT the Rollarena at 6:00 p.m. as promised, I called her house at seven and then again at eight but got no answer. "They probably just forgot to pick you up. I've done that before with my kids." Bernie put the phone back under the counter before handing me the key to the vending machine and telling me to help myself to a Coke and a bag of Fritos.

At nine, Bernie locked up and drove me home. I'd already told him Grandma had gone to Seattle to see Uncle Frankie. Now I added, "They weren't after my uncle. They came for Paco. He's a draft dodger. Uncle Frankie tried to get him to Canada, but something went wrong."

Bernie shook his head. "I'm okay with it. If anyone knows why a kid shouldn't go to Vietnam, it's Frank. Too bad they'll send Paco there after a stint in prison."

"Jeez, I hope not. His real name is Patrick Richardson. He's from Spokane, and he's nineteen. The cops beat him up. It was scary."

"It's an awful thing we're asking from these kids. I don't know what I'd do if I had a son old enough to be drafted. Probably the same thing Paco's mom and Frank did," Bernie said. "Hey, I gotta get home, but you're always welcome at the rink—on the house."

There were no lights on, and Grandma wasn't in the living room sitting in the dark watching TV like I thought she might be. I ate a bologna sandwich in front of the TV, trying to get interested in *Room 222*.

"We didn't forget you," Grandma said when I answered the phone not long after 10:00 p.m. "There was an incident at the jail, and Frankie died. I had to stay to identify his body. We'll be home in an hour or so."

"What did you say?" But she'd already hung up.

I went to my room, but I didn't put on my pajamas, and I didn't get into bed. I sat on the windowsill, watching for the Studebaker and trying to breathe away the knot in my chest.

WHEN I HEARD GRANDMA COMING UP the stairs at midnight, I ran to meet her. She was still wearing her coat, her purse was on her arm, and her face was red and puffy.

She tried but couldn't turn the doorknob, so I reached out to help, putting my hand over hers.

"Just go to bed. I can't talk about it," she said.

I started to cry. "But why is he dead?"

"I don't know. I really don't," Grandma mumbled and closed the door.

It was getting light out when I became aware of sounds downstairs. I tiptoed down and saw Grandma bent over the dining room table, polishing it with Crisco shortening instead of bee's wax. When she spotted me, she sat down in a chair and slumped forward. "This table is so greasy. You know he didn't have shoes. He should've had shoes. His feet were cold." She sounded frantic.

"Should I run to his house and get them?" I asked.

"I've got to find them." Grandma was shaking her head.

"I'll go, Grandma. You stay here. I know where he keeps his shoes. I'll be back in five minutes."

"No, no. Not now. Later. I need to see Viv. You'll have to drive."

"It's really early. Visiting hours don't start until eight. I'll make a pot of coffee, and while it's perking, I'll run upstairs and get dressed. Then, if there's time, I'll go to Uncle Frankie's and get his shoes."

GRANDMA WAS LYING FLAT IN AUNT Vivian's chair, staring at the ceiling, when I returned with Uncle Frankie's favorite boots. When Hal and Hubert began playing a song called "Ave Maria," Grandma sat up.

"Open the door," she said. "I want to hear this."

The music gave me chills, and we were both sobbing as I helped Grandma into the car. I drove without crying or talking and without making one mistake, and since it was Saturday, there were plenty of parking spaces. I took two.

We were fifteen minutes early, but when I told the nurse at the front desk why, she looked up and said, "Go ahead, girls, it's okay."

Aunt Vivian was sitting up in bed, drinking coffee, when we walked into her room. She seemed shocked to see us and then scared when Grandma slumped against the wall. "Oh, Viv," she wailed, "our poor boy is dead."

Grandma needed to sit down, but there wasn't a chair in the room, so I ran to the nurse's desk to get one. When I returned with a chair and a nurse, Grandma was on the bed, holding Aunt Vivian, and they were sobbing. I knew if I kept looking at them, I would, too. I couldn't let the sadness about Uncle Frankie sink in any more than it already had. If I did, I might not be able to drive Grandma home.

I looked out the window at the gray sky and took a few deep breaths, praying the nurse would tell us to leave. Eventually, Grandma released Aunt Vivian and got off the bed. The startled look on their faces told me they hadn't realized anyone else was in the room. Aunt Vivian must have been embarrassed because she almost screamed at the nurse that her nephew hanged himself in a jail cell because of the goddamn war.

Hanged himself? That can't be. I'd been thinking that one of the other prisoners had beaten him for something he said or did. I looked at Grandma for a sign that Aunt Vivian had been wrong, but she was sobbing too hard for it to have been a mistake.

"He was a regular American kid who did what he thought was his duty. He came back from that place so beat up, frightened, and hostile, it was hard to be in a room with him. And now he's gone and done the worst thing," Aunt Vivian said.

I pressed my back to the wall, slid to the floor, and shuffled over to Aunt Vivian's bed so I could pull the corner of her bedspread over my face and become invisible.

When we got home from the hospital, Grandma tried to call Dad in Saigon but had to leave a message. The following day, someone from the army called and said Dad wouldn't be available for weeks. Grandma told the person to tell my dad his brother had died, and she needed to know what to do about his funeral.

"That man on the phone was rude. He said he wasn't a messenger, and I should call the honor guard agent at Fort Lewis Army Base with Frankie's name, rank, and number. I'm not going to," Grandma said when she hung up. "I think a military funeral service is the last thing Frankie would want. I don't even know where his dog tags are."

Later, when Grandma went to her room to rest, I walked to the garage to call Mom. I was crying when I told her what Uncle Frankie had done. She was quiet for a few seconds and then said it was a shame he never got help from the VA hospital. Then she asked me if I'd called Louanne with the news. When I said no, she said I'd better get off the phone and do it.

The next voice I heard was Teddy's. He told me about his new friend, Bobby, and how they'd trained Leroy to catch a stick, chase a car, and dig a hole. Mom didn't get back on the phone.

I DIDN'T CALL LOUANNE AS MOM HAD suggested. I wasn't ever going to. I wanted to forget about her. But a day or so after Uncle Frankie died, when Grandma said Louanne needed to know, and she didn't have it in her to call, I felt like I had to.

On my way to catch the school bus the following day, I grabbed the spare key to the garage to call Louanne from there. I started by telling her Velvet liked parsley more than lettuce, then burst into tears and blurted out that Uncle Frankie had killed himself.

"So soon," she said.

"What?"

"I had a feeling he'd do it. I used to have the same feeling about myself until I met Dr. Lars." She was crying.

Before our call ended, Louanne said she wanted to come to the funeral. "I'd like to say goodbye to my little brother. I'm tired of being mad at him. He should be with our parents and our sister, Kathy, in the Stevenson cemetery. He loved Kathy. I'll arrange a plot for him. Can you tell Willa that, please?"

"Sure," I replied. It seemed a long way for her to come to say goodbye to a brother she didn't like.

HAL HAD OFFERED TO DRIVE GRANDMA to the hospital to pick up Aunt Vivian that day. I was happy that she was coming home because Grandma was getting weary and more and more confused, and I didn't know what to do. Just the afternoon before, someone called, and I heard Grandma shout down the phone, "I don't want a dead body in my house!" Whoever was on the other end calmed her down, and I heard her say, "Peace be with you, too," before saying she'd call them back the next day with an address of where to send his body.

"I just can't stop seeing his bruised and bloody face whenever I close my eyes," she said.

"I keep expecting him to walk in and wink at me or complain about Dad," I said.

"Me, too," Grandma said. "Me, too."

Aunt Vivian was on the living room couch, and Grandma was in her lounge chair when I got home from school. I knew they hadn't heard me come in, so I stayed in the kitchen to listen.

"A casket, a burial plot, and a funeral service are going to cost a fortune," Grandma said.

"What about the box of cash from Frankie's house you told me about? It's not as if we're going to hand it over to the police now, is it?" Aunt Vivian said.

Grandma let out a tired sigh, and I moved closer to the living room so they could see me.

"How ya doing there, Too Tall?" Aunt Vivian waved me over. "I heard you might not want to call me Aunt Vivian. And what's with you wearing a bra, now?"

I was so glad to have her back that I didn't care if she teased me. She was the only one who could calm Grandma down, the only person Grandma relied on. Even with her leg in a cast, I knew she'd organize everything for the funeral.

"I've decided you can call me Aunt Vivian or Your Royal Highness. I'll answer to both," she said.

"Not Mrs. Pigge?" I asked, not sure of what I'd just done.

Grandma tipped her head back and roared. A second later, Aunt Vivian laughed, too, and for a moment, the dreariness that had been in the house disappeared.

"WE'RE NOT PUTTING AN OBITUARY IN the paper, and we don't want an after-funeral gathering in the café. Viv says we'll have something at the funeral home. And don't tell anyone how Frankie died," Grandma said the next morning.

"I've already told my mom and Louanne." I swallowed hard. "But I won't tell anyone else—I promise. Oh God, Grandma, I forgot to tell you that Louanne is coming for the funeral. And she's getting a burial plot for Uncle Frankie in Stevenson so that he can be with their parents and sister, Kathy."

"Oh, that's awfully good of her," Grandma said. "I'm feeling stronger now that Viv is home. I'll call Louanne. You might need to clean the basement room for her."

I didn't want Louanne to come. And I didn't talk to my friends about Uncle Frankie; I thought they'd ask how he died. If I told them the truth, Grandma might find out, or they might think it was gross and stop coming to Eat and Get Gas or tell their friends to stop coming. And then Grandma would go broke, and it would be my fault.

FRANKIE'S FUNERAL WAS HELD ON THURSDAY, June 1. Hal drove Grandma and Aunt Vivian (and her crutches) to the Hoquiam funeral home in the Studebaker, and Hubert took me in his truck. Not very many showed up for the service. Just Fisky and his wife; Mrs. Fine and her sister, Bella; four of Uncle Frankie's girlfriends; three poker friends; the postmaster; Mooch; and Louanne and Dr. Lars Larson.

"How about you sit next to Louanne?" Grandma said.

"I'd rather sit next to you," I replied.

"I understand, but just sit with Louanne this one time." She patted my hand.

The man Aunt Vivian recruited to perform the service, Chester Tuffin, called the bingo games at the Eagles Hall. Aunt Vivian liked him; Grandma didn't. When Chester started the service by saying Uncle Frankie could pump gas faster than the attendant at the Aberdeen Phillips 66 and was unlucky at bingo, but very lucky with the ladies, Grandma said, "Oh, for God's sake!"

Chester didn't notice or didn't care. "Francis Arnold Stewart's contribution to our great nation was his willingness to protect all Americans from the evil Communists. We all owe a thank you to President Nixon for his outstanding leadership."

"That's it, service over. Cake and coffee in the other room," Aunt Vivian said loudly, motioning me over to come back and help her up.

After the coffee and cake were gone, Dr. Lars invited me to have an early dinner with him and Louanne at Lee's Chinese restaurant. I still wanted to try Chinese food, but I wasn't sure I should go. What if they wanted to talk about Louanne being my birth mother?

"I would if I could, but Grandma and Aunt Vivian need me at home. Maybe another time," I said with a fake smile.

"I think we'll be okay without you for a few hours,' I heard Grandma say from behind me.

So, I went. Dr. Lars was a bad driver, even worse than me. He parked in front of the restaurant with a front tire on the sidewalk.

They ordered ten different plates of food for us to share, but I ate most of it. I couldn't help it; everything tasted so good, and I was starving. It wasn't until we were in the car heading back to Grandma's that Louanne said, "I understand from Willa that you saw a letter I left for Frankie. He shouldn't have left it laying around. But I shouldn't have left it for him in the first place. I'm sorry I did," she said.

I kept my head down and picked at my nails.

"I don't want to be your mother, but I'd like to be your friend. But only if you want that," Louanne continued.

"Maybe that would be okay. I'll have to think about it."

When we got back to Grandma's, Dr. Lars opened the back door for me. "Come back to Boston with us. It will be good for you and us. And I'll make sure you get to Canada when your mother's ready for you, I promise. We're leaving next week, once Frankie is resting with his parents and sister."

"I'll have to think about that too," I replied. Even if I wanted to go, I didn't have enough money for a plane ticket, and Mom and Dad would never give it to me. But the thought of spending the summer somewhere other than Grandma's sounded good.

Louanne waved goodbye from the car window for way too long, and I felt, as her potential friend, I should wave back for the same amount of time.

"We're on the edge of our seats here," said Aunt Vivian when I walked into the living room.

"Louanne just wants to be my friend." I sat down on the couch next to Grandma. "She doesn't want to be my mother. She told me that twice. And Dr. Lars invited me to go to Boston."

"Well, that was nice of him. And isn't it great Louanne just wants to be your friend?" Grandma said.

"God knows no one needs two mothers," Aunt Vivian added.

"A month or two in Boston might be a nice thing for you," Grandma said. "I still have most of the money Gene got from selling all those clams. Let's use some of it for a plane ticket, huh?"

"I don't think I should. Mom might come to get me now that the roads are clear," I said, though I knew, as well as they did, that it wasn't going to happen.

"Sleep on it. You might feel different in the morning. And I'll handle Gene if you decide to go," Grandma said.

SOMETIME IN THE MIDDLE OF THE NIGHT, I decided I'd call Mom in the morning and ask her if she was coming home soon or if I could take a bus or a train to Edmonton in the next week or two; I'd hang around Eat and Get Gas and clean Uncle Frankie's house if she was. But if she said it would be September, I'd go to Boston with Louanne and Dr. Lars for the summer.

Adam answered on the first ring.

"Why are you there? Dad told me you don't live with Mom. Is everything okay?" I asked.

"I'm okay. Teddy's okay, but Mom's not okay. And no one knows how the hell Dad is. He's coming back with his girl-friend in a few months. That's what Mom says," Adam replied.

"Yeah, Grandma said something like that, too. She tried to reach him a few times last week. You heard about Uncle Frankie, right?"

Adam said he hadn't, so I filled him in.

"I've got nothing but admiration for a guy who risks going to prison to keep guys like me out of Vietnam. I'm sorry he killed himself. That's fucked up," he said.

"Can I talk to Mom?"

"Didn't she tell you she's having surgery today? She has something on her brain. The doctor said it's been growing for years. She's not gonna die, but it'll be a long time before she's back to her old self."

"She didn't tell me. No one ever tells me anything." I could hear my voice rising. "I'll take a train to Edmonton. I have the schedule and enough money for a coach-class seat. I can be there when Mom gets out of the hospital to help with Teddy."

"She's got lots of help here. And there's no room for you. I'm not kidding," Adam said.

"Yeah, Dad told me that, too. You know they sold our house and they're getting divorced, right?"

"Yeah, I know. It sucks. And I feel bad that you're stuck there. But what can I do? I'm only here to keep Teddy in check until Mom gets out of the hospital. I've got a job, a new name, and a girlfriend up north in Red Deer. But we live in a small trailer—there's no room for you. You'll just have to be cool until Mom gets better."

I couldn't believe he was telling me to be cool. "I've been invited to Boston for the summer by Frankie's sister. Do you think it will be okay with Mom if I go?" I asked as I swiped away tears.

"Sure, it will. And it sounds like fun. Hey, I've got to go. Teddy's outside waiting for me."

"Tell him I miss him, okay?" I said.

WITH HER LEG IN A CAST, AUNT VIVIAN couldn't get into a car to attend Uncle Frankie's burial service in Stevenson, and Grandma couldn't leave her alone all day, but she let me skip school and go with Louanne and Dr. Lars. Dr. Erik Larson drove us, and Louanne sat in the back seat next to me. It was quiet until Dr. Lars turned the radio on and found a classical music station. After two songs, I told Dr. Erik about Hal and Hubert and how they played the same music on pianos at their house. I don't think he believed me until Louanne said she'd seen them play. "They had a recital last Christmas. It was magical—the best thing about living at Eat and Get Gas."

When we arrived at the cemetery, Uncle Frankie's casket was next to a deep hole across from the graves of his mother, father, and sister. I put my hand on top, wondering if he was really inside. It didn't seem possible, and I couldn't stop the tears I'd been holding in for days. I cried and coughed until I almost threw up. Louanne moved closer to hand me a handkerchief. "It's sad knowing they'll shovel dirt over him when we leave," she said.

Standing at one end of the casket, Dr. Lars almost sang a poem he said was the "Prayer of Divine Mercy." When he finished, he stepped back and motioned for me to step forward. I didn't know any poems by heart, so I didn't move until I felt

Louanne's hand on my shoulder. "It's okay," she said. "Just anything will do."

I said the only thing I could think of, hoping no one would notice it was lyrics of "Close to You." Louanne said it was sweet, and then she read her tribute from a book she'd brought along. It was a poem called "Because I Could Not Stop for Death." When she finished, she threw into the grave the dozen white roses we'd brought along. I stepped closer to see them, and Louanne grabbed my arm. "It's not your turn," she said, sobbing. "It wasn't his turn, either."

When we'd finished at the cemetery, Dr. Erik took us to a roadside diner for lunch and then to Louanne's old neighborhood. We walked a couple of blocks, and when we got to her old house, she described the rooms inside, only crying a little and not for long.

SCHOOL GOT OUT FOR THE SUMMER THE next day, and I went to two parties and still ended up at the Rollarena, skating with Marie and Carla. They told me they'd be working all summer at a 4-H camp in Olympia, and I told them I was going to Boston.

Marie said I should leave my honeybee bracelet with her. "Just to make sure you come back."

EPILOGUE

WHEN I RETURNED FROM MY PIANO LESSON, I found two letters in Dr. Lars's mailbox. They were both from Grandma. The letter to me had general news about Aunt Vivian and Velvet, and information about Paco. He was in prison for another five months and wouldn't be going to Vietnam because he broke his jaw in the scuffle with the FBI.

Louanne's letter had another inside. There was no return address, just a postmark from Campeche, Mexico. When she opened it, the dog tag I once saw in Uncle Frankie's house fell out. Louanne clutched it to her chest as she read the letter out loud:

September 30, 1972

Dear Louanne,
I heard the news about Frank last month. I'm sorry.
He was one of the good guys. He helped a lot of boys
stay out of the war.
I won this in a poker game. Frank was supposed
to win it back.
Sympathies,
Dan Blaser

END

ACKNOWLEDGMENTS

THANK YOU TO MY FUN AND FUNNY HUSBAND, Peter, inspirational daughters Lindsay and Chelsay, wonderful grandson, Eli, beautiful parents, Lois and Walt, kind and witty sisters, Juli Ann, Wendi Ann, and Lori Ann, brilliant sponsor of thirty-eight years, Pat M., and especially Anna Rogers (editor) and Brooke Warner (publisher).

ABOUT THE AUTHOR

J.A. WRIGHT is the author of *Eat and Get Gas* and *How to Grow an Addict*.

Author photo © Johannes van Kan

SELECTED TITLES FROM SHE WRITES PRESS

She Writes Press is an independent publishing company founded to serve women writers everywhere. Visit us at www.shewritespress.com.

The Fourteenth of September by Rita Dragonette. $16.95, 978-1-63152-453-0. In 1969, as mounting tensions over the Vietnam War are dividing America, a young woman in college on an Army scholarship risks future and family to go undercover in the anti-war counterculture when she begins to doubt her convictions—and is ultimately forced to make a life-altering choice as fateful as that of any Lottery draftee.

Don't Put the Boats Away by Ames Sheldon. $16.95, 978-1-63152-602-2. In the aftermath of World War II, the members of the Sutton family are reeling from the death of their "golden boy," Eddie. Over the next twenty-five years, they all struggle with loss, grief, and mourning—and pay high prices, including divorce and alcoholism.

Hard Cider: A Novel by Barbara Stark-Nemon. $16.95, 978-1-63152-475-2. Abbie Rose Stone believes she has navigated the shoals of her long marriage and complicated family and is eager to realize her dream of producing hard apple cider—but when a lovely young stranger exposes a long-held secret, Abbie's plans, loyalties, and definition of family are severely tested.

Our Love Could Light the World by Anne Leigh Parrish. $15.95, 978-1-93831-444-5. Twelve stories depicting a dysfunctional and chaotic—yet lovable—family that has to band together in order to survive.